THE FLIGHTLINE II:
GENERATIONS

Written by T.M. Lander

The Flightline II: Generations
Copyright © 2024 by T.M. Lander

Cover art illustration by: William Lander

All rights reserved. No part of this publication may be reproduced, distributed, or transmitted in any form or by any means, including photocopying, recording or other electronic or mechanical methods, without the prior written permission of the author, except in the case of brief quotations embodied in reviews and certain other non-commercial uses permitted by copyright law.

Without in any way limiting the author's and publisher's exclusive rights under copyright, any use of this publication to "train" generative artificial intelligence (AI) technologies to generate text is expressly prohibited. The author reserves all rights to license uses of this work for generative AI training and development of machine learning language models.

This is a work of fiction. Any characters, businesses, places, events or incidents are either the product of the author's imagination or are used fictitiously. Any resemblance to actual persons, living or dead, events or locales is entirely coincidental.

Printed in the United States of America
Hardcover ISBN: 978-1-965253-12-0
Paperback ISBN: 978-1-965253-13-7
Ebook ISBN: 978-1-965253-14-4

**Canoe Tree
Press**

Canoe Tree Press is a division of DartFrog Books
301 S. McDowell St.
Suite 125-1625
Charlotte, NC 28204

www.DartFrogBooks.com

*"Know thy self, know thy enemy.
A thousand battles, a thousand victories."*
Sun Tzu, The Art of War

Acknowledgments

For my great, great, great, great, great grandfather, Johannes 'Justus' Lander. The one who boarded a ship named the Argus from Germany in 1832. He was accompanied by his wife and eight children to arrive in New York City. Thank you, Justus! I think we are here to stay. God bless America!

Key Players

The Dirtbag Dozen

Avionics: Sam Kirkland and Justus Johannes
Crew Chiefs: Patricia York and Burrt Wilhelm
Electro-Environmental: Lenny Bronson and Seth Harvard
Engines: Maisie Elton and Manny Eastern
Hydraulics: Phil Merrick and Jack Flange
Weapons: Pete Ward and Simon Ward

Spaceships and nose art

0026: Theodore "Bully" Roosevelt
0086: Grim Reaper
0310: Train Engineer
0341: Student
0721: Blackjack Dealer
1895: Cowgirl
3034: Beach Babe
5050: Magician

Prologue

"Sam, wait, don't go!" screamed five-year-old Aaron York as he ran through the maze of white and gray corridors.

"Hurry A-A-Ron!" twelve-year-old me yelled.

"I'm trying!" Aaron whined.

I could see two military members in camo uniforms following behind Aaron.

One demanded, "Hey kids, you're not supposed to be here!"

I knew this place well and was betting on the odds that we could outmaneuver them.

"Follow me!" I yelled, as I continued to run through the corridors that I had memorized. I turned down several directions, each time looking back to ensure Aaron was following. I turned down the next one. Finding the back door to the cafeteria, we ran through the kitchen area. The cooks gave a surprised look as we passed by several prepping stations. We escaped through the next door fast.

"This way!" I told him as we passed by several offices. I stopped at one point, wondering why the specialists in that office had their feet on their desks, then shook my head and looked back as Aaron was trailing behind me. A couple military policeman turned the corner and followed us.

We ran through the enormous parts warehouse full of racks that contained boxes as far as the eye could see. There were automated forklifts moving about carrying crates. After the long stride, we escaped through the next set of doors and reached a long corridor with an elevator at the end of it. Running to the end of the hallway, I jumped into the open lift and hit the 'up' arrow. I was waiting with my head outside the elevator, breathing hard, ready to hold the doors open if needed. Aaron was running as fast as his little child legs could manage with two MP several paces back. The lift's doors began to close. I grabbed Aaron's outstretched hand and pulled him in just as the doors closed behind him. We collapsed onto the floor laughing.

The lift approached the top floor. Exiting, I guided little Aaron down a long path. I stopped at the door I knew and entered an empty office room, closing the door behind us. It was dark. I walked slowly to the end of the room. I stopped and glared out the enormous window in extreme awe, as I had done many times before.

Aaron, right next to me, asked, "What's out there?"

"Look."

We stood side by side and looked out the enormous office windows to see the wonder. For Aaron, this was his first time. This office, among many, oversaw the expanse of spaceships parked underneath the clear dome overlooking the vastness of space. We were on Space Station Prime overlooking the Flightline.

Rows and rows of spaceships were parked and maintenance trucks were driving around them, with men and women walking with toolboxes going to and from the BC-76s, a bomber-cargo hybrid.

"What are they doing with that high thing?" Aaron asked.

He pointed to one on the right side where a couple maintainers were high up on a cherry picker crane.

"They're probably checking on a part. That's the vertical stab they are looking at. There's a communication antenna and coupler up there."

"How do you know that?"

"One of my dad's workers told me. Max was his name; he even showed me this room for the first time while he was babysitting me. He said he would work high up there sometimes changing radio parts."

"Totally rad! What about that one?" Aaron said as he pointed to a ship to the left.

"Looks like they're replacing an engine."

"What's wrong with the old one?"

"That, I don't know. These things break from time to time."

"That's totally weird."

I pointed. "Hey, A-A-Ron, look at the driver getting out of the truck. You see it? Next to the third ship down that row—count: one, two, three. Do you see her talking to the flight crew?"

"I see her."

"Do you recognize her?"

"Is that...my mom?"

"It is."

Aaron's mom, Sharyn, got back in the truck and drove off to a parking spot in view of the ship. The Crew Chief marshaller then walked to the front of the enormous spaceship.

I told Aaron, "I think they're about to launch that one out."

We watched as the marshaller waved his wands and the ship crept forward. It went into a turn and started its slow trek to the runway.

Aaron exclaimed, "That's so awesome!"

The ship stopped at the edge of the runway and waited. Then we heard an alarm, a continuous yet muffled ring of chimes echoed though the Flightline and into our room. All the maintenance trucks stopped; even the maintainers halted. Aaron and I watched as the maintainers checked their harnesses that were attached to a rail system. They all put on oxygen masks, then crouched down and waited.

The alarm tone changed to an even louder and more prominent one. I pointed to the giant window at the end of the runway as it opened to the vastness of space. Then the spaceship blasted across the runway. We could feel the window in front of us start to shake. The ship lifted with ease and made its way to starry night. The space station's giant window closed, the tension dropped, and the alarms ceased. I could see Aaron's eyes wide open.

He looked across the Flightline, seeing multiple ships ready to launch. "Are they all going up now?"

"Not all, but a bunch of them. My father says their doing a *generation* this week."

"What's a gen-e-a-son?"

"A generation is like an exercise to practice launching lots of ships all at once. If you look over there, you'll see they are loading some with bombs."

"Are they gonna blow something up?"

"Not today...just for practice. My father said it's to prepare, just in case we need take a lot of troops to one of the moons or need to use the bombers."

"Is your dad out here? Where is he?" Aaron looked all around.

"I don't think so, he's probably in a meeting."

"What's he do?"

"He helps the maintainers, tries to make things easier on the Flightline."

"Cool. Is he the general?

"Nope, just the Maintenance Group Commander.

ACT I

CHAPTER 1

Big Black Boots

My old suitcase is one I have had as long as I can remember. I sat in the crowed airport terminal and stared intently at this small carry-on. I was wondering why people call it a *suitcase*, since this small thing wouldn't do much good holding a suit. I'm not sure if I'd ever be used to how people talk or do things on Earth.

I've taken this suitcase on many trips, and it has always had sentimental value since it was my mother's. She taught me so much growing up, especially in the unique environment that it was. I was born on Space Station Prime, eight light-years away from Earth.

That space station was my home; I knew of nothing different. I still picture the play areas with the cushioned floors and climbing structures that I explored as a toddler. I had a blast in grade school with our tiny class sizes among all the other military brats. We knew all the places that were off-limits, but still had a blast going up and down the lifts and playing hide-and-seek through the endless white and gray corridors.

We took a couple family vacations to the moon of Viridis. I was truly amazed by its oceans and sandy beaches. My mom was at peace there. I still carry a picture of her sitting on the sand with the purple ocean in front of her. I was twelve years old when my parents and I traveled to Earth. Twelve years old years old before I first saw the Sun and stepped foot on Earth's actual soil...now I am twice that age.

They scanned my boarding pass on my tablet, then I walked down the aisle of the airplane. This was *day one* of my new adventure. I am about to depart from Sky Harbor Airport. That's the one in Phoenix, Arizona.

I found my aisle seat, 14-C. There was already a passenger in 14-A, a middle-aged, *very* large man next to the window who was spilling into seat 14-B. I quickly put my old suitcase in the overhead compartment and took my seat. There wasn't a lot in my luggage. They said you do not need much. Anything else required they'll provide me when I get to Space Military Boot Camp.

This morning was difficult as I said my goodbye to father. He knew this day would come, since it was all I ever talked about. I am just excited it's finally happening. He took it as well as could be expected.

I was thinking about our last two years together when I heard a voice. "Seat 14-B," said a muscular guy of average height. He looked younger than me and had tall, wavy blonde hair. He pointed to his seat and repeated, "Seat 14-B."

"Yes, I'll get up to let you pass."

"Hey man, no worries. Just shove over."

"It's good, really. I prefer the aisle."

14-B put his duffle bag up. He looked at the large man in 14-A, then looked back a row. "You know what? Take your seat. I found a better one."

I watched as he swaggered back one row and across the aisle next to a couple of attractive girls his age. He sat in the empty aisle seat next to them and started a conversation with the pretty girl with black hair. I thought, *well, let us see how long this lasts. Then again, if Johnny Bravo here has moves, I may have a little extra elbow room on this flight.* More and more passengers were taking their seats.

I overheard the conversation behind me as I turned to my right to watch it ensue.

"Sir, you're in 15-D. That's my seat," said the tall one standing in the aisle.

A tall lanky guy our age was staring at his ticket when *Johnny Bravo* looked up at him and said, "Look dude, there is an empty seat right there, 14-B."

"Yes, but this is my seat. I must sit in my assigned seat."

"Listen, kid, it doesn't matter."

I continued watching. The girls were smiling, looking somewhat embarrassed. The blonde looked around as we caught eyes. I just smiled back and shrugged my shoulders. Other passengers seemed to get agitated as they were trying to pass the tall one blocking the aisle who wasn't going to let this seat situation pass. Finally, a stewardess came by to resolve the whole thing. I saw *Johnny Bravo* stand up.

I got up as well, pointed to our seats, and said, "After you 14-B."

He slumped into his middle seat looking defeated.

I sat, then asked him, "You're heading to Boot Camp, also, right?"

"Yep."

"Well, at least you can get a second chance with those girls."

"Why's that?"

"They were at the Processing Center as well."

"Oh, I didn't notice. I was so hung-over during all that processing."

"I notice everything. **Sam Kirkland** here," I said reaching out my hand.

"**Justus Johannes**."

We shook hands, then Justus asked, "So how many of us on this plane joined the Space Military?"

"There are eighteen in our group."

"Well, this is going to be *fun*."

"We better enjoy this flight while we can."

"Hey, you wanna get some drinks?"

"That would definitely *not* be a good idea, trust me."

"You're probably right...I not sure if can pass as twenty-one here."

The flight attendants went through their little safety briefing. It wasn't long before we started to slowly taxi. After sitting there for a bit, we felt the sudden acceleration as we sped down the runway and climbed higher and higher into a steep climb.

Justus turned to me. "You alright man?" he said, looking down at my hands.

I didn't notice until he said that, but my knuckles were tight as I had a firm grip on each seat handle.

I loosened my grasp. "Yes, fine. I just get nervous about flying."

"Wow, man. There's nothing to it. We can go up, down, this way or that way..." he said as he waved his arms all around.

"Okay, enough. I got it."

The flight was boring and uneventful. The man in 14-A never talked as he leaned up against the window trying to sleep. Every now and then Justus asked me to turn around and see if those girls were looking at him. The answer was same each time: "Nope."

They announced we would be landing soon. I gripped my handles once more as this plane slammed into the ground then suddenly decelerated. After waiting for others to deboard, as one does, we grabbed our luggage and started walking through the tunnel towards the terminal.

Justus asked me, "Where do we go, once we get in?"

"Your guess is as good as mine," I answered. "There should be sign."

There was definitely a sign. Right as we entered the terminal seating area there were two sergeants dressed in Space Military camouflage uniforms.

Justus walked up to the sergeant, "Yo, dude! Do we meet here for the Boot Camp thing or what?"

The sergeant responded harshly, "'Yo, dude?!' How dare you, you piece of sludge! You will address me as Sergeant Bevington! Stand here, don't move and shut up!"

Justus looked wide-eyed and in shock.

Sergeant Bevington stared at me with a scowl, "You! Stand directly next to *Yo Dude*...on his left side!"

More recruits were approaching. The two sergeants continued to bark orders. I could see the girls from row 15 approach as well.

"Eyes front, newbie!" Sergeant Bevington yelled at me.

They had the other recruits line up directly behind us, then the sergeant commanded, "Everyone! Drop your bags on the floor.

Now pick them up with your *left* hand." He then laid into Justus. "I said left hand!"

Justus responded, "I know man. The bag was on my right; I was just transferring it to my left."

The Sergeant got in his face. "Don't argue with me! You were told not to speak! Even if I allow you to speak you will address me as Sergeant Bevington." The Sergeant then addressed the rest of the formation, "Yo *Dude* here has a problem identifying his left and right. Everyone will drop their bags again! Now pick them up with your *right* hand this time! Good...now drop them again and pick them up with your *left* hand!"

The Sergeant got back in Justus' face. "Do you know your left from your right now?!"

"Yes, sir, Sergeant Bevington, sir!"

"Good, now follow me. Formation! Forward, 'arch!"

The group of us in two lines *attempted* to march through the crowded airport. I could hear the other sergeant blurting orders towards the rear of our small crew. I could see other airport passengers staring at the sight of our group in colorful civilian clothes being escorted by these two in camo.

Sergeant Bevington yelled at me again. "Eyes forward, newbie!"

In front of me I saw a couple more sergeants with another colorful group of recruits. They were all standing in a large formation, four across. As we approached, Sergeant Bevington said, "Join that group! Stand directly behind the last person. Heel to toe, heel to toe!"

I couldn't believe he meant this literally. We had to stand with our shoes bumped up against the ones in front of us as more joined behind me. Talk about being too close for comfort. Carry-ons or duffle bags still in our hands, we stood there for a while.

One of the sergeants yelled, "Formation! Sit down!"

Immediately we all sat, very awkwardly as we were already so close to each other. We were all trying to adjust in this uncomfortable formation with our luggage and legs and feet trapped under and over each other's. It seemed we sat there for over an hour while another couple of groups approached and joined our collage of recruits. These other groups must have come from different flights across the country.

It was another awkward moment as we all stood up after being given the command. My foot had fallen asleep. We were then escorted outside. I saw the night sky and felt the hot, humid Texas air surround me while hearing the repetitive chirp of cicada insects. We were led into a blue military bus. The driver, another dressed in camo, barked orders to have us fill every seat starting from the rear. No one dared to speak, knowing if anyone did, we'd all be screamed at. We were all shuffled around. I had no idea where Justus or those girls were. I sat cramped, holding my suitcase in front of me, staring out the window watching the vehicles and traffic lights amongst the darkness.

It was very late at night when we drove through the military guarded gate and made our way to a building. There was more yelling as we were told where to line up and where to go. We were put in a room where they assigned flight numbers. Afterwards, we were escorted outside and told specifically where to stand in rows and columns. There were only males in our new formation of about fifty recruits. We waited there for some time before another sergeant approached us. This one was wearing what they called a Smokey the Bear hat.

The new sergeant stood in the front of the formation and addressed us. "I am **Drill Sergeant Stone**! You are about to encounter the worse weeks of your lives! I have never seen a group with this many pathetic losers! I own you now and I will not hesitate to send you back. Please just give me one reason and you'll be back on a plane to your old sorry life! Welcome to the House of Pain!"

Drill Sergeant Stone was not a big man; he was not overly tall, nor physically intimidating. Yet, there was a certain evil meanness to him that made us all shake with fear whenever he spoke. It was how he spoke with sharp authority and confidence. I was terrified...yet impressed.

There was a barrage of insults as this drill sergeant approached us. "Hold your bag with your left hand—are you deaf or a complete idiot? Who told you to use your right?!" He marched up and down our columns yelling, "Stand up straight. Is this really how you stand naturally? Have you been slouching your entire life? Eyes forward! Don't fidget!"

Then Sergeant Stone got right in my face. I could feel his large, brimmed hat against the short hair on my head. He stared right into my very soul. I tried to remain perfectly still and look past his piercing eyes. Then he yelled, "They warned me about you at the Processing Center! You're a troublemaker! Do you really think you can act that way around here? I'll be watching you. You make one mistake and you'll pay—you'll all pay!"

The Drill Sergeant continued his assault on unsuspecting recruits. An interesting calm came over me as I replayed the event that just transpired and used logic to deduce it all. Sergeant Stone has no idea what my name was. I didn't have a name tag yet. We'd never met. No one from the Processing Center had told him anything. Even if they had, I never did anything there that would cause trouble. This was all a game. One big head game to weed out the weak. All I needed to do was play this game for eight weeks and I would be home free. I was actually smiling on the inside at this point, yet I didn't dare show it.

"Forward, 'arch!" bellowed the Drill Sergeant.

We were marched to our new living quarters: rows and rows of bunk beds. Each of us was assigned a bed and a small locker. I looked next to me and saw that Justus Johannes had the bunk on top of mine. It made sense, since they most likely arranged us alphabetically. It was late, well after midnight. I am not sure if I even slept that first night.

———————

The bright lights came on and there was more yelling. Sergeant Stone was at it again. It had to be well before five in the morning. We were lined up to wash in the communal showers followed by speed shaving. Speed shaving is a process where men with sharp razors must shave their faces while being screamed at to *hurry up* by someone without a razor. Some were intimidated by this. I saw a dozen leave the washroom with an array of cuts and nicks with blood running down their faces. Nope, I would take my time with this one. What were they going to do? Tell me I have exceeded my shave time?

After an extremely quick breakfast at the chow hall, it was back into a large formation led by Sergeant Stone. "Your left, left, left right left!"

Our first stop was the barber shop. I already had a short crew cut. I didn't think they would take much off...I was wrong. They were shaving our heads almost to the scalp. The look on Justus' face was priceless as they mowed through his big, blonde surfer hair.

The next building was beyond interesting. One by one we were given shots. Not just one shot in the arm, but multiple shots by several medics. I felt like we were products in an assembly line. Then we were told to take off our shoes and enter a chamber one at a time after giving them our names. This small one-person booth was cylinder shaped. We had to stand on the foot markers and put our hands flat against the circles on the wall in front of us. We were then told to look into a goggles eye frame, bite down on a stick, and stand perfectly still. The outer mechanism rotated around us doing a scan.

The random specialist said this device had just recorded our shoe size, pants size, shirt size, fingerprints, eye exam, and had even taken dental x-rays. The specialist then gave me a small printout with all my information.

I will never forget the smell of the next room. It smelled like clean mildew, the smell of new military uniforms. A dozen stations were set up, starting with giving us a very large duffle bag. I gave my uniform sizes to the workers as we were given our physical training uniforms and Military Dress Uniforms, which are the nice ones with button shirts, slacks, a coat, and a tie.

We were also issued our camo uniforms, boots, and temporary name tags. Putting on my military camo for the first time brought forth a new emotion in me. It was the boots that hit me with a strong sensation, the last item in my uniform. Wearing those boots made everything seem real. It was those boots that spoke to me on that day: *this is it, you made it, this is real. Sam Kirkland is officially in the US Military.* If only my mom could see me now. From that day forward I felt like a different person every time I put on those big black boots.

CHAPTER 2

On Top of the World

Boot camp was about survival. I knew deep down I would pass. Most responsible people with common sense do. However, the challenge was to get through it by the path of least resistance. In life, we all try to take the smooth way to avoid obstacles that will create discomfort or stress. That's Boot Camp.

The only goal was to take it step-by-step and try to avoid a Drill Sergeant getting in your face. It's inevitable that will occur. The next trick is to do everything you can to minimize the length of exposure, which I have found is to agree with whatever they say and not give them a reason to continue. It was not so easy for others.

On day one, Drill Sergeant Stone started to assign duties to each of us. I knew all I had to do was stay under the radar, get through this whole ordeal without being noticed. The sergeant started going through the list, taking volunteers for miscellaneous jobs. He would say a task and see who would raise their hands. If no one did, he would start yelling until someone did.

The key would be to pick one that had almost no exposure. I listened to the first set of duties: Latrine Queen, Hallway Crew, K.P., Guidon Bearer, and Fire Monitor. I had looked up all the positions before I joined. The previous jobs were coded for those in charge of the washroom being cleaned, sweeping the halls, cleaning dishes after meals, carrying the flight flag, and taking out the trash.

I knew exactly what job I was waiting for; one I knew I could excel at: *Academic Monitor*. This position was to ensure people studied for the end of course exam. It was an easy task with very little responsibility and with little to no interaction with the Drill

Sergeants. Sergeant Stone went through job after job. I did all I could to avoid eye contact.

"Academic Monitor," Sergeant Stone said finally.

My hand shot up fast. *Almost too fast*, I thought.

The sergeant looked directly at me, "No, Recruit Kirkland. I have a special job for you."

"Yes, sir."

He picked another volunteer and continued down his list of assigned duties. *What just happened? Did I just get singled out?* I didn't dare raise my hand again. All I could do was wait.

Sergeant Stone addressed me last. "Recruit Kirkland, stand up."

I stood. "Yes, sir."

"Everyone...Recruit Kirkland is your Dorm Chief. You will report to him if you have any issues, and he will report directly to me."

Well, so much for staying under the radar, I thought. The Dorm Chief is the leader the entire flight, the one responsible for everything. This was not going to be easy.

Sergeant Stone took me aside, alone, into a little office within the barracks.

I stood up straight as he spoke to me.

"Recruit Kirkland, do you know why I picked you?"

"No, sir."

He approached closer, his voice was loud at first, then it dwindled down to an eerie whisper. "Don't you dare lie to me! I think you are smarter than you pretend to be. I also believe you already know why you were picked as Dorm Chief. Let's start over. Do you know why I picked you?"

"Because I am older than the rest of the recruits, sir."

"And...?"

"And because I have some college, sir."

"Some college? You have a bachelor's degree! You may be smart on paper, but you're dumb as they come. You could have skipped all this and gone in as an officer."

Sergeant Stone then leaned in real close and whispered slowly,

"Now you're stuck with me. You *will* lead these recruits and ensure everyone stays on task when I'm not around. Not only that, if you *choose* to screw this up, I will assign a new Dorm Chief. Do you know what will happen to you then?"

I thought for a second, then answered slowly, "You will make my life a living hell, sir."

"Maybe you are smart. You are *very* correct. I *will* make your life a living hell."

———————

I will never forget that next breakfast. Justus was in front of me, walking with his tray in hands immediately after receiving his food. I believe his first mistake was making eye contact with the Drill Sergeant. I stopped in my tracks when Sergeant Stone leaped out of his chair fast and approached Justus.

Sergeant Stone was right in his face. "Recruit Johannes! Are you smiling? Why are you smiling?"

"I don't know," Justus answered as five other Drill Sergeants at the front table leaned in simultaneously and listened intently.

Stone continued, "Are you smiling at me? Do you like me?"

"No, sir."

"Oh, you don't like me."

"Yes, I like you, sir."

"Oh, now you *do* like me. How much do you like me? Do you want to take me to the prom?!"

Justus didn't answer.

"Well, do you? Answer me, Recruit Johannes!"

"That all depends, sir. Will you wear a dress?"

I stood there motionless with my tray in hands, shaking. I could see the other Drill Sergeants laughing.

Sergeant Stone looked at Justus. "Boy, you have balls of iron. I do believe you earned yourself a new job here, Chow Runner!"

The next couple of days consisted of physical training, more in-processing, more briefings, more marching, meals in-between, and back to the dorm for more yelling. Sergeant Stone explained exactly how our uniforms are to be worn and how to organize them in our lockers. We spent a few hours attempting to get things perfect. We learned very quickly and harshly how many small details we missed.

"Your left, left, left right left!"

It was only our third day in. We woke before dawn as usual to be shuffled outside with our PT gear on. These consisted of generic running shoes, mid-calf socks, tight T-shirts, and short shorts over our tighty-whities. An attractive ensemble, I'm sure. *Just play the game*, I kept reminding myself. We marched to the field, did a series of strenuous exercises, then were told to run around the large track.

"So what's Dorm Chief like?" Justus asked, running next to me.

"I'm responsible for making sure every single assigned job gets done. If anyone screws up, Sergeant Stone puts all the blame on me."

"That sucks."

"He told me when there are no Drill Sergeants around, I need to ensure no one screws up and if they do, I need to report any incidents to him."

"Are you really going to do that?"

"Look, I don't want this job. I'm not ready to be a leader. I'm going to need help with this whole Dorm Chief thing."

"Dude, you got it made. You don't actually have an extra duty. As long as everything is cool, you'll look good."

"That's what I am afraid of."

"At least you're not the Chow Runner!"

"How is that going for you, Justus?"

"How's that going? It's hell! It's pure, unadulterated hell."

"Do tell."

"Alright, you know how you're all formed up outside the chow hall before each meal?"

"I would not call it a meal, but yes."

"I'm the first one that gets sent in. I gotta march in looking all professional or whatever. Then I gotta approach the Snake Pit using what they call 'short choppy steps.'"

"The Snake Pit is where all the Drill Sergeants sit, right?"

"Yeah. I think this is their favorite time of day. They get to sit there and see who can make fun of me the best, like it's some sort of competition between them."

"What do you mean?"

"I gotta stand right in front of them and say a specific phrase: 'Sir, Recruit Johannes reports as ordered. Sir, Squadron 323, Flight 332 is prepared to enter the Chow Hall from the west side.' Then one by one they screw with me. They say I didn't say it right or say I'm not standing right. Sometimes they ask me trick questions trying to mess me up."

"What kind of trick questions?"

"They ask if I was really coming in from the west side. Or ask me what my flight number is, trying to convince me what I told them is wrong. Just this morning, right in front of Sergeant Stone, another Drill Sergeant asked me if Sergeant Stone was easy or hard on us."

"Wow, that is a conundrum. I believe there is no correct way to answer that. What did you say?"

"I said, 'Sir, Drill Sergeant Stone is the only lead Drill Sergeant I have. I've got nothing else to compare him to.'"

"What happened then?"

"The one that asked the question said I was a brown noser and my uniform looked like a duffle bag."

"Well, what can we do? How long do you think they'll keep us running?"

"As long I'm not getting yelled at, I'll run all day. Better out here than anywhere near Sergeant Stone."

One step at a time. We were in our daily routine. Back to the barracks, communal showers, changing into our camos, and stuck in a formation marching to some unknown place. Every time a recruit was out of step or swinging their arms wrong, two things happened:

they were screamed at, then I was screamed at for allowing it to happen. I was even asked why the Guidon Bearer couldn't keep our flight flag straight. **Lenny Bronson** was the guidon's name; he was that tall kid that kicked Justus out of his seat on the plane. Good kid, just really quiet. I knew I would have to work with him to get his flag movements right.

"Your left, left, left right left!"

Most days we were led to classrooms to learn all about the Space Military and our chain of command, customs and courtesies, military history, rank structure, and other random facts. This was going to be a cake walk. I had already learned most of this from my parents and absorbed what I could on the space station.

I knew the Space Military already dumbed down the ranks from the other branches. They went from the standard E-1 to E-9 enlisted grades to only four ranks: specialist, sergeant, senior sergeant, and chief. Not that it made much difference; fewer ranks meant more time stuck in each one. The officer side still had your standard ranks; they just omitted a few. The current ones are: lieutenant, captain, major, colonel, and then the four general stars, sometimes a fifth. The next step was to ensure the rest of my flight studied and memorized all these classroom lessons. That part would certainly be a challenge.

Nighttime in the barracks was a time to attempt to catch up on things without the drill sergeants hovering over us; however, time was limited.

One night, I brought everyone from our flight together and said, "Listen up, guys. We only have so much time during these evenings. We need to clean the barracks, organize our lockers, prepare our uniforms, and study our class material. Bronson should also practice his movements with the guidon flag. Those with marching issues should practice their steps. We all know some of us have problems doing push-ups and sit-ups. However, the extra time we spend honing in on these skills equals less time sleeping. This will be a balancing act for sure. Are there any suggestions?"

Ziskey said, "We can all pitch in and help with the cleaning duties while those that need to work on things like studying can concentrate on that."

I agreed, then asked, "Anyone else?"

"It'd be good if someone looks over our lockers and uniforms to find the discrepancies before they do," Oxberger added.

"Good. What else? We need to stay one step ahead of the Drill Sergeants."

"We should get in small groups of who needs help with PT or anything else," Recruit Winger suggested. "I can definitely lead the marching routine."

"Perfect. For now, we forgo our assigned duties at night. Everyone helps. Those that are struggling with the study material, marching, or PT, focus on that. The rest of us will pick up your slack. Half of us will stay up real late cleaning and checking each other's lockers while you sleep. We will start with my half of the barracks. The next night the other side will do the same to allow the rest of us to catch up on sleep and so on. We'll trade off each night. Remember, it is us against the Drill Sergeants. How does this sound?"

Most of the flight agreed, although there were a few that just did not care or wanted to do their own thing. Overall, I thought this night was productive.

"Your left, left, left right left!"

One would think *eating* should be an important thing to do while in a training environment. Doing all these physical exercises, marching, and trying to stay focused in class takes a toll on the body. However, nutrition and sleep seemed to be the last priority here. I was thinking this through as I was going through the motions to get my food. Every single meal we were lined up and told exactly how to stand, where to look, and where to march. The workers slopped food on our trays as we were given three tiny glasses of water. Then, like cattle, we go to the first available table and wait for it to fill up so the four of us could sit in unison. The next step is the most critical part: we had to scarf down the food as quickly as humanly possible while being screamed at to hurry up. Like half-starved zombies we marched to the trash, threw most of our food away, and gave the empty trays to our overworked K.P. robot brothers to clean. Every...single...meal.

"Your left, left, left right left!"

Here we go again. PT, Chow Hall, marching, classes, and back to the barracks with very little sleep. One day we did that whole obstacle course thing, which at least broke up the monotony. Running, climbing, crawling, jumping over things and under various monkey bars was fun, but I believe the movies and streaming shows hyped it up too much.

One obstacle, we had to shimmy across a rope with our hands while our ankles were crossed over the rope as well, all while dangling over a pool of water. Of course, a handful of recruits fell into the water. The very next obstacle was the monkey bars. They ordered all the recruits that fell in the water to go first, leaving all the horizontal bars wet for the rest of us. This claimed a few more victims for the mud underneath.

Tired, sweaty and filthy dirty, we formed up ready to march back to the barracks.

Drill Sergeant Stone hollered, "Forward, 'arch! Double time! Your left, left, left right left! Repeat after me...I don't know, but I've been told!"

We all repeated in unison as we jogged marched: "I don't know, but I've been told!"

> *"Living in space is really cold!"*
> *"Send me to the moon of Nix!"*
> *"All the girls there...need their fix!"*
> *"It's too cold for all those chicks!"*
> *"Let's stay inside and see some tricks!"*
> *"Your left, left, left right left!"*

"I don't know, but I've been told!"
"Living in space is really cold!"
"Send me to the Viridis moon!"
"Laying on the beach all afternoon!"
"All she wants to do...is spoon!"
"Hang on babe, let's get a room!"
"Your left, left, left right left!"

"I don't know, but I've been told!"
"Living in space is really cold!"
"Calidum is hotter than hell!"
"Never mind...she's an infidel!"
"Your left, left, left right left!"

It was finally our last week. Sergeant Stone let us know what jobs we would be assigned going forward. This was huge! This determined our fate as to which Technical School we'd attend next, and would guide the choice of which base or station we may end up at.

The recruits were assigned various jobs such as Military Police, Food Services, and Medical. One guy got Firefighter; others included desk jobs like Personnel or Finance. I knew I joined with a guarantee in Flightline maintenance, but I had no clue what my job would be. This could be anything from Aerospace Ground Equipment to an engine mechanic.

Sergeant Stone was nearing the end of his list. "Recruit Lenny Bronson, Electrical-Environmental. Recruit Justus Johannes, Avionics. Recruit Sam Kirkland, Avionics."

Boot Camp was not so bad. Things seemed to get easier as the weeks went by, although the eight weeks felt like four months. It is amazing how much you learn about others when you spend every single hour of the day with them. Some struggled with the PT test, others almost failed the end of course test. Overall, we all passed.

Graduation day came. All of us in our Space Military Dress Uniforms marched across the parade grounds in formation. I never did get fired from being Dorm Chief; in fact once it was all said and done, Drill Sergeant Stone actually told me I didn't suck at Dorm Chief. Not much of a compliment, but I'd take it. I could cross Boot Camp off my list. Next stop, Technical School.

CHAPTER 3

Going to Wichita

A large group of brand-new specialists wearing our Military Dress Uniforms uniforms waited with our bags and luggage. Everyone who'd just graduated Boot Camp was divided by career fields and would be sent on different buses to a range of Tech Schools across the country. Most would be taken to the airport first. Our maintenance troops were lucky enough to drive a short trip north.

A skinny specialists arrived and asked, "Is this bus seven?"

I answered, "Yes. Are you a spaceship maintainer as well?"

"Yeah, Crew Chief."

"Sounds good. I'm Sam and this is Justus. We'll both be Avionics."

"**Burrt Wilhelm** here. Is everyone at this stop for spaceship maintenance?"

"It appears so. That's Lenny over there, Electro-Environmental."

Wilhelm replied, "Well, no one else from my flight was maintenance, so I'm gonna hang with you guys. Is that cool?"

"Absolutely."

A few more specialists showed up.

I asked Justus, "Hey, are those the two girls from the airplane?"

"Yes, they are," he replied, swaggering towards them.

Wilhelm and I followed him.

Justus smiled at the girls and said, "Let me guess. You are a couple of the US Military's newest, finest spaceship maintainers?"

The one with black hair responded sternly. "Really, you're going to call us *fine*?"

"I called the spaceships fine, but if you wanna go there…"

I jumped in. "You'll have to excuse Justus here; he was traumatized in Boot Camp. Nice to meet you. I'm Sam Kirkland, and this is Burrt Wilhelm."

The blonde replied, "Well it looks like one of you has manners. Thank you, Sam. I'm **Jen Thompson** and everyone calls her **Pepper**."

"I take it you both got maintenance jobs, as well?" Wilhelm asked.

"Yeah, I'm Avionics," Jen answered, "and Pepper got Crew Chief."

"Looks like our bus is here," I said.

As soon as it parked, the storage doors at the ground level opened. We all squashed our luggage and duffle bags that contained all our uniforms in there. Two doors opened. We entered from the rear, and found seats close to each other. As the vehicle hit the open highway, everyone was talking and laughing. Finally, we all had a sense of some freedom. There was not a sergeant around. Then I noticed there was *no one* around. We were on one of those driverless buses. *Who is in charge in case anything happens? Where is the order? Why I am worried about these things?*

I had to tell myself to calm down and just go with it.

Justus, Wilhelm, Pepper, Jen and I talked the whole way there, sharing Boot Camp stories. Someone towards the front started to play music from their tablet. Just hearing that was an absolute joy. We hadn't heard any music for the last eight weeks. We talked about how much we missed the simple things that were deprived of: eating without being told to rush, watching movies, wearing regular clothes, taking long, hot showers...alone.

We arrived at our new base and new barracks. One of our Military Training Leaders lead us through the process. Although strict, this was nothing compared to the insanity of Boot Camp. We were issued rooms. Most of our group was on the second floor. These tiny rooms contained a bunk bed, desk, and closet. I'd be rooming with Lenny.

After dumping off our bags we were led to the Chow Hall and told to meet in the auditorium in an hour. I sat at a table with Justus, Wilhelm, and Lenny after we went through the cafeteria-style line.

Justus spoke up. "So what do you guys think? Think I got a chance with Pepper?"

Wilhelm answered, "Dude, she hardly talked to you on the bus."

"That's because she's playing hard to get…Trust me."

"Actually, if anyone has a chance, Jen was looking at Sam hard."

"What?" I answered.

Justus asked, "What do think Lenny? You don't talk too much, do you?"

"I dunno," Lenny said.

"Come on, Lenny. You need to say more than that."

"I think you need to give it a few weeks. We just spent eight weeks around only dudes, living in tight quarters in uncomfortable conditions. The first two girls you see, you go crazy."

I replied, "Wow, Lenny. That is a good observation."

"How do you think the girls' Boot Camp was?" Wilhelm asked.

Justus answered, "I saw their flight a few times out marching or in the Chow Hall. They had it way worse than us."

"Why is that?" I wondered.

"First of all, they couldn't wear makeup the whole time, so there's that. I saw it all at the Snake Pit. Their Drill Sergeant would scream at them and at me like nothing else. She was way meaner than ours."

Wilhelm asked, "What's the deal with them running at PT in the blazing heat? We're all in shorts and the girls are running around in their long track pants."

I scratched my head. "That was weird. I have no idea."

"Really?" Justus said. "You guys don't know? It's obvious. They wore long pants because they didn't have time to shave their legs."

I looked at the time on my tablet. "Hey guys, we need to go. We need to be in the auditorium soon."

The four of us found seats in the auditorium along with the all the new maintainers. To our surprise, Jen and Pepper sat directly behind us and gave us a quick pat on our shoulders to let us know they were there. Someone walked out on stage.

"I am Senior Sergeant Mast, the lead Military Training Leader, or MTL. Welcome to Tech School. You will all be on a strict schedule Monday through Friday. There is a day shift, swing shift, and mid shift. All of you here will start on the day shift. Your day will start with Squadron PT, then breakfast, followed by marching to your classes in formation. You will march to and from the Chow Hall at lunchtime. After each day in class, you will march back to the barracks."

Mast continued, "There are separate barracks for males and females. Under no circumstances are you to enter the opposites sex's building! You will be responsible for keeping your uniforms up to standard, as well as keeping your rooms in tip-top shape. You will have a several MTLs in the barracks to ensure you stay on task with many random room and uniform inspections. You will have a curfew to include the weekends. It is very simple: if you choose to abuse the rules or get in trouble, you will be assigned additional duties during the weekend."

Senior Mast continued to explain the rules and expectations for some time. I could see others doing all they could to try to stay awake.

The next morning, we got in our camo uniforms and formed up outside the barracks. That was after we'd already done PT, showered, and had eaten a quick breakfast. We saw many groups of all sizes forming up; they were the various classes that had been here for a while.

All of us newbies had to form up at the end. It looked like everyone from the bus was there, about fifty of us. We then marched to our place of instruction. As soon as we arrived at the schoolhouse, we were all sent to a large classroom where all fifty of us sat.

The Senior Sergeant in front of the class addressed us. "Good morning. I am Senior Sergeant Kanan, this school's superintendent. To my right are a few of your instructors. As spaceship maintainers, your Tech School Training will be conducted in three phases. Phase One lasts one month. You will be in this large class of fifty. As you can see, it includes all career fields. You will learn everything about Flightline safety, the ship's maintenance logs, and basic tool usage."

He continued, "Phase Two is three months long. There you will be broken up into your individual career fields and meet in separate schoolhouses. This may be Engines, Hydro, Avionics, Crew Chiefs, etc. There you will learn about your unique systems and troubleshooting. After Phase Two, you will receive your preliminary orders to your new assignment's location and specific spaceship model. You may end up on any one of our bases here on Earth working on ships, or be sent to one of our Space Stations orbiting Earth. If you're lucky enough, you may end up on going to the Stella System through that Kirkland Bridge wormhole."

Justus looked at me after Kanan said *Kirkland Bridge.*

Kanan resumed. "Phase Three is a month long, where you will be given a quick overview of the particular spaceship to which you will be assigned."

After a quick break, we all stayed in this large classroom to start Phase One. Many were happy to get started since this felt so different than Boot Camp.

Sergeant Structo walked in and gave us an overview. "Welcome class. I'll be your main instructor for this first phase. It will be broken down into four areas. We already sent you the lessons on your tablets, so you'll have something to study in the evenings. First, we will cover safety on the Flightline. This will include everything from wearing proper protective equipment to securing your tools. We will also cover utilizing ladders, maintenance stands, generator charts, heaters, and AC units. The track system and wearing an O2 mask will also be covered, just in case you end up on a space station."

Sergeant Structo continued, "The next week we will focus on the maintenance logs. Every time you work on a ship, you will need to document everything. Let me give you an example. Let's say I'm going to change that lightbulb above you. The first step is to pull the circuit breaker, then get a ladder, then remove that light cover, then remove the light bulb, install a new one, then push in the breaker, check to see if the new light works, then install the cover. Prior to each of these steps you will need to document the action in the ships' maintenance logs. Afterwards you'll document what the fix was, how it was fixed, the condition of the problem, when it was fixed, how many people, how many hours, the type of maintenance, and so forth."

Justus' hand shot up.

"Go ahead Specialist...Johannes," Structo said, trying to read his name tag.

Justus asked, "So, it seems like we are spending ninety-five percent of the actual fix on documentation?"

"Welcome to the US Space Military! There's more. Then you need to fill out condition tags to put on your old part, which is then turned in to be repaired, tested, and put back on the shelf at Parts Supply. In the case of the lightbulb, it may just be destroyed or recycled."

I could see Justus was getting agitated.

Sergeant Structo continued, "The third week we'll continue to use maintenance logs and apply it to removing and replacing various generic parts in our spaceship trainers. The last week, we will go out to one of the retired ships outside and put all the lessons together, going through various scenarios."

Wilhelm raised his hand.

"Go ahead."

"Sir, which ship will we be working on that final week?"

"It's an old C-345. That's a cargo ship, which you should have figured by its designator."

"Was that one you worked on?"

"I have. I spent my first four years working on Space Station Lunar, working the C-345. I never did go through the *Kirkland Bridge* to Stella."

A few people looked at me. I just keep looking straight ahead.

———

At dinner at the Chow Hall, Justus, Pepper, Jen, and I found a table.

Jen asked me, "So how did you end up as the Dorm Chief in Boot Camp?"

"I was the oldest recruit in our flight," I answered.

Justus put his hands behind his head and leaned back in his chair. "This ought to be good. Go ahead, Sam, explain your situation to the girls. Why don't you start with your age...your *real* age."

Jen and Pepper looked at me with a blank stare.

"I already told you," I said. "I lived my first twelve years on Space Station Prime. Things got complicated when we moved to Earth. You learned about all the Space Bridge problems, right?"

Jen asked in a way that could only be pictured as Padme meme, "You mean the Kirkland Bridge? Strange coincidence...right?...right?"

"Well..."

"Yeah, we heard about the delays," Justus said, "but that's good now? They got that fixed like ten years ago."

"Actually, it was fixed seven and a half years ago."

"Go on, Sam," said Jen.

"When my parents and I traveled to Earth, we were frozen in cryo-sleep for almost sixteen years."

"What?!" Pepper exclaimed.

"It's true. Not counting the time I was frozen, not aging, I am twenty-four years old. Now based on my birth year, I'm like forty or something. In fact, my ID card has two ages listed for legal reasons."

"That is insane!" Jen said. "Are you okay? How did you...how did you cope with all that?"

"I took it much better than my parents. I never knew any other family members except for all the friends I made on the station. I was sadder about leaving them. Earth was Earth. I never knew of it prior. I had nothing else to compare it to."

"What about your parents?" Jen asked.

"That was tough...still is. My mom was never the same. She was deep in a depression. She sought medical help, but..."

"And your dad?"

I was drifting off in thought.

Jen repeated, "Your dad?"

"Sorry, yeah, my father, Henry Kirkland. He retired as a Colonel. After his service, he became obsessed with the Space Bridge and got a job working for the DOD under an R&D division. He was able to obtain all the information on that wormhole, so to speak. He spent hours upon hours watching videos of the vessels taking that journey eight light-years away. He was trying to figure out how the trips were delayed. Even though those transports were on autopilot there were still video recordings of every trip. He was locked away in his room for hours upon hours, hardly slept and didn't eat much. I was pretty much on my own through my teen years."

"We know this is hard... but continue," Pepper said. "It's good to get it out."

"Then one day he was teaching me to drive. I missed our exit on the interstate and the GPS immediately rerouted us down another road. I was on some random country road when he yelled, 'Stop the car!' I hit the brakes fast and we just sat there. That is when he got a huge smile on his face and ordered me to drive home. I wasn't sure what happened at the time, but it was the first time I had seen him smile in a long while. He had figured out the Space Bridge problem."

Jen smiled. "So it's named after your dad."

"It is. He explained to me that it's like a tree. Going from our Solar System to Stella is like starting on the top of a tree and making a path down the limbs to the base. There is typically only one way to travel, yet sometimes it gets off course. It was the GPS that reminded him of this. When you get off course, the GPS will calculate the next best route to go. This is why some transports took a little longer to get to Stella," I told them. "On the way back to Earth, it's more complicated. This is like going from the base of a tree to one particular limb. There are multiple paths that open, and any time the transport sways off just a little, it may take the wrong path. Then the GPS, or autopilot in this case, tries to correct itself. My father explained that these transports coming back sometimes get so off course it would take years to go through the new paths formed to get back on track. But eventually they always got here."

Pepper asked, "So how did he prove this? How was it fixed?"

"In the early days, the first few transports that went through had few problems. That was because they were manned by pilots that could keep everything on track and ensure the vessel stayed its course. This was troublesome because it took eight weeks or more. They had two crews continually trading off. If they were delayed too much, there was a fear the pilots would go crazy spending years in space unfrozen. They needed to go fully automatic. However, once they went full autopilot, they experienced more delays."

I continued, "Using the video footage, my father was able to show how to stay on course and where the wrong paths were. He convinced the US Military to go back to manned vessels. He even taught the new flight crews what to look for to stay on target. They used this new method, along with a faster engine system. They were able to reduce the *Kirkland Bridge*, as it's now called, into a thirty-day trip, cutting the time in half. After that, there were almost no more delays."

"That was seven years ago," Pepper said. "What about the recent stage booster tech? Can't they go even faster now?"

"See, that's where it gets weird. My father warned about going any faster. He said the wormhole could potentially pose a hazard—something about going way too fast and creating an irreversible *rift*."

"*Rift* sounds bad. What's that mean?"

"I don't know. I know he thinks it's extremely dangerous. The current speed is about as fast as it'll let us go."

We continued Phase One. Weeks went by fast. I had to help Justus fill out the maintenance logs. There were several nights I helped him study the course material, especially the nights before the tests. He was trying, but just had problems concentrating or memorizing the facts. Perhaps he was distracted by other things...

Justus and Pepper were getting closer and even started dating. Justus kept asking me what I thought of Jen, but I kept telling him I didn't have time for all that here. I kept up with course work and couldn't wait to see what we'd learn next.

The classes seemed easy, except for the hands-on portions. Justus had to help me with part removals. I understood the mechanics of it all, but working with hand tools was new to me. I could figure out the basic ones, but when they threw in safety-wire plyers, vice grips, torque wrenches, soldering irons, and pin insertion tools, I was all thumbs. I got it eventually. It was a definitely a new experience being the slow one in class.

CHAPTER 4

Gonna Fly Now

Phase Two began. There were only eight of us in class. Justus sat to my right, Jen to my left, and there were five other Avionics students.

Our instructor, Sergeant Leonard, addressed us. "Phase Two! Now time to have fun. You may not enjoy this first month, but I guarantee you'll need it. Everyone, look at your tablet and bring up page 87. What do you see? How about Specialist Thompson?"

Jen answered, "Sir, all I see is a maze of lines and strange symbols."

"By the end of this first month, you will be able to read all of this. These are schematics or wiring diagrams. These outline your entire system. This first month, we'll cover basic electronics and how they apply to Avionics. After the first month, each lesson will follow the same flow. You'll get an overview of how the system works, which parts are involved, and how it is all tied together in these wire diagrams. In between the classroom lessons, we'll go back and forth to the spaceship trainers and mess with these systems firsthand by identifying parts, running through the operations checks and troubleshooting. Then it'll be on to the next system, repeating that same process. Any questions so far?"

"Are these the same parts we'll see on our spaceships?" Justus asked.

"Yes and no. Some will be, but you'll learn the basics, which are going to be the same on any ship. A receiver is a receiver, a control panel is a control panel. They may have different buttons and some different functions, but they are basically the same. We will cover the different radios, different navigational systems, radar, guidance and control and defensive systems. When you're all done, you'll have just enough knowledge to be *dangerous* on the Flightline. The real training will be once you get to your next assignment and do your on-the-job-training."

––––––––––

"Sam...Sam...Wake up. Sam." Lenny was trying to get me up.

"What time is it?"

"0400. You agreed to this."

"I need more sleep."

"No, man. Justus and Wilhelm are waiting the hallway."

"Alright."

I got up. All four of us were wearing PT clothes.

Wilhelm whispered to Justus, "Why does it have to be at 0400?"

Justus said quietly, "We already went over this. 0400 is the perfect time. Dayshift won't wake up for at least another hour, swings won't still be up at this time, and the graveyard shift is still at school. No one should be around at this hour." Justus reached into his plastic bag and gave us each a screwdriver. He gave a second plastic bag to Lenny. "Come on, let's go."

The four of us snuck upstairs to the third floor of our barracks and slowly peeked around each corner. Justus went into the first washroom, then came out shortly.

"It's clear," he said. "Wilhelm and I will take this one. You guys start hitting the other ones. We'll meet at the last set of stairs."

Lenny and I walked stealth-like to the next washroom. He made sure it was clear. I went to the first shower stall, and using the tool, unscrewed the shower knob marked with an "H." Lenny and I proceeded to the next few stalls to grab the rest of the "hot" knobs. We put them all into the plastic bag. I slowly opened the door and saw a sergeant in camo coming down the hallway.

I panicked and whispered, "Lenny, MTL. Get in a toilet stall."

The door to the washroom opened. I could see his boots as he walked by both our stalls. Sitting there in a scared state, I didn't dare make any noise. My heart was racing. We heard him flush the urinal, then could hear him walking toward the showers. He used the sink, then left out the door. A couple minutes passed, and we both figured it would be safe.

Lenny and I hit the next few washrooms removing all the "H" knobs from all the showers. We finally met up with the others.

Justus told us quietly, "Okay, give me your bag of knobs. I'll put these in a safe spot. Go separate ways and head to your rooms. We'll meet at PT."

During PT, after our exercises, we jogged as I asked Justus, "Where did you stash the knobs?"

"I put them in the first-floor rec room behind the all-purpose monitor. I'm sure someone will find them...eventually."

After PT there was a mass panic. We had a handful of third-floor residents coming down to use our showers. Wilhelm, Justus and a few others refused to let them in; in fact, all of the second floor stood their ground. We overheard so many of them talking about the cold showers during breakfast, but the four of us kept our best poker faces on.

About once a week on various nights, the four of us would meet at precisely 0400. We called ourselves the "Four O'clock Committee." We figured we would stay on the third floor for these shenanigans. We didn't want to prank ourselves and if we "got" the first floor, they may catch on to who was doing the pranks. There was the Vaseline on the doorknobs to their rooms prank. The Saran wrap under the toilet seats. We locked each bathroom toilet stall from the inside and crawled under on the floor to get out. We would rearrange their rec room furniture. Another night, we pulled the circuit breakers to their rooms. Once the MTLs were getting serious about locating the elusive pranksters, we decided to lay low for a while.

———————

We were almost done with Phase Two when all fifty of us were called to the auditorium. Well, almost fifty. There were a handful that had to retake classes and a few that just could not hang on. They were to be reclassed into a completely new career field. I heard they got put into the Food Services field or Military Police.

Senior Kanan addressed us from the stage. "In two weeks, you will start Phase Three. I have all your current orders as to where you will be stationed and which ships you'll be maintaining. However, I won't give these until you finish Phase Two. Some of you may want to reconsider after you hear this next briefing. I have **Senior Sergeant Marston** here with a very important proposal for you. If you choose this new opportunity, and qualify for it, I will cancel your current orders and you will take this new route. Senior Marston, the floor is yours."

Senior Marston looked a little rough around the edges, but in a dignified way. He was tall, with a solid build and had short black and gray hair. He walked with confidence as he looked over the crowd.

He spoke with that same confidence. "In about two months, I will be leading an ADVON team. That's a team that arrives first with new equipment. We will be delivering a group of our newest and finest spaceships to their base of operation to be put out in the field for the first time. I have a crew of twenty experienced sergeants and a couple senior sergeants that have been training on this new ship throughout its production process and testing phases. We have also been working closely with over a dozen experienced flight crews that have transitioned over to fly this marvel of a ship."

"Our next goal is to take volunteers to be the first specialists to work this ship and test the Tech School training aspect," he continued. "You will be the very first to go through this new course. Over the next month, we plan on taking a few from each career field and giving you an overview of your systems. This will also be your primary ship once we deliver them to our next destination. This new ship is...you know, I think I'll just play the video."

Marston stepped aside and the video played on the theater's big screen. Music rumbled through the auditorium as the new spaceship was revealed coming out of a large hangar.

The narrator spoke slowly in a deep baritone. "Introducing the newest and most advanced spaceship in the known universe. Stealth capabilities, extremely maneuverable with its low-level terrain following systems, four super-ion engines that can be switched from air to space mode in an instance. An extremely powerful precise targeting tail gun. The most advanced computer systems including A.I. technology. Behold...the brave, the bold, the beautiful, the badass...B-43 bomber."

The video then showed a better look at this marvel, including videos of it in space. With its swept back wings, it almost had a fighter look to it; however, it was massive. It looked even larger than the B-X3.

We saw the inside as the narrator continued. "The flight deck consists of the two pilot seats with the newest technology of flight controls to include the advanced heads-up display. Behind them are the classified defensive countermeasures and the tail gunner crew positions. The lower deck contains the navigator and bombardier station."

There was another view of it flying, this time low level. Then it showed a series of vehicles, buildings, and hillsides being completely decimated by its guided bombs.

"Look for it! The new B-43 may be flying over your neighborhood soon!"

I was in awe. Goose bumps covered my arms.

Senior Marston walked back on stage. "There is a catch. There's always a catch, right? If you *qualify* to be accepted for this, you will accompany my team and the flight crews through the Kirkland Bridge to the Stella System. You'll still be able to return to Earth, on leave, every five years. That will also mean you will be required to extend your current enlistments. This is not a decision to be taken lightly. Senior Kanan, anything to add?"

Senior Sergeant Kanan walked on stage. "You have a big weekend coming up. If you want to apply for this, let your instructor know on Monday and we'll see if you qualify by the end of Phase Two. Are there any questions?"

Justus stood up.

Kanan sighed. "Yes, Specialist Johannes?"

"Can we decide *after* we see our original orders?"

"That's not how this works. No, we only want serious candidates."

Another specialist stood up.

"Yes, Specialist Harvard?"

"Sir, what are these qualifications?"

Kanan looked at Marston.

Marston answered. "We can only take a set number from each career field. I will personally look over your records and determine who I deem eligible."

That Friday, after class, we went to the local café. Justus was out; he'd failed the last end of block test and had to stay over to get remedial training. Jen, Pepper and I sat at our regular table.

Jen asked me, "Sam, what's this I hear about you having a bachelor's degree? Why am I always hearing things second hand?"

"What's your degree in?" Pepper asked.

"Aeronautics. I didn't think it was a big deal."

"You could have gone officer!" Jen said.

Pepper asked, "Why didn't you?"

"I told you my father retired as a colonel, right?" I responded.

They replied, "Yeah."

"I want to be an officer, like him."

Jen said sarcastically, "Well, you're off to great start, *specialist.*"

"No, really. I have heard so many stories from my father and he always told me the best officers were prior enlisted. Those that have walked in the boots of specialists and sergeants really understood everything better and made great leaders."

"Yeah but look at all the extra money you could've made!" Jen said.

"The way I see it, I get free room and board either way. I'll do four or five years, make sergeant, then transfer to officer."

Pepper sighed. "I wish I had my life figured out like you got yours."

Jen then asked, "So, are we going to discuss the elephant in the room?"

I was confused. "I do not understand that expression."

"That new bomber, trip to the cosmos, all that nonsense. Who would even volunteer for that? Being stuck light years away, only coming home once every five years."

"Yeah, but those new bombers look so freaking cool," Pepper said. "Imagine being in space launching from a space station."

"It sounds like you want to go," Jen said.

"Well, yeah. Besides my brother is out there on one of the Stella stations. He's five years older than me. It'd be great to be stationed near him."

Jen turned to me. "Sam, you're quiet. What's up?"

"Nothing," I answered. "I am just excited to return home."

"Huh?" Jen asked.

"I already made my decision. I am a B-43 maintainer."

"How do you even know you'll qualify?"

"My grades are the best in the class. Listen, you all can make your own decisions, but I belong there. I loved living on Station Prime."

"What was so great about it?" Jen asked.

"The lack of options."

"Explain."

"There is just too much on Earth. Too many people. Too much drama. This may sound crazy to you, but I like only eating at one place. I can just go to the cafeteria, look around and pick what I want. I don't want to think about what I should eat every single day. My grade school class sizes were small; I knew every kid my age. Everywhere I walked, I would see people I knew. I could go to the movie theater on station and probably name half the people in there. That small community was a paradise. No worries, you didn't have to drive anywhere, there was almost no crime. There was order. Most people respected each other. I just want to go back to that environment."

Jen looked frustrated. "Well, it'll be different now. Now you'll have a job and real responsibilities."

Pepper was smiling. "You know, everything you're describing sounds cool, real cool."

Jen looked at her. "So I guess you've both made up your minds."

"Do you keep in touch with any of these kids you grew up with?" Pepper asked me.

"Not really, not after my sixteen-year delay."

"Oh, yeah. I forgot about that, sorry."

Pepper was doing math in her head and then asked another question. "Did you know a kid named Aaron York?"

"I don't think so. I didn't know a lot of their last names. Did he have any siblings?"

"No siblings at that point. His parents were Sharyn and Marcus."

My face lit up. "Yes! A-A-Ron, we called him. He was seven years younger than me. I watched him grow up. I only remember his parents' names because I used to babysit him."

Pepper turned her head fast and spit out her coffee. "Shut the front door!" She stood up with her hand over her mouth.

"What's going on?" Jen asked.

"Pepper, what's your full name?" I said.

"Patricia York. Pepper's just my nickname."

Jen asked, "You okay?!"

"Aaron's my father!" Pepper said. "You babysat my dad!"

Jen looked confused. "How is this even possible?"

"Space bridge," I explained. "It took me sixteen years to get back. A-A-Ron left when he was six. He must have gotten lucky without much of a delay. During all those years I was frozen, he grew up. After that he got married, then had Patricia's brother...and her."

Pepper sat down and said, "This is insane."

"How is A-A-Ron now?" I asked.

"First of all, stop calling him that. Aaron, my dad, is great and still married to my mom. He works for a construction company. He doesn't remember a whole lot from space, but I have heard all sorts of stories from my grandparents, Sharyn and Marcus. You know they actually met and got married up there."

Another morning, another PT session. Sam, Justus, Wilhelm, and even the twins, **Pete and Simon Ward**, all jogged together.

Justus asked Wilhelm, "How was Phase Two in the land of Crew Chiefs?"

Wilhelm answered, "Going great. First, we learned all the mar-shaling signals; that took a bit to memorize, and included a detailed test over it all. We even had to go through a practice run outside where an instructor drove a truck to simulate a ship taxiing in and out. We covered all the pre- and post-flight inspections, fueling procedures, servicing and so forth. I'm enjoying it, and just can't wait to do it for real."

"Same here. What about you two, Ward twins? I hate that I don't know which of you is which?"

Pete answered. "It's simple. I'm Pete, the smart one."

"Smart ass," Simon said. "He may be book smart, but I'm stronger and wiser. Simon here."

Justus asked, "So how is Weapon's training?"

"We're busy every day," Pete answered.

"Can't be too hard. All you do is load the bombs, right?"

"Are you kidding? There is so much more. Knowing all the different bomb types and correct loading configurations. Learning to drive and coordinate those jammers was a challenge. We need to approach the ship carefully while our other team members spot us in. Then you must use the controls with precision to get them to the exact spot to lift the bombs. They say we need to practice so many times that it becomes second nature without thinking, an extension of us. After that, we also need to know how bomb integration works, attaching everything to the ships so they can communicate with all avionics systems."

Simon added, "Pete, don't forget the C.R.A.T.E.S."

"What are crates?" I asked.

Pete answered, "C.R.A.T.E.S. stands for Cargo Relocate Air Transport Equipment System. These huge containers can be loaded into the bomb-bays with our jammers, when there are no weapons loaded. They're used to transport cargo."

"So, they are huge boxes to store stuff in. Why not just call them crates?"

"We do call them C.R.A.T.E.S."

"Why do they even need them? Just send a cargo ship."

"It's so they don't have to rely on the cargos."

Justus asked, "So, then what about the bombs? Will the cargo ships deliver them?"

"I don't know. We just learned about it."

The rest of Phase Two wasn't bad. We all helped Justus pass the written exams while they all helped me with the physical maintenance aspect.

TRAINING MONTAGE, cue the Rocky music...

In the flightdeck simulator with headsets on
System checks on the simulators
Hands being raised in class

Studying in the barracks
Uniform inspections
Classroom lectures
Running during PT
Marching to class
Taking tests
Changing the Satellite Antenna
Hooking up power to the ship
Checking wires for voltage
Looking at wire diagrams
Studying at the chow hall
Marching in the rain
Safety wiring parts
PT sit-ups
An instructor drawing a complex system on the smart board
Sam teaching Justus the same system in the barracks
Stealing all the third floor's toilet paper
More looking at wire diagrams
More part removals
More marching
More studying
More running
More tests
Sam and Justus racing fast up the steps of the base library, got
to the top, arms in the air...slow it down, then freeze

CHAPTER 5

Real World

At the schoolhouse, Senior Sergeant Kanan addressed all of us. "I will display each set of orders, and which ships you will be assigned to. After which you will go to your new classrooms and start Phase Three. These are locked in, no going back."

The senior continued, "First is the brand-new B-43 bomber course. Since this is an experimental course, they are only taking two from each career field. From all those that applied and qualified, here are the names." He displayed them on the big screen. "Those that are on the list need to report to classroom A317 to start Phase Three."

On the screen:

B-43: (Orders: Space Station Prime, Stella System)
Electro-Environmental: Lenny C. Bronson and Seth J. Harvard
Engines: Maisie F. Elton and Manny F. Eastern
Weapons: Peter C. Ward and Simon P. Ward
Hydraulics: Phillip S. Merrick and Jack T. Flange
Crew Chiefs: Patricia B. York and Burrt S. Wilhelm
Avionics: Justus M. Johannes and Jennifer P. Thompson

Report to Room A317.

We all looked at the list. The others were silent. I stared at the list a second time, reading the names again. *How is this even possible? This can't be right.* I kept reading the list, but I could not make the name Sam Kirkland appear. I had to rethink everything. Justus, Pepper, and Jen looked at me with the same look of surprise and shock. The new B-43 maintainers left.

Kanan displayed the C-345 new maintainers, then those specialists left. Then was the C-113s, after which there were only a few of us left in the room. I finally saw my name on the very last slide. My new job would be to repair and maintain a fleet of old BC-76ers that operated out of North Dakota.

I was surprised they still flew those dinosaur ships. I was told which classroom to report to. The five of us in the class made our way across the schoolhouse to a tiny classroom at the end of the hall. Then an old civilian instructor walked in. He was wearing shorts, and everyone noticed right away he had a robotic leg. He introduced himself as Mr. Tom Jackson.

The day was boring as we were given our course work and received a general overview of these BC-76 bomber-cargo hybrids. We found out the only time we'd go to space was during an off-chance we would have to fix one up there if it was stranded. *This was not what I predicted. How did this happen? I did everything I possibly could to get to space. Why did Jen and Justus get in? I nearly aced all the end of block tests.*

"Specialist Kirkland. Kirkland!" shouted Mr. Jackson.

"Sorry, sir."

"I asked you a question. What do you know about avionics?"

"Sorry, sir. avionics are the electrical components used for aerospace vehicles. In our case, it's the career field that inspects, services, and repairs communications, navigation, automatic flight controls, and electronic warfare systems."

"Okay, thanks for the book definition. But what does it mean for us?"

"Sorry, I don't know what answer you're looking for?"

The lesson continued as he asked the other students the same question and then started breaking down each system into smaller subsystems. Lunch time came. The other four filed out.

I said, "Mr. Jackson, I don't feel too good. Do you mind I if I skip lunch and stay here and look over this course material?"

"Sure, no problem."

The rest of the day was not much better as we covered more

of that old ship. We marched back and I did everything I could to avoid talking to anyone.

The next morning, Justus met up with me at PT while we jogged. "Hey Sam," Justus said, "you okay? I haven't seen you."

"What do you think?"

"Listen I just want to you know, Jen and I talked with Senior Marston. I begged him to pick you. Hell, even Jen said she'd give up her orders for them to pick you over her."

"What'd he say?"

"He went on and on about how these things don't work this way. He picked the crew for a specific reason and can't just swap orders around because people are butt-hurt about it."

"That figures."

"Man, I don't how I got in. This doesn't make sense. What orders did you get?"

"North Dakota."

"Ah man, I'm sorry, dude. Hey, maybe we can still fight this one."

"What's done is done. I can wait it out a few years, make sergeant, become an officer, then do what I can to get to space."

"Who knows, maybe you'll go to Stella and work with me. Actually, I'll be working for you. I'll tell you right now, I'm not gonna salute you."

"Yeah, you will! Race you to the end!"

"You're on!"

We got cleaned up, ate a fast breakfast, and formed up into our marching flights at the barracks.

Senior Sergeant Mast addressed us. "Does anyone know the whereabouts of Specialist Jen Thompson?"

We all looked at each other wide-eyed. Pepper looked concerned.

Senior Mast continued. "No one will get in trouble. We just want to make sure she is okay. No one has seen her since last night. If anyone has information, please let us know."

It was another morning of my small class learning our ship. I found out they had a decommissioned model here at Tech School that we would be practicing changing out parts on. The instructor said the infrared scanner was tricky to change, but we'd learn the process.

At lunch, I met up with Pepper and Justus in the Chow Hall. Pepper was almost in tears as we sat at the table.

She told us, "I talked with Jen last night. She was upset, she was crying. She kept telling me how scared she was to go to space. She was terrified of the whole cryo-freezing process. Afraid she'd wake up losing countless years of her life. Jen was at the point of hyper-ventilating. I did everything I could to calm her down. The only reason she signed up was for us. She didn't think she'd be selected. She even told Senior Marston that she was done. He told her there was no backing out. The only way she could back out was to be reclassed to another job and start the whole Tech School process again."

Pepper looked around the Chow Hall to see if anyone of authority was within earshot, then said quietly, "Jen asked me how much trouble would she get into if she just left and went back home. I didn't know what to think. I kept telling her things would work out."

"You think she ran?" Justus asked.

Pepper replied, "Yes, yes, I do. I even tried messaging her and calling her...no answer."

The next two days were more of the same. We still had not heard from Jen. Towards the end of the third day, we were talking in class about the A5009 junction box when Mr. Jackson got a message on his tablet.

He looked at me. "Kirkland, Senior Marston needs to see you in his office."

"Yes, sir."

I approached the office and gave a reporting statement and he had me sit down across from his desk.

Marston started. "First things first, your friend Jen Thompson is safe. She was found halfway between here and Arizona. I'm sorry, but they don't treat these AWOL situations well around here. I don't expect to see her again. Secondly, I am *considering* putting you into the B-43 course."

"Yes, sir, I would love that!"

"Hold on. I said I am only *considering* it. There are other candidates. I need to ask you; do you know why you weren't selected?"

"No, sir. My grades were top. I really don't know."

"That's just it. You don't know. Grades aren't everything. I've worked with some of the best maintainers out there and am a pretty good judge of what works. The last three years, my team and I learned every possible thing we could about that new bomber and worked hard developing this course. Now I am going to take this crew to the outer reaches of space. We'll be the only ones out there that understand this ship. There will be no one else to turn to."

The senior continued. "I need maintainers that can think for themselves, not just memorize words on a page. I need those that can troubleshoot unique solutions, not just what is written in black and white. Our lives may depend on it out there. You're a smart kid, I'll give you that. I've been reviewing everyone's records, and you are just too linear. Too by-the-book without considering the best option for each unique situation."

"Sir, is everyone on your team able to think outside the box?"

"Of course they are. I handpicked them."

"Sir, maybe now you need someone to think logically to balance it all out."

The next morning, I arrived in my new B-43 class along with the other eleven specialists from various career fields. It was strange. There were no chairs or furniture in this large room except one instructor desk. We stood around a sizable area with multiple large squares outlined on the floor with tape. I saw the team of B-43 instructors who were part of Marston's ADVON team, as well as a few of our Phase Two instructors there.

I asked Justus, "What are those instructors doing here?"

"They're students, like us."

"What?"

"No, really. They are learning how to teach this class. Once the ADVON team leaves, it'll be up to them to continue teaching all this for the next group of students."

Sergeant Carlson instructed us, "Listen up, class. I need everyone to go through the next lesson, wherever you left off from yesterday. Johannes, show Kirkland what to do and where to find lesson one for Avionics. I'll be monitoring all your progress. Feel free to ask any instructor if you have questions."

I was surprised to see a set of Virtual Reality kits in the closet. We each grabbed one and Justus showed me how to operate the VR set and which controls did what. I put on the goggles and gloves. After selecting "Lesson One," I was in.

I was in a different world. In front of me was a B-43. I could look in every direction by turning my head. I followed the hint arrows as I approached the ship and entered from the lower hatch. I was in the navigator's station. Following the instructions on the screen, I was able to bring up a navigator's computer. The instructions were identical to the technical data we would be using for real.

I went to the maintenance screen on the nav computer and typed in the correct circuit breaker numbers for my task that I would have to open electronically. The instructions then showed me a picture of which part I would be changing. Behind me was an entire rack of components. I looked at the instructions again and had to select the correct part before the program continued. *This was amazing*, I thought. For a second, I took off my goggles and looked around the room.

Everyone in the class had the VR sets on as they were all going through various motions for their career fields. I donned the set again and was staring at the electronics rack. I followed the instructions and disconnected various electrical plugs. When it was time to use hand tools, I looked down at a virtual toolbox and had to select the correct tools to remove the hardware, then the part. Once I put the bad part on the floor, it disappeared, displaying a new part. Going through the reverse actions, I installed this one, then "sat" back at the nav's station. I "closed" the circuit breakers and proceeded to run through the operational check following all the instructions button for button.

We spent all day on those bombers. Lesson after lesson. Many of the lessons were explained thoroughly by Senior Marston in the VR. The first two days, I had to stay after class in order to catch up to the rest of them. The Crew Chiefs learned to do pre- and post-flights, and various other tasks to include refuels and servicing. E&E, Hydro, and Engines were learning all their components, removals, and ops checks. The weapons team had separate simulators; they sat in a stationary jammer with their VR as they "drove" to and from the ships to remove and install munitions.

That Friday, our whole B-43 class went out to the local café. I looked around the table. Justus and Pepper sat next to each other, as always. The Engine troop **Manny Eastern** was eating his second dinner and was, by far, the largest member in the group. **Maisie Elton**, the other Engine maintainer, was talking with Hydro's **Phil Merrick** and **Jack Flange** as they were all showing each other their tattoos. They all agreed to get a new one the next day. The E&E tech **Seth Harvard** was in a deep conversation with Weapon's Pete concerning which comic book hero had the most money. The other Crew Chief and Weapon's troop, Wilhelm and Simon, were discussing last week's football games. Like E&E's Lenny, I just sat back and listened to it all, trying to predict what would come next for our new team.

———

Time flew by; we only had one week left. We all felt pretty good about this new bomber and the new course, learning all we could through the VR. Our last Friday night before graduation came as we met back up at the café, as usual.

Wilhelm asked, "Where's Pepper and Justus?"

"Oh, you didn't hear?" Maisie answered.

"No..."

"They got busted! An MTL caught Justus coming out of Pepper's room late last night."

"No way!"

She added, "Yeah, they lost their off-base privileges and have to work all weekend cleaning the barracks."

"That sucks," Lenny responded. "Sneak in *one time* and they put the hammer down."

Maisie laughed. "One time? He's been sneaking in there for weeks. They just finally got caught."

———

Monday morning PT is where I caught up with Justus as we jogged. "Hey, how did your work weekend go?"

"Hell. It started with a room inspection and uniform inspections...multiple. I even had to get in my Service Dress for the first part. Then it was an all-day affair of cleaning every area of the barracks. They even took us over to that park where everyone hangs out on Friday and Saturday nights."

"Oh, PDA park?"

Yeah. Talk about a mess of trash and whatnot. I'm actually happy about getting back to class."

"How did Pepper take it?"

"The same. She was out there as well, cleaning and getting yelled at. We stayed apart for the most part, otherwise the MTLs would have been all over us."

"So, you can still finish the course, right?"

"Oh yeah. At first Senior Mast said we'd be washed back a few weeks. Then I think he may have talked to Senior Marston. The next thing you know, we were back in."

"Good to hear."

———

We made it to the classroom, where Senior Sergeant Marston addressed us. "Although, we can't work on an actual Bully, we do have something tangible for everyone."

Wilhelm raised his hand. "Sir, you said *Bully*. We've heard that term before..."

"That's the nickname for the bombers, the B-43 *Bully*."

Maisie responded, "I like it. We bully the enemy, then blow 'em up."

Senior Marston shook his head and clarified. "No, that's not it. The term bully originated as 'being brave' or 'great job'. It's a term that takes us back to those first years of flying with the Wright brothers."

"President Theodore Roosevelt," I added.

"Bully for you, Kirkland! Let's move on, everyone. This lesson is for all career fields. The Digital Verifiers or DVs are essentially the black boxes on the Bullies. Although these are maintained by the Avionics Techs, you all need to be familiar with how they work. These will record everything the ships do. They even record errors or glitches that the pilots may not even see. The DVs will be your guide to diagnose the systems. They will give you a run-down of faults, and even have Artificial Intelligence."

Marston continued, "The DVs will calculate all past errors and estimate the best possible solution as to where to check or which parts to change. I can't stress this enough: in no way do they replace good old-fashioned troubleshooting! However, they're a good place to start. You can use them on the ships, or physically bring them to your respected Debrief office to download. Sergeant Carlson, will you do the honors?"

The instructor left the room and returned carrying a small remote. Rolling behind him on its own was a shiny, pristine, orange and black rectangular box with four small wheels. Its shape was similar to carry-on luggage as its dimensions were about a foot wide on each side and almost two feet tall. Sergeant Carlson handed the remote to Lenny and told him to walk around. Everywhere Lenny went, the DV followed a couple paces behind him.

"DVs each have a name," Senior Marston continued, "dependent on which ship they belong to. For example, this one is assigned to Ship 5050, its name is DV5050. We have DV1895, DV26, DV310, and so forth. Once on location, you can program it to do a slew of options. For example, you can walk it from the ship's parking spot to the location of your Debrief office. Debrief is where it can download all its flight information and findings to your maintenance computers. Once programed to that specific location, it'll roll there by itself and will even find its way back to the ship. Since we will be on a space station, they even have a lower adapter that will connect to the track system. Because they record vital information, the ships can't launch without them. The DVs are installed under each ship just aft of the bomb-bays. They are uplifted to their slot, connected to the ship and remain there during the flight."

Justus asked, "What are those silver soda can things on its head?"

"Good question. One is the UAB, Underwater Acoustic Beacon. It lets us locate it if the ship crashes and is submerged in water. The other canister is the SAB, Space Acoustic Beacon. This will activate a signal if exposed to extreme pressure changes, as in the vacuum of space. There is another identical set of these beacons on the B-43 ship for redundancy. I want you all to load the DV program on your VR. This will show you how to physically load these into these units to ships, as well as how to do the digital downloads and fault isolations."

———

It was finally graduation day. We arrived at the schoolhouse in our Military Dress Uniforms. Our entire class would be leaving for space in less than a week. Other students that were in various classes a few months behind us were in attendance as a *rent-a-crowd*. Senior Sergeant Kanan and Marston were handing out our course completion certificates. After receiving mine, I looked out and saw my father standing off to the side clapping for me. I couldn't believe he came out here for this. I was in shock! I immediately went over to him to thank him for coming. He gave me a big hug.

Senior Kanan then addressed us. "Congratulations to the very first B-43 Class!" After the crowd's clapping, he continued, "We have a special guest today—the man who figured out the mystery of the space bridge, allowing fast and safe travel for us all. Mr. Kirkland, retired colonel. Thank you so much for joining us."

They all clapped, yet there were many surprised looks from those that never knew the connection between us.

Afterward, our entire class went out to dinner; my father insisted. Well, everyone except Justus. Apparently, he was mouthing off to an MTL a couple days ago and was put on another clean-up duty and base restrictions.

My father picked an expensive Italian restaurant and paid for it all. Everyone was asking different questions about space and the Stella System. I didn't mind. I just sat back and enjoyed every moment of it. Pepper even asked him about her grandparents,

Marcus and Sharyn. He told us all about a crazy maintenance response team that her grampa was on that rescued a stranded ship in space. Apparently, they found an EMP bomb hidden inside a food crate. Then they had to figure out how to get power back on this stranded ship. Pepper just nodded and laughed, as she had heard this story a few times from her grandpa. It was all laughs and fun throughout the meal. I thanked my father for coming out for this as he wished me the best of luck. I really couldn't have been happier.

The next week, we all departed for space. We would leave the Earth's atmosphere then be transported to a massive vessel that would carry hundreds of us on it. These vessels would be carrying the eight B-43 bombers in the aft cargo hold hangar. Even all the new flight crews for the new Bullies would be coming, along with Marston and his ADVON team of maintainers. Once on the massive transport vessel, we would be put into cryo-sleep, not aging nor waking for about a month until we arrived at the Stella System, eight light-years away.

ACT II

CHAPTER 6

I Ain't Happy

I'm feeling glad. *Those damn birds continue to squawk.* My eyes opened a bit. Everything was cloudy. Lights were flashing rapidly across the room. Alarms were blaring with a constant pulse. *Those aren't alarms; those are birds. I am flying.* Maybe I should get up. *No, I can't get up. I'm flying with the birds. If I get up, I will surely fall. More damn birds squawking, over and over again. Will they every stop? Wait, am I up? I think I am in a chair. I need more sleep. Where are the birds?* Alarms continued. I was slumped over, sitting in a chair wearing only my underwear. *Where's my bed? I'm cold, I need a pillow and blanket. The squawking continued...*

I heard a stranger speak. "Hey! I'm going to give you a series of shots."

I was poked in the arm multiple times. Then a man's face appeared through my narrow vision. *Is he flying, too? Why didn't he fall?*

He looked at me and grabbed my hand. "Here, take this bottle. Drink the whole thing." He put my other hand on the large Thermos, as well. He continued, "After you finish the entire drink, go to the that room." He pointed across the way to the room with flashing lights. "Do you understand?"

I tried to answer with slurred drunk-like speech. "Um, drink... can I sleep?"

"No, this is an emergency! Drink it, then go to that room."

"Okay then."

I turned slowly to see the nice man attending to a different guy in his underwear who was lying face-down on the floor next to me. People in front of me were stumbling and falling. I laughed.

I heard screams, lots of screaming. *People are crazy*, I thought. I saw a woman run completely naked across the cold blurry area in front of me. *This has to be dream.* I sipped my fake drink amidst the chaos. *What's going on? This can't be real.* I closed my eyes. The birds continued to squawk. I was flying next to them. I heard more voices. "Get up! Get to the supply room!"

Maybe this is real.

I took another swig of the purple-colored drink. The taste did not agree with me this time. I tried to stand up as the room started to sway to the left. I fell onto a table that partially caught my fall.

"Excuse me, Mr. Table," I said. *Maybe I was the one swaying.* I tried to walk towards the room with the flashing lights. People were all over, running and stumbling all around me. Lots of unnecessary yelling and those alarms going off. I entered the room and my blurred vision made out a gamut of men and women in their underwear rummaging through supply crates.

The place smelt of clean mildew.

I said, "Ah, new uniforms, ha! Smells like Boot Camp."

People were frantically scrounging through the clothes and getting dressed.

I felt someone catch me as I was falling. "Sam, it's Justus!" he said, as he grabbed me and caught my drink.

"Hello there," I slurred happily.

"I dunno what's going on. Here, drink the rest of your stuff." Just as Justus handed me my purple liquid, he threw up on the floor all over both our bare feet.

I laughed. "Ha! It's purple."

He wiped his face with his arm. "Sam, have you seen Pepper or the others?"

"Nope, not here."

A female voice bellowed from across the room. "This is an emergency! There has been an accident! You are still on the transport vessel. I need everyone to get dressed. There is no time to find your personal gear. Just grab some random camo or coveralls. Put boots on. Then follow the green arrows on the floor to the staging area... You need to hurry!"

"Come on, Sam." Justus grabbed me as we stumbled to a random crate.

People were grabbing clothes like crazy. It was a sea of flesh, white bras, panties and underwear in every direction. Justus and I each grabbed a set of coveralls. We made our way to the crate of boots. The first two sets were too small. I found some that might fit. They were too big, but who cares.

The voice yelled again. "Hurry! Get something on and follow the arrows. Get a move on!"

Justus and I headed out. We stumbled as we walked.

Then I slurred, "Hey, I'm swaying right and you're swaying left. We should hang on to each other to keep centered."

"That's a great id—" Justus tried to get the words out but he vomited again all over his left leg.

We hung onto each other and followed the massive crowd as the alarms continued to ring. Justus kept looking around to see if he could find Pepper in the gaggle of camo-dressed young men and women all falling over each other after being stuck in cryo-sleep for who knows how long. I looked down at the two of us: boots not tied, no socks, coveralls zipper partially down, no undershirt. Drill Sergeant Stone's head would explode at this sight.

The crowd stopped as we were led into a huge open area. Hundreds of us were in there. Some were wide-eyed and pacing back and forth. Others hunched over, throwing up. I saw a few dozen sprawled out on the floor as if they were passed out. The alarms finally stopped ringing. Justus and I stood there trying to make sense of it all. More people were shuffling in as a man climbed a ladder towards the front of the crowd.

The man spoke. "Listen up! Listen up!" He was holding a microphone and we could hear him throughout the vessel's intercom system. The crowd's noise died down to an eerie silence. He continued. "Listen! I am Brigadier General Eastwood. There was an accident as soon as we entered the Stella System. We were hit! I don't know by what, maybe asteroids, maybe enemy fire. That doesn't matter right now." General Eastwood's head lowered. "We lost several cryo-bays in the blast...A lot of people are dead."

Justus was in a severe panic looking around for the others.

The general continued, "I am going to be very direct since we don't have time. This vessel is losing life support functions as we speak. We have a plan to get every single one of us to safety. I need everyone to remain calm and focus on this current plan. Right now, I need all the B-43 flight crews, ship maintainers, and any other Flightline maintenance functions to stand on the left section of this area." He pointed to his right. "All medical, firefighters, and military police in the middle. Lastly, shuttle pilots and everyone else to your right. It doesn't matter if you just got out of Tech School. Go to your assigned section."

We shuffled to our left as everyone was crossing each other. The general continued. "We have already called for help from the space stations. They will be sending cargo ships for us. However, we are on the other side of this system, so it'll take them a few days to reach us. There just isn't time to stay on this sinking vessel. We aren't that far from the moon Viridis, and we will rendezvous there. Captain Leslie, raise your hand. Everyone on the right, follow the captain. You will start to board the small escape shuttles. Maintainers and flight crews follow Major Warfield. The emergency crews will stay here for now and help clear the rest of us off this transport, then board the remaining shuttles."

We followed our group through the hallways and continued to hear General Eastwood through the echoing intercom speakers. "Those tiny shuttles have enough oxygen for a while, but it is only a temporary solution. The shuttles can't make it through the atmosphere to land on the moon. The B-43 flight crews and maintainers will head to the main hangar and board the ships. We'll pack those bombers with as many people as we can and head to Viridis. As soon as they land on that moon, they'll dump off the passengers and return to space to get more from the shuttles. Pilots, I hope you all remember the shuttle linking system. These bombers will dock with the shuttles and transfer the passengers through the hatches. Then the B-43s will repeat this process until everyone is saved. We need to work together on this one. Our priority right now is to get off this dying transport!"

There were eight B-43s lined up in this top hangar of the massive transport vessel. Each one was secured via a locking mechanism on their landing gear. As we were waiting, we found the rest of our class. All twelve of us were there. Justus gave Pepper a very long hug. I could see tears of relief in his eyes. Then a lieutenant started counting us off into groups of ten and directed each group to whichever bomber they were assigned to.

I was in a group with Wilhelm, Maisie, Lenny, and a few others. Climbing aboard the B-43, we headed up the ladder. With the crew aboard in all the seats, we had to find a place to sit on the floor between the pilots and defense station. A couple had to stay on the lower level behind the navigators.

We sat there for a while, cramped next to each other, looking wide-eyed at everything. The crew was going through a series of checks fast. It wasn't long before I heard the massive ion engines engage. I felt the vibrations as the ship shook. I could hear the other bombers echoing in the hangar of this enormous transport vessel. Straining my head, I could barely see out the pilots' window. There was a ship in front of us. Then a massive door opened revealing the expanse of space behind it. Our ship continued to rumble. The B-43 in front of us took off like a bat out of hell. I watched as our pilot raised his hand and released the locking mechanism. The acceleration was so fast that I fell back fast, landing into Wilhelm hard. I thought he would have screamed, but he just made an "uff" sound as we tried to hang on. Once we were in space, there was an eerie calm as we continued our journey to Viridis.

Before we entered the moon's atmosphere, the navigator came up the ladder and yelled, "Take these and strap yourselves down by any means possible!"

He handed out a bunch of cargo straps. We thought he was joking at first. We did as we were instructed. We wrapped these straps across and around anything we could find to include ourselves, securing them tight. As we entered the atmosphere. The shaking was intense as we were all being pulled hard. The bunch of us strapped to the floor were hanging on to each other waiting for the insanity to stop.

―――――――――――

The bombers landed on Viridis and made a short taxi to a spot. We deboarded the ship and stood looking around, trying to figure out our next course of action. The sky had a purple tint to it with a slight cloud coverage. It was hot here, but not too bad. In the not too far distance, we could see the vast, never-ending expanse of the water. There was a calm ocean breeze that had a certain smell that took me back to the vacations I'd had here. It was the same scent I sensed whenever I imagined that photo of my mom sitting on the beach. I felt home, yet at the same time as far away from it as possible. If my mom could see me now...

The other ships had landed and people were departing them fast.

Justus yelled to our other maintainers, "Over here!"

We found the rest of our class and the twelve of us grouped together. Justus had his arm around Pepper. Half of us were wearing maintenance coveralls, the others were in camo pants and button shirts. A few only had the pants and T-shirts. We were relieved to be safely off that transport. One thing was for sure, the haze of drowsiness and cloudy effects of the cryo-freeze seemed to be gone.

Maisie turned to Manny. "I'm surprised you found pants that fit."

"It did take me while, but these are *really* comfortable," Manny answered.

"When's she due?"

"What?"

"You know you're wearing maternity pants, right?"

"Oh, what the hell!"

We all started laughing.

Pepper said, "Hey we should definitely hit that beach later."

We all agreed.

A man in a flight suit approached us and spoke fast. "Are you maintenance?!"

We answered, "Yes sir."

"I'm **Major Warfield**. I'm a pilot...and for now in charge of this mess. Where is Marston and his team, the ADVON team?"

Pepper answered, "We haven't seen them at all."

"Damn, they might be on the last ship. Listen, we have way too many shuttles in space full of passengers. We need to send these ships back up to retrieve them fast before they run out of oxygen. There are even more people waiting from the dying transport to get into a shuttle once we retrieve the others. It's going to take us many trips. The Viridis people here are letting us use their airfield. Right now, we need to launch these first four ships back up there. We need a Crew Chief on each spot to marshal them out."

"We only have two Crew Chiefs," Pepper said.

The Major spoke with frustration and authority. "Let me be blunt. Figure it out. Right now, I need four of you to hit those first four ships."

Pepper, Wilhelm, Maisie, and Manny went to the ships. I could see Pepper trying to explain to the Engine Troops what to do.

Major Warfield continued. "All these ships have their bomb bays full of the C.R.A.T.E.S. Do we have anyone that can download those?"

Pete and Simon raised their hands. "We can. That is, if there are any jammers, you know, weapons loaders."

"We used to operate out of this airfield years ago. See what you can find. There is a vehicle yard over there. Those crates contain food, water, medical supplies, tools, spare parts and other equipment. We need them downloaded fast. You don't need to download all the crates, just the ones we need."

The Major continued, "Start on the next set of bombers. Once those essential crates are down, we'll need to launch the second set of ships. We also need someone to get with the locals here and coordinate the fuel trucks. We can make one more trip up there, but after that, we'll need to refuel."

We all agreed.

Major Warfield then said, "One more thing. Once that ADVON team comes, things will get much easier. I gotta go and coordinate the rest of these flights. If you need anything I'll be in that building trying to talk with the locals in the Control Tower."

The major ran off.

I told the group, "We need to prioritize and split up."

Pete jumped in. "We learned that the DVs on each ship can tell us what's in each of the C.R.A.T.E.S."

I answered, "Great. Find out which ones have the tools and parts first."

Pete and Simon ran towards the ships to check the DVs.

Then I asked, "Who wants to find the fuel trucks?"

Our E&E team stepped up. Lenny and Harvard headed to talk with the locals at the airfield about the fuel trucks.

The remaining four of us ran towards the area that contained the vehicles. It was just Hydro and Avionics left. Merrick, Flange, Justus and I were running. We watched the first ship taxi out of its spot. Pepper was waving her arms directing it out, then gave the indication for the turn; lastly, she gave it a brisk salute. Then she ran over to the next spot to ensure Manny did it right. We could also see the next set of bombers landing.

We entered the vehicle yard that was full of old trucks and generator units. I was glad we didn't have to mess with those power carts, since our new B-43s were self-contained and didn't require them. Right away, we spotted a weapon loading jammer.

Staring at the short, forklift-type vehicle, I said, "Maybe we should have brought a Weapons Troop."

Justus jumped in the seat of the jammer. "How hard can it be?"

He pressed the start button…nothing.

Flange noticed something. "The fuel gauge, it's empty."

I checked one of the nearby trucks. "This has fuel."

Merrick asked, "Whatcha thinking?"

I answered, "We can transfer the gas. All we'll need is a four-foot clear hose, rubber gloves, a gas can, an air pump, and possibly some adapters for the pump…"

Before we knew it, Justus had found an old plastic tube, opened the gas cap, put the line in, sucked the gas out and let it siphon into a bucket. We filled the jammer, then Justus drove it out to the ships.

As soon as we approached, Wilhelm ran up and yelled, "Ship 0086 has a hydro leak!" Merrick and Flange ran to the Bully with Wilhelm.

We met up with Pete and Simon. They were correct; the DV units told them exactly what each C.R.A.T.E.S. contained. We made the one with tools our priority. Pete guided Simon as he carefully approached the ship and engaged the crate in the bomb bay with the jammer. He made sure all the connections were correct and guided Simon as they downloaded this large crate, bringing it to the side of the Flightline.

Merrick came back shirtless with only his camo pants and boots on. He yelled, "Did you get those tools yet?"

"Where's your shirt?" I asked him.

"Right here." He held up his wet and dirty T-shirt. "I had to use it to clean the hydro leak. I need a wrench."

Justus answered as he had the first crate opened and was locating boxes. "Yeah, I think I got a toolbox, yep."

Merrick opened the toolbox, grabbed a wrench, and ran off with his shirt in his hand.

While going through the crates, we found a case of headsets. I quickly grabbed a bunch and ran from ship to ship giving them to our marshallers. I got to Maisie; she was already wearing a spare headset she got from the flight crew.

Maisie said, "Just in time. They got an engine problem on this one!"

"But you're Engines!"

"I know. Stay here and monitor ground. I'll check the engine. Set your headset to station three."

She ran to the ship and went up the forward hatch.

I thought, *monitor ground? What am I even doing?*

Then I heard the flight crew over my wireless headset's interphone. "Ground, we're starting engine one, are we clear? Hello... are we clear? I'm talking to you in front of the ship!"

"Sorry. Explain. What am I looking for?"

"Engine one is the first one on the ship's left, your right. Is there no one around it? I'm about to start it."

"Yes, you are clear. Good to go, sir."

The enormous beast of the engine started right away. The pilot asked again, "Ready to start the rest; are we still good?"

"Yes, sir, all are good. You are clear."

Justus ran up and handed me a couple of marshaling wands, then ran off to the other ships. Not long after that they had all four engines going. Maisie ran out and joined me. The pilot said he was ready to taxi. Maisie guided me through the marshalling process.

After my ship taxied, I saw the twins had already downloaded two of the C.R.A.T.E.S. from Ship 3034. There was now a fuel truck parked next to it.

I approached Pepper and Seth and asked, "I didn't think these needed fuel yet?"

"They don't, but we are going to top this off for practice," Pepper said. She introduced me to the fuel driver. "This is Filmu. I think that's his name... He showed us the process to hook this hose up. There is a bit of a language gap."

"How much of a gap?"

"Do you speak Viridis?"

"No."

"Well...there's that much of a gap," she said. "Anyways, Wilhelm is up in the flight deck monitoring the fuel transfer. The flight crew is doing their walk around. Once done, they'll be the next to go up."

Major Warfield approached us. "Has Marston's ADVON team arrived yet?"

We looked at him and shook our heads no. He quickly boarded the ship. Once we were done fueling, Pepper disconnected the line and secured the panel. We walked around to the front of the ship, thinking of what was next on our list. Just then, the major came storming out of the ship and threw his headset clear across the parking spot. I could see it hit the ground as broken pieces flew off it.

Warfield screamed, "Aaaah! Noooo!" He fell to the ground on his knees. Pepper and I ran to him as he stared up to the sky.

Justus ran over as well. The major tried to compose himself but couldn't. He just sat down on the concrete as Pepper gently grabbed his arm. A couple more flight crew members came out.

Pepper consoled him. "Tell us what's wrong."

The major just stared straight ahead as if he was looking past everything. He had tears in his eyes and spoke slowly. "I just got off the radio...They're dead, all of them. Marston and the entire maintenance ADVON team. Their entire cryo-wing, along with some medical and support personnel...The blast, the initial blast...They're gone...just gone."

With no time to think, we continued to work, shaken by the news, unsure of the future, knowing no relief was coming. The next three ships went up without much of an issue. The last ship was having a problem. They called Engines out, but Manny and Maisie couldn't figure it out. I ran up there with Justus.

Manny told us, "Engines won't start. It won't let us try to start it. We keep getting this error code."

We looked at it as the pilot's screen that read:

DV310: ERR CD 12 - A.H.U.D./242/.

Justus looked at me. "What's that mean?"

"I don't know."

"What do mean, you don't know? You know everything."

At this point, both pilots were looking at us.

"I need our tablets. That's I need. Without the tech data…"

Justus said, "We don't have them. We couldn't find any yet. Stop thinking and just do."

"Alright, let's break this down. DV310. We're on Ship 0310, right?"

"Yeah."

"Okay, so it's trying tell us something."

"I think that means error code twelve."

"Yeah, we just need to find out what code twelve is."

Maisie asked, "What's that number 242?"

"That might be a circuit breaker," I said.

I quickly brought up the maintenance page and found the circuit breaker list:

242 – AFT HTC UNIT DR.

I was still confused.

Justus said, "Aft hatch unit. The DV *is* trying to tell us something." He quickly went down the ladder as we followed.

We all saw the issue. The panel aft of the bomb bay securing the DV unit was slightly ajar. As I was trying to remember the correct procedure to close the door, Justus made a fist and smacked the bottom of it. It snapped back in place. We checked; the error code went away. Manny had the crew try the engines again and it started right up.

We launched the last ship. The Flightline was finally quiet and empty of ships. Looking across the Flightline was a disaster. C.R.A.T.E.S. and their contents were everywhere. We had a number of toolboxes laid out. Other personnel that weren't maintenance seemed to be helping get things sorted out. At least that's what we thought at first, but they were just seeing if they could get to the ration packs and water bottles that were in one of the crates. We cleaned up what we could and were about to find shade to sit in when Lenny pointed up. Another set of bombers were about to land.

The twelve of us lined up at the edge of the Flightline awaiting the barrage of work that was to come. Simon sat ready in his jammer with Pete next to it, waiting to snag a couple more crates. The rest of stood next to each other with our headsets on; some had toolboxes. Although we tried to look professional, you couldn't look past the hot, sweaty mess of us all.

Merrick still had no shirt since his was used as a hydro rag. Flange had a new set of rags, a bucket and a large wrench. Seth and Lenny had tools ready for any E&E work and camo pants and T-shirts. Pepper and Wilhelm had their marshalling wands ready to guide the Bullies in. The Engine troops were crossing their fingers that there would be no engine troubles. Manny was still sporting his stretchy maternity pants, while Maisie had her sleeves rolled up and coveralls zipped down to her tight abs as she only had a sports bra underneath. Justus had no shirt on, with the top part of his coveralls off and tied around his waist and the purple vomit stain on his left leg. I had my toolbox and headset ready, taking a deep breath and telling myself, *we got this.*

CHAPTER 7

It's the End of the World

I feel fine, as I see our maintenance team working fast together. Lenny Bronson was not afraid as he quickly directed the newly landed passengers to the nearby building. They seemed still in shock from the space trip. The first set of Bullies was down, and we were on it. We talked to flight crews to see if anything was broken. Pepper and Wilhelm started the thru-flight inspections. We checked each DV's download to see if there were any additional errors. The Weapons Troops were all over those C.R.A.T.E.S. as Simon drove and Pete was securing them.

We barely ate or drank, and if we did, it was during the refuels or running up any systems that seemed off. The crew didn't have any major issues, but it was the constant turnaround. Each ship left and came a few times, each one full of nine or ten passengers. Some people arrived in bad condition as the medical teams were assisting them. The chaos continued as our tiny group bounced between ships trying to keep up with the launches and unexpected problems. We could see it in our eyes how drained we were. The flight crews had the same look of defeat as they slowly climbed back in their seats for each trip into space.

Another ship landed. I could see it was Ship 5050 due to its nose art: a picture of a pinup girl dressed in a magician outfit with a top hat. One hand held a magic wand while the other was flipping a coin.

One of the flight crew walked out to us and said, "Hey, I'm Captain Reynolds. I'm a pilot. Listen, we got some serious radio problems."

Justus and I stepped up as the captain explained. "The entire time we were flying, comm was going in and out. While we were trying to dock with shuttle, it got so bad we almost had to call it off.

You see, we need to talk with the shuttle pilot to ensure we are at the right spot for docking and our pressurization is synced exactly."

I asked, "Which radios were you using? Was there a certain frequency range causing more trouble?"

"It's everything, all radios and interphone. All positions were having trouble, not just mine."

"Got it. We'll take a look," Justus replied.

"Hopefully soon. Once this thing is refueled, we gotta go back up for the rest of them. There is only a handful of packed shuttles drifting out there and they are losing oxygen fast. We only have one more shot at this. Hey, you guys know where there's food and water for my crew?"

Justus pointed. "That second crate's got a bunch."

"Thanks. We'll be back soon."

I stood there thinking.

Justus turned around. "Come on, Sam! We've got work to do."

"Yeah, I was just thinking..."

"Don't think, do. Ain't nobody got time for that."

Justus sat at the navigator's station. I climbed up the ladder to the pilot's seat and donned my headset. Sitting next to me was Pepper, helping with the re-fuel. She was monitoring the various tanks to ensure the fuel transfer was correct.

I heard Justus in my headset. "Hey man, are you there?"

"Roger. I copy five-by-five. How you? Over."

"I hear you fine."

"Roger...one, two, three, four, five...five, four, three, two, one. Over."

"Dude, the interphone is good."

"Copy. Try other crew positions, over."

We tried the other positions and I even brought up the DV on the screen. I told Justus, "I brought up DV5050. This is not showing any communications issues from their last flight. We should do a radio check, over."

"Alright Sam, I'll go the ship next door. Set yourself on the standard UHF frequency; the one we always used at Tech School."

"You can just say UHF. *Frequency* is redundant."

"Whatever, just tune to the frequency."

"Wilco."

"What?"

"Wilco. It means I *will comply*."

"Dude, you are so freaking weird. I'm outta here."

After a bit, Justus said over the UHF, "Ship 5050, this is Ship 310, radio check, one, two, one, two, roger, wilco, whiskey, tango, foxtrot, test, test, testes, testes, over?"

"I copy you loud and clear. Are you making fun of how I do radio checks?"

"Do I really need to answer that? And by the way, you didn't say *over*, over."

"Hold on a minute...Hey, most of the crew is on board now, going through their pre-flight checks. What do we do if we can't find anything wrong with this ship?"

"Man, I don't know. Just be honest and tell the crew everything seems good. Let them decide if they want to take the ship."

"Roger. I do not like this, over."

"Hey Sam, Wilhelm just told me that Ship 1895 just landed some video issues. I'm going to see what they got."

"Copy."

I approached Captain Reynolds and told him, "Sir, we couldn't find an issue with the comm. There were no faults on the DV unit. The radio checks were good, as well as the interphone."

The pilot shook his head. "Listen, I know you're trying, but if this goes out again that last shuttle will *not* survive. We don't have much time. I'm telling you that once we got into space this thing was acting crazy. This is what we're going to do. Get some tools or parts or anything else you think you need. You're going to join us on this flight."

"Yes, sir."

I quickly ran to Ship 1895. Looking up at the nose art, I could see this was the "Cowgirl," as it depicted a girl in old western attire straddling a dropping bomb and waving her hat in the air.

I found Justus. "Hey, they want me to fly with them in case the problem comes back. I need the tools."

"Hold on. I gotta change out the pilot's video monitor; just give me the tiny flathead. Take the rest of the toolbox. You probably won't need it, but who knows."

I ran back to Ship 5050. Pepper was getting everything ready and would be marshaling us out. I told her the situation.

She replied, "Good luck...have fun."

I climbed aboard with my toolbox. The crew told me to sit in the small seat right behind the pilots and set my wireless headset to channel one.

Captain Reynolds spoke. "Welcome back. I already informed my crew of the situation. Hey, I'm sorry; I didn't catch your name?"

"Specialist Kirkland, sir."

"Oh, like the bridge, right?... I'm sorry, I bet you get that a lot."

He has no idea, I thought.

Once we were ready to go Captain Reynolds said to the tail gunner, "Hey Louie, why don't you give Kirkland the introductions while we taxi?"

Louie's scratchy voice came over the interphone as we started to taxi. "No problem. Time to meet the band. The two up front there on the idiot sticks are on vocals. Those are your pilots, Reynolds and Wrexham. Down in the drum section is your navigator Cricket, who's going to locate this last shuttle of stragglers. He'll also point us in the right direction to land back on this moon. Next to him is The Bird. Her job is to blow shit up, but she's basically worthless today since we ain't got no bombs, just a reserve nav, I suppose. Why did you even come, Bird? Anyways, directly behind you is your guitar section, if we happen to come across any bad guys. Next to me is Luigi, your defensive guy that will throw all sorts of nasty stuff at the enemy to jam their crap or deflect a missile. That leaves us with yours truly, Louie here, on bass guitar ready to shoot anything I don't like. I got control of that huge gun at the tail to take down anyone that wants to play."

Reynolds came back up. "Thanks, Louie. Wrexham, take us up."

We barreled down the runway and climbed fast and high for what seemed like forever. The ship was shaking as I was staring straight ahead through the pilots' windows as we departed the Viridis atmosphere. I could make out the head-up display as they had their nav system displayed on the windows. We finally reached space. I was in awe seeing the expanse of stars and taking it all in...

Wrexham spoke. "Cricket, brin...coor...stran...uttle...opy?"

"Say aga..."

"Any...hear...It...n...wo..."

Then both pilots turned around in unison and stared right at me.

I nodded my head. *I can't believe this is happening. Okay. Think.* I was racking my head around everything. I pictured the interphone diagram in my head. All the wires going to each component. *What could cause this? Why is not working now? It was good before...*

Louie yelled across the ship, "Well, you gonna do something or just sit there?"

I took off my headset. "Yes, I'm thinking!"

I got up and started to move down the ladder to the nav station and stopped. *What connects to everything? What does all the comm have in common?* Then it hit me: *the I.J.B.* I went back up the ladder and asked the pilots, "Interphone Junction Box; where is it?"

Reynolds turned and said, "The what?"

"Interphone Junction Box."

"Hey, you see all these control panels and displays. That's what we know. Random boxes...that's your job."

Okay, think. I can see it on the wire diagram in my head. But that doesn't tell me where it is physically. The VR training never showed us it. I was pacing back and forth between the very small section between the pilots and the defense station.

Louie yelled, "Will you get a load of this guy!"

Then I remembered in class. Instructor Carlson was talking about changing avionics parts and farting in the hell hole near the nav station. I grabbed my toolbox and went down the ladder fast. Then I got the bombardier's attention.

She turned to me as I said, "I need to find your hell hole!"

"Excuse me?"

"The hole, it has the avionic parts. I think it is called the hell hole?"

Cricket answered. "Maybe the wine cellar. There is a bunch of stuff down there."

"Wine cellar?"

"Yeah, get down real low next to me. Hands and knees."

Bird questioned, "What are you having him do, Cricket?"

Cricket continued. "See where my foot is pointing? Crawl through there. I don't know what's down there, but I've seen Marston's teammates go in there a bunch."

I grabbed a light rod from the toolbox and crawled through the tiny space. Once inside, in front of the nav station, I could sit up a bit. I looked all around me. Wires were everywhere, lots of parts. I read each one as I didn't recognize any of the numbers or acronyms. Then I saw it, staring right in front of me. I.J.B.

I looked at the panel. Cricket crouched down. "Hey, if you need a tool from your box, let me know."

"Yes, I need a one-fourth socket wrench. No, wait, three-eights."

I received the wrench and took off the bolts and washers as I carefully put the hardware in my pocket so I wouldn't lose them. Then I took off the face plate and looked in the box as hundreds of wires were going in every direction. Each wire was connected to a screw via an eyelet.

If I had a wire diagram and a meter, I could test each wire. Why would a wire be bad? This worked fine on the ground. What's different? What changed? Altitude, temperature, pressure, turbulence... What would Justus do? He'd say, 'Stop thinking and just do.'

Then right in front of my eyes I saw a flicker. The eyelet that connected one wire to the box was shaking due to the ship vibrations. I gently grabbed the wire and wiggled it. The screw that attached it was loose, causing the continuity to be intermittent.

I yelled for Cricket. "Can I get the flathead screwdriver, the tiny one?!"

"I don't see one in here!"

Justus has my tiny flathead. Okay, now what? Screwdriver, screwdriver... I reached into my pocket and took out a tiny washer. I turned the screw with it and the wire was secure.

I yelled back, "Try the interphone!"

After a few seconds I heard Cricket say, "Yes, all seems good now!"

I reattached the cover, secured my tools, headed back to the flight deck, and put my headset back on.

Reynolds said over the interphone, "Great job, Kirkland! What was the fix?"

"I tightened a screw, sir."

"That's it?"

Wrexham said, "Well, you gotta give him credit. He did have to know which one among millions. None of us could have figured that out."

I then heard Bird's concerned voice come up. "Guys, there are a few other ships out here and I don't think they're ours."

Luigi confirmed, saying, "I see them too, on my screen. Two of them bogeys!"

"Keep an eye on them," Reynolds said, "as I coordinate with the shuttle. We're getting close to it."

Wrexham said, "Okay, the shuttle is connecting now...Hey team, this is definitely the last shuttle out here."

"How do you know that?" questioned Louie.

"General Eastwood's on this one!"

"Oh boy," Louie said.

"Pressure is matched," Wrexham said. "All ready for transfer. Hey Kirkland, everything is secure. Grab the hatch above you. Undo those locks, then pull that lever and grab the hatch towards you."

I took it off and saw another hatch on top. Just then it opened. I helped the shuttle passengers aboard. They all crowded around, sitting anywhere they could on the ground. Some went down the ladder to find room to stand or sit.

Luigi spoke in a panic. "Those foreign ships are getting closer!"

"Okay," Reynolds said. "Tell those passengers to move faster, and let me know when we got them all. There will be twelve of them."

"Twelve?" asked Louie.

"Yeah, the shuttle pilot is on here, as well. They really crammed that thing full. The other Bullies got the rest. We're just going to jettison that shuttle away."

The remaining passengers arrived. General Eastwood was the last aboard. I got up and gave the general my seat.

I finished securing the hatch. With my headset still on, I said, "We are good to go. We got them all!" Then I found a crammed place on the floor to sit.

Wrexham said, "Shuttle is jettisoned! We're outta here!"

Reynolds addressed his crew. "I tried various radio channels and none of the foreign ships are responding. Luigi, keep tracking them. Make sure all your systems are up and running. Anything out of the ordinally, prepare to engage. Louie, get that tail gun ready!"

"One step ahead of you, boss," Louie replied.

We had the passengers strap themselves down with cargo straps, as well as me. The next few moments were intense. I heard the traffic through the interphone system as I sat, strapped down and looked around.

"Crap!" Luigi yelled. "It just fired on us! We gotta tracker, spike on sector four, five...and six. I'm deploying anti-missile chaffs!"

Louie came up. "Oh, don't fire that shit at us. Captain! Am I free to engage?"

"Yes! Yes! Kill the bastard!" Reynolds shouted.

Our ship swerved left as I continued to hear the panic on my headset.

Luigi screamed, "There's another one! Two on us!"

"Do you see how that's moving?" Bird yelled, monitoring her screen. "I've never seen ships move like that!"

Luigi said, "Look at that! That thing is all over the place. How do they do that?"

Wrexham was in shock. "I just got a visual as it flew in front of us. Guys...you're not going to believe me."

"At this point I'll believe anything," Louie responded.

Wrexham continued. "Yeah...it's a flying saucer."

"What?" Bird asked.

"You know, round on all sides, circular, vertically short, saucer-like."

Louie spoke fast. "Hold on, I think I can..."

"Yes!" yelled Luigi. "We got one! Louie took one out! Blew it up! She gone!"

"Yeah, but what about the other one?" Louie said.

Just then Cricket saw something new on his radar. "Nice! I see two sets of XF-94 fighters out there. They're on our side."

"Where?" Reynolds asked. "How far? I'll see if I can radio them."

Louie chimed in again. "We don't have much time. This second unknown is right on us!"

"Listen, we are on approach to Viridis, entering now," Reynolds said. "His instruments will be useless when we go through the moon's atmosphere."

"Yeah, but so will ours," Luigi responded.

I could see panic on the other passengers' faces, yet I knew they had little clue what was going on since they couldn't hear the interphone conversations. The crowd of scared passengers were just trying to hang on as we started to enter the atmosphere.

I was looking behind me when I heard Luigi yell, "Oh no! NOOOO!"

Then I felt an enormous shockwave. The entire bomber shifted with an unnatural force. I felt the pulses in my bones. Then I saw it. To my horror, the entire top panels above the gunner station were ripping away rapidly, everything was breaking completely apart as the...

CHAPTER 8

November Rain

Justus felt like he hadn't slept in days. "What time is it?" he asked Pepper. "How long is this fucking day?"

"You need to rest, drink some water."

"Can't rest. Too many ships to fix."

"I don't even know if the sun sets here. I think we've been awake for at least two days, maybe more."

"Really?"

"Here, drink the water."

"Don't we need to refuel those that landed?"

"The crew said they were done for now. There are only three more ships up there. They are getting the last passengers from the shuttles."

"Now what?"

Pepper pointed. "I see one entering now."

Justus looked up as well. They both saw it at the same time, a plume of smoke stretched across the entire skyline.

"What the hell?" Justus yelled.

Major Warfield ran out of the building and looked up to the sky. The entire maintenance team gathered, staring at the debris spread across this moon's sky. It looked like a thin stream of dark smoke stretched across the purple sky and over the water.

Warfield said in a solemn, slow, shocked voice, "I was listening to the other ships the whole time from the tower. I can't believe it. I'm sorry...I'm so sorry. That was Ship 5050."

Justus yelled, "Sam!"

Justus and Pepper collapsed to the ground and sat there. The rest of the team was in shock.

Pepper asked, with tears in her eyes, "What was it? How'd it happen?"

Warfield was shaking his head. "Enemy fire. There's someone out there."

They could see the other two B-43s come through high in the air, being escorted by a few XF-94 fighters. Wilhem and Manny grabbed some marshalling wands and headed out to the spots.

Justus sat in a daze along with Pepper. Dead to the world. Dehydrated. Hungry. Thirsty. Tired. Just done. He finally got up and in his zombie state approached the first B-43 that landed. He could see dark rain clouds in the sky start to creep in. After watching all the panicked passengers get off, Justus approached the crew of 721.

"Any issues?" he asked. "What needs fixed?"

The crew gave him a list of write-ups. Justus went to the next Bully, 310, and received a list of their problems, each time seeing if there was anything additional on the DV downloads. It started to rain, a relief from the star light, yet a hindrance to work.

The rain came down hard as Justus addressed the rest of the tired maintainers. "Let's get these post-flight inspections done first. We can worry about the rest later."

Everyone felt out of it. Justus got a ladder out and started to help Maisie and Manny with the post-flights by inspecting each ion engine as they had shown him earlier. After an hour or so, Justus was on the last ship, inspecting the engines. Soaking wet, tired and defeated, they saw a C-345 cargo ship land, then another one soon after. The rain seemed to lessen into a light drizzle. These new ships had their own set of Crew Chiefs jump out and marshal them in.

An older, short, plump man who had just departed one of the C-345 made a beeline to the B-43s. Justus could see him coming. When he got closer, Justus made out the chief stripes on this man's perfectly pressed sharp camo uniform.

Chief Cogstorm laid into Justus. "What are you doing?! Put your shirt on, for God's sake! Why are there tools lying around?! Where is your technical data, young man?"

Justus slowly stepped down from the ladder and looked at Chief Cogstorm.

The chief continued to yell. "Who is in charge here? No one has their technical data out! Why is that girl without a T-shirt with her coveralls half down? Oh my, oh my. Hey, don't turn away from me!"

Justus calmly grabbed his ladder and moved it to the next engine.

"Oh, don't you dare!" the chief said.

Justus stopped and said calmly, "You have no idea what went on here, or what we went through."

"How dare you question me! Don't give me that crap! There is no excuse for your lazy team's shitty maintenance!"

Justus ignored him and grabbed the ladder. He was about to step up when the chief grabbed Justus' arm. Justus pulled his arm away quickly and without thinking, reached back and punched the chief with force, right in his jaw. Chief Cogstorm went down fast, collapsing on the hard ground. A crowd of others saw it happen and ran over to check on the chief.

Justus was about to walk away when two Military Policeman approached him.

The MP Sergeant said, "Sorry, you gotta come with us."

Pepper saw it happen and ran up and asked, "Justus, what the hell were you thinking?!"

Justus' rights were read as he put the top part of his coveralls on. Then the younger MP zip-tied Justus' hands behind his back. The two MPs led Justus into a small office next to the Flightline and told him to stay there. He paced back and forth across the small room, trying to wrap his mind over everything. *Why was this happening? What will happen next? How could they lose Sam?*

After about twenty minutes, the office door opened and the two MPs entered, along with Chief Cogstorm and **Lieutenant Michaelson**. Justus could tell Lt. Michaelson came with the chief on the cargo ship due to his nice clean uniform and fresh crew cut on his slender build. The chief approached Justus as they were both standing, squared-up on each other. Cogstorm had a bloody napkin in his hand and was using it to clean up his fat lip. The left side of his face was puffy and bruised.

The chief looked directly him and demanded, "What is your name?"

Justus snapped back, "Specialist Johannes."

"When I get done with you, you won't be a specialist! I found out there is nothing, nothing documented on those ship's maintenance logs! There was no tool accountability. I won't accept this cowboy maintenance from a bunch of dirtbags! Were you even qualified to do half of those tasks?" As the chief ranted, blood dripped down from his lip. Justus acted like he ignored the drips staining the chief's clean uniform shirt, but deep down he was enjoying the site of this. The chief continued, "Who was in charge of that gaggle of dirtbag maintainers, anyway?"

Justus stood there staring at the chief's face, not answering.

Chief Cogstorm asked again, "Where is the ADVON team? Who was in charge?"

"We're all exactly the same rank."

"That's not possible. Who is the ranking maintainer? Answer me!"

"If you really think you need a specific name, Specialist Kirkland outranked us, but only by his age."

"Oh really. So where is this *Kirkland*?"

Just then the Lt. approached the chief. The chief took a couple steps back as the Lt. whispered something to him. Then the chief said, "This isn't over! You're in lockdown. Stay here while I try to fix all the shit your team of dirtbags fucked up!"

The MP Sergeant clipped the zip tie, releasing Justus' wrists as they all left the room. Justus looked around the office. There was a desk, yet he couldn't read any of the script on it. *Must be Viridis*, he thought. The rest of the room only contained a couple of chairs and something that resembled a couch. After a few minutes of passing back and forth, he tried the door handle, and to his surprise, it turned. He peeked open the door a few inches and looked out.

Right outside the door was the young MP sitting in a chair.

Justus closed the door, sat on the floor with his back against it and said, "You know this door isn't locked."

The MP answered, "Oh, I know. We can't lock it from the outside."

"So, I could just leave and make a run for it."

"You could, then I would have to *try* to tase you."

"Try?"

"You know what? I came off that destroyed space transport also. I'm probably as tired as you are. I may be able to get a shot off, but you *just* might have a chance."

Justus said sarcastically, "You sound confident."

"Have you been tased before?"

"No."

"It sucks. The initial hit puts pain throughout your whole body, then you helplessly fall on your face. I'm not sure which is worse— the shock or the pain you'll receive from hitting the ground. In your case, though, the shock will hurt way worse."

"Why's that?"

"The intense pain is worse on those with more muscles, as the muscles try to contract."

"Then what?"

"That's it. You'll be incapacitated. Then I'll just drag your ass back to the room. But seriously man, even if you got by me, where would you go? You just going to roam this moon forever?"

"I see your point."

"Then we'd both be in trouble. No one wins in that plan."

"Hey, what's your name?"

"Specialist Roland, but everyone calls me **T-Rex**."

"You didn't look scary."

"Nah, inside joke. They were making fun of my short arms."

"So, you gotta sit here and guard me, T-Rex?"

"Yep."

"The way I see it, you got it worse than me."

"Why's that?"

"We are both in the same position, we can't leave. Only I can curl up on that couch thing and get some sleep."

The two of them talked for a couple hours through the door. T-Rex explained about being one of the last groups to the leave the dying transport. He was with a team making sure everyone got out safely. Justus talked about his maintenance team and the ship that was destroyed on re-entry.

T-Rex said, "Sorry, Justus, but my relief is here. I hope it turns out okay for you."

"Thanks, man."

Justus had no interest in talking with the next guard. He curled up on the couch-like piece of furniture and fell fast asleep.

———————

Lt. Michaelson came in six hours later and woke Justus. He handed him a couple water bottles and a ration pack. "Chili mac. It's supposed be the best one."

"Thanks, LT. Where's the chief?"

"Chief Cogstorm is busy with other things. I don't know how this will end for you and I don't want to get into it. We'll set you up with the Legal Office when we get to Space Station Prime."

"So now what?" Justus said, opening his food packets.

"Now we need to get off this rock, but we have a bit of a problem. We have a group of C-345 maintainers here and your little team of Tech School grads. No one is qualified to fix the bombers."

"That *is* a problem."

"We've been in communication with the general at Space Station Prime. They don't want to leave these new bombers here and we can't stay. The priority is for us to fix these last few bombers and launch them out of here as safely as possible. We will be pairing your team up with the cargo maintainers. Although not familiar with your systems, they do have maintenance experience."

"So, what about me?"

"For now, you will be escorted by a couple of MPs and paired up with a C-345 Avionics Tech. He's going to need your help trouble-shooting your fails."

"And if I don't comply?"

"You can choose that. The way I see it, though, the more you help, the easier it'll be for you to explain this alleged assault thing."

"Alleged?"

"Hey, I'm not your lawyer. Don't say anything. I just know the more you help, the better you come out with this case. Come on. Finish your food and let's head out."

Justus ate, then headed outside with the MPs. The rain continued steadily. While they walked, he noticed one of the cops was T-Rex. From across the Flightline they watched the first C-345 launch. The MP Sergeant explained that most of the passengers boarded that first cargo ship.

Another sergeant approached them and said, "Hello, I'm Sergeant Scheels. I'll be helping you with the avionics problems. First things first: they can't find one of the toolboxes. Do you know anything about that?"

Justus could still feel the small screwdriver in his pocket as he answered, "Yeah, that box was on Ship 5050."

"Oh, I see. I'll let the others know. For avionics problems there were only a couple."

Scheels led them to Ship 3034. "This one won't display any faults from the previous flight. Plus, the system seems locked up. The other maintainers tried to reset it, but they couldn't figure it out."

The picture on Ship 3034's nose showed a pinup girl on the beach in a bikini. Justus and Scheels sat in the lower section in navigator and bombardier seats.

Justus brought up the faults screen and said, "Normally when I retrieve the download, it will show up here. I'm getting nothing, like the DV isn't talking at all. This says DV3034 is online and ready, but it's not responding, and it seems to be locking up some of the other systems."

"What components would cause this?" Scheels asked.

"DV3034 gets all the commands from various systems. It could be something internal to the ship, but I think the DV unit may be bad."

"How can we check that? Can we swap DVs from a known good ship?"

"We could, but the flight info is specific to 3034, and will only display to this ship. It'll still show a blank. However, we should be able to have another DV diagnose it."

Justus and Scheels went to the outside panel aft of the bomb bay. The two MPs were standing out there as well, following along. Justus pulled the release lever and activated the lowering mechanism. DV3034 slowly lowered to the ground.

Justus disconnected the cables attached to its head. "So, now we gotta bring her to another ship."

"Okay, but first we need to document this panel and part being removed," Scheels instructed.

"Really?" asked Justus.

Once the maintenance logs were filled out, Scheels said, "You bring that DV. It looks heavy. I'll grab your tools."

"Deal."

Sergeant Scheels started walking, carrying the awkward toolbox. He looked behind him as Justus was walking with his hands, and remote, in his pockets. DV3034 followed along behind him. T-Rex laughed. Scheels just shook his head.

They arrived at the next Ship, 0721. Justus lowered DV721 and pulled out a comm cable and hooked the DVs together. On the remote, he activated the test function.

The small screen on DV721's head read:

DV3034...FAILURE...INACTIVE FUSE...A7.

"Nice," said the Sergeant. "Where are the fuses?"

"Uhh...I dunno."

They both looked up and down the unit. They found a few small, suspect panels. The second one they unscrewed and opened contained a set of fuses. Scheels asked for the multimeter from the toolbox to check the fuses.

"Here you go, sergeant," Justus said. "It's the setting with the horseshoe thingy."

Scheels stared at Justus with annoyance and spoke slowly. "Yes…I know how to do a continuity check. That's an omega symbol, also known as an ohm."

"Sorry."

He checked it. "Yep, it's bad. Do we have another?"

"We can check the crates. I'm not sure if we have that particular fuse. Can't we just do a temp fix unit we get to the Space Station? We can find a piece of metal to fit in the fuse slot, right?"

"See, that's what you need to learn. Why did it break the first time? Power surge? Volt fluctuation? The fuse did its job. What if that comes back? What you're talking about is a good way to start a fire or cause multiple problems. So…no; we need to find a fuse with the same rating."

"Okay."

"But first we need to finish up on 0721. Put that DV back, update the maintenance logs, then we'll need to retest this ship and document it."

"Really?"

"Yes. Did they teach you anything in Tech School?"

They went to nav's station and brought up the DV721's test page.

"That's weird," Justus said. "Everything is testing good, but the last two flight downloads are missing."

"What do you mean, *missing*?"

"They're just not here, see? It has all the other flights, just not the last two. Not much of a problem; we already got the info."

"Okay, let's just move on for now."

They both went to the C.R.A.T.E.S. that contained the spare parts, along with the MPs that looked bored out of their minds. After searching, there were no fuses.

Scheels then said, "What about these other parts? Do any of these carry the same fuse?"

Justus was trying to think. "I don't think so. Let me ask my other guys."

They meet up with Wilhelm, Seth and Lenny. Justus held up the fuse. "Ever see one of those?"

Wilhelm looked at it. "I think our microwave in the galley has a fuse like that."

Sure enough, it did. Wilhelm took it from the microwave, and they popped it into place in the DV. After loading DV3034 in the ship, Justus brought up the faults page with ease. Everything seemed to be working well. The faults from the last flight only showed a few engine fluctuations along with something else...

Justus looked perplexed. "What the hell? This has the faults from 3034, as well as info from 721's last two flights. This DV3034 must have stolen this data when she was connected to DV721. Thirty-thirty-four is a dirty-dirty-whore!"

Wilhelm laughed, then left to go find Manny or Maisie to look at the newly discovered engine faults.

Manny arrived and looked at the fails. "I may need to make a few adjustments. Then we need to run the engines and check the faults again."

They told the C-345 Engine Troops about the faults and engine run.

The cargo ship sergeant said, "I can't run those engines up. This is a completely different ship."

Manny said, "Yeah, this is way above Tech School level, but we learned the theory behind it. I may be able to figure it out..."

Sergeant Scheels stepped in. "Stop! We are *not* running the engines! We'll get a couple B-43 pilots to do it."

The Engine team was looking to coordinate the engine run with a flight crew. Scheels made sure Justus documented the ship's logs correctly for the fixes and even showed him how to document the 'now inoperative' microwave.

There was other avionics work on Ship 0341 that consisted of a bad satellite receiver, which they found a replacement for in the C.R.A.T.E.S. It also had a defective interphone box at the co-pilot's station. Since there were none of these around, Justus and Scheels swapped it with the one at the seat behind the pilots. After the operational checks, Scheels made sure Justus documented everything correctly in the maintenance logs.

They all continued to work throughout another extremely long day. Manny and Maisie made a couple engine adjustments and, along with a couple pilots, successfully ran the engine. Greg and Seth replaced an AC valve on one ship and changed the gravity generator whose faults indicated a potential problem. Even the Hydro team was busy, as Merrick and Flange tightened a couple lines and ran through their systems. During all this maintenance, Simon and Pete finished loading the C.R.A.T.E.S. on the rest of the bombers. Justus still had not seen Chief Cogstorm. *Perhaps he left on the first transport*, he thought.

Justus also barely saw Pepper. He knew she must have been busy like the rest of them, but he was getting agitated that she didn't even attempt to see him after his whole ordeal with the chief and being in lockup. It didn't help that he kept replaying the event in his mind when she yelled at him for striking the chief. *Was she on his side?* Justus felt hurt, mad, and confused from it all.

One by one, they marshalled out the B-43s and the Flightline was almost empty. To their surprise and relief, all the Bullies launched without issues. No Redballs. The rest of them on this barren airfield on Viridis finally boarded the second C-345 and made their way to Space Station Prime.

One thing was for certain, the crew of Bully maintainers slept well on that flight in the cargo hold, but only at first. Then it was the waiting. Eating ration packs, sleeping, waiting, and thinking.

Justus sat next to Pepper and Seth on the C-345. He asked Seth, "What's the deal? Sam talked to me about his beach trips to Viridis. He said it took less than a day to get there from Station Prime. Now we're having to endure this three or four-day day ordeal."

"It's the orbits. These moons and the Space Stations are different distances from the planet Centrum, and everything revolves at different rates. They probably went at the time of year they are the closest together."

"I'm not sure if I agree with you, but I'm too tired to think too much about it."

"Just go with it. Nothing makes much sense lately."

Eating ration packs, sleeping, waiting, and thinking. Justus kept thinking about Sam. He'd had his whole career planned, and now this. Nothing about this seemed right. He was also wondering what would happen next for him after the confrontation with the chief. He hardly talked with Pepper. Justus didn't know what to say. He didn't want to show her how hurt he was. He didn't know how to express it. He just wanted to be alone with his thoughts. He could tell she was getting upset. However, the more she got upset, the more he didn't want to talk to her. This seemed like the longest flight of his life.

ACT III

CHAPTER 9

Fly Away

The group peered through the windows of the C-345 and saw the expanse of the Flightline as their cargo ship touched down on Space Station Prime. While taxiing they saw rows and rows of ships: their seven B-43s in the first section, then a few dozen B-X3 bombers. They found out that the XF-94 fighters were all on Space Station Bravo, while the C-345s came from Station Delta and would head back soon.

Once they arrived at a parking spot, the ramp in the aft opened and they all quickly boarded a bus. Looking up, Justus and Pepper noticed a giant dome covering the entire Flightline. Seeing the immensity of stars was beyond astonishing.

The bus took them through an Entry Control Point to a terminal. They got some food and were issued new camo uniforms, maintenance coveralls and what they call a track uniform. The track uniform was a comfortable uniform they could wear while at the gym or off-duty. They all received new tablets that had all the Space Station Prime's information pre-loaded on them. The eleven maintainers, still in their wretched uniforms, all waited in a small room with their new gear in bags next to them.

Lt. Michaelson stepped in and addressed them. "Listen up. I know you have all been through an insane experience. You have only been trained to work on the B-43, yet none of you are qualified. There should be a new crew of qualified maintainers arriving here eventually to help you out and get you qualified on your tasks. I was told you all have two options at this point. Based on your experience getting here, you have the option of taking the next transport vessel back to Earth. Then you will be reassigned to a different unit and ship, yet it may be some time before that happens. You are not obligated to stay out here in the Stella System."

The Lt. continued. "The other option is to stay here and do miscellaneous tasks until the new crew of B-43 maintainers comes to help you out. Tomorrow you will all report to the BX-3 bomber unit at 0600. I pinged it on your maps, on your tablets. Let your supervision know tomorrow if you want to head back. That's all for now. Get cleaned up and get some sleep; you all deserve it."

The Bully maintainers were all issued rooms in the Texas Barracks.

Standing in the courtyard in the middle of the horseshoe-shaped barracks, Lenny said, "Hey everyone. There is a coffee place near here. Let's all meet there in about an hour or so. What do you say?"

They all looked at the location on his tablet and agreed. Justus found his room on the second floor. He was relieved to find he had a room to himself. His whole body was in pain as he sat down. He took off his boots, relieving his aching feet. It was a good thing he just received new boots. He was sure these current ones were too small. His feet hurt to the touch and he could see that multiple blisters had already formed. He threw his stained, reeking coveralls in the corner near the small waste basket and limped to his washroom.

The shower felt blissful as he put his head under the hot water, washing away the blood, sweat, tears, dirt, hydro, fuel, grease and vomit from his broken body. He was clean but couldn't wash the thoughts that were going through his mind. He put on his track clothes and comfortable socks and lay on his bed. After about twenty minutes, he woke up and thought to himself, *Stay awake. I need to meet with the others.*

Justus splashed water on his face and took a good look at himself in the mirror, wondering how he was going to get through all of this. He made his way through the vast hallways and grimaced at the sight of the stairs as he forced his hurt feet and aching body to endure it.

Justus found the others at the little coffee shop called *Green Beans*. The eleven of them had pushed a couple tables together. They ordered coffee and all looked relaxed, tired, and just out of it. One thing was for sure, this situation on the space transport and Virdis had changed every single one of them in a different way. Lenny was going on and on about the Redballs and each E&E fix. He couldn't believe what a bunch of brand-new Tech School kids did on their first mission. The Ward twins sat back looking relaxed, and Flange and Merrick were talking about all the hydro work they had.

Then Seth, after looking at his tablet, said, "Hey guys, you know we could go up another level and hit the bar they have here."

"Bar?" Simon asked.

"Yeah, it's eighteen and older."

"Hell yeah," Merrick exclaimed. "What are we doing here?"

Lenny was looking at his tablet. "Really? I don't see it. What's it called?"

"I don't know, some sort of space bar," Seth answered.

Maisie responded, "I'm not drinking anywhere called the *Space Bar*...stupid name."

Lenny was still scanning his tablet. "Hey, I got it now," he said. "One floor above us. It's called *The Shack*."

Everyone headed up another set of stairs to *The Shack*.

It was not your regular bar. The confused looks on everyone's faces gave that away. They were surprised by a giant, bright sign that said, "*Welcome to the 1980s!*" Neon lights were everywhere. The bar and tables had slick surfaces, and everything was purple, pink and green with stripes and triangles everywhere. There were several display screens mounted on the walls playing music videos, which they could hear throughout the bar.

They looked at each other with hesitation as they found a table and received their drinks. Everyone missed Sam, but no one wanted to bring it up.

"Hey, isn't your brother on this station?" Maisie asked Pepper.

"Would you believe my luck? He just deployed to Nix," Pepper said. "Won't be back for a while."

Simon asked, "Which one is Nix?"

"That's the cold one," Seth answered.

"Oh, I hope we don't go there."

Maisie asked, "What's with this music here? *Like a Virgin?*"

"You don't know Madonna?" Pepper said, looking surprised. "It's 1980s music. My grandparents made me listen to it all the time. Michael Jackson, Metallica, Guns N' Roses, Van Halen, Mötley Crüe. It was the age of modern rock, pop music. It was the last decade before the internet messed everything up!"

Seth smiled and raised his mug.

"Hey guys, we made it," Lenny said, speaking fast. "I think we need to address the big question."

"What's that?" Wilhelm asked.

"Are you all staying here, or are you done? Is anyone choosing to head back to Earth?"

"You first," Wilhelm said.

"Oh, I'm all in. Whatever hit us up there, we can't let them do that. I'm totally in."

Pepper said, "I don't care about that, but I am here to see my brother when he comes back, so I'm here to stay. What about you, Justus? Justus...what about you?"

Justus took a long swig of beer, almost finishing his mug, and said, "It would kill that chief if I stayed. So, of course I'm in."

It was unanimous. They all agreed to stay, at least until their five-year mark was up, then they'd call it quits or relocate or continue on.

"We need a name for our little group," Lenny said.

Justus stared straight ahead and said, "That chief called us dirtbags, doing cowboy maintenance."

Lenny proposed, "Cowboy's Eleven."

"No!" Justus said immediately.

"Why not?" Lenny asked.

"There were twelve of us. Don't leave Sam out."

Seth declared, "The Dirtbag Dozen!"

Pepper nodded. "I like that."

"Now what?" Merrick asked. "We do menial tasks for a while, while they figure out when we can become real maintainers?"

"This is bullshit!" said Maisie. "I want to actually work, not sit around waiting. We can do it."

Everyone experienced the rest of the night differently. Lenny, Maisie and most of the others raised their glasses, toasted and enjoyed being free. Pepper was confused and hurt as Justus nearly ignored her.

Justus had too much on his mind. Sam was gone, his career was in the balance, and he really had no set direction moving forward.

After the last round had been drunk, the Dirtbag Dozen, minus one, found their way back to the Texas Barracks.

Pepper caught up with Justus outside the dorm. "What's going on with you?"

"What do you mean?"

"You've barely acknowledged me. I know you went through a lot; we all did. But that's no reason to shut me out."

"Whatever."

"I'm trying to talk to you!"

"I'm...tired. I don't want to get into it."

"You weren't the only one that got hurt on Viridis."

"I know."

"Fine. See you around."

"Okay."

"Okay?! Listen, you wanna feel bad by yourself, go ahead. I was just offering my help. You know where my room is."

Pepper stormed off and Justus kept walking towards his new room, ready to finally sleep in a real bed.

The next morning, in their new camo uniforms, Justus and the others found their way to the BX-3 work center on the top floor of this marvel of a Space Station. They approached the roll call area with hesitation as other maintainers stared at them with uncertainty. A Senior Sergeant formed everyone up.

Towards the end of roll call, **Senior Sergent Ection** from the Resource Office addressed the new group. "We have with us a few new maintainers that arrived with the new B-43s. Welcome. After roll call, stay behind so we can discuss your future. That's all. Shift, dismissed to your Expeditors!"

Senior Ection brought the group into the Production Superintendents' office. It was a large room with a few office desks and a large table. Justus instantly recognized Lt. Michaelson. They were introduced to their First Sergeant, **Senior Sergeant Smith**, as well as the Production Superintendent, **Senior Sergeant Wrangler**.

Pro-Super Wrangler addressed the maintainers. "Hey guys... and girls. We heard all about your ordeal. Thanks for all you did on Viridis, really. I keep hearing more stories come through and find it just outstanding. I like speaking honestly to my troops. We are in a dilemma. You might even call it a slow burning dumpster fire. The B-43 flight crews want to fly, they really do. We need them to, those amazing bombers are supposed to replace our old BX-3s. But we just don't have qualified maintainers, at least not by Space Military standards. Hell, we don't even have tech data. I know they are working on sending us digital copies of it through the Kirkland Bridge. I'm hoping to have it soon so we can download it on your tablets."

Senior Wrangler continued. "According to our commander, they will plan on training already experienced maintainers in your career fields on the new B-43 course back on Earth. But I know that will take time, plus the time it'll take for them to get over here via one less transport vessel. Hell, even the spare transport vessel near Earth is undergoing major depot level maintenance and I know those take a while. Along with all the supply delays, I don't when we'll have another operational transport. There was an idea to train our current BX-3 troops to learn your ship, but then again, who would train them? Believe me, we are working on a solution. Until then, Lt. Michaelson, would you like to address our temporary plan?"

Lt. Michaelson stepped up. "The B-43 flight crews need training, which they will get. We are going to treat this like a generation. The crews will come out every day and night and run up the bombers. They'll go through a gambit of operations running up every system and scenario. We'll even load bombs and go through every test phase. However, we will not fly. Not until we can convince the higher-ups we have a crew of fully qualified maintainers. Until then, you will work hard with these flight crews. I'm sure their systems will encounter problems. With that, you will be there getting these bombers ready, troubleshooting, and fixing what you can when the time comes up. We are asking a lot. I am really pushing for all of you. In fact, as your new Maintenance Officer, I have been assigned to oversee this whole effort."

Senior Wrangler added, "These next five days I want everyone to work together. I am assigning **Sergeant Theo Malone** here to work directly with you. He'll take you to get the rest of your in-processing done. The rest of this week he will guide you through everything about this Flightline: Tool Counter, Debrief, Parts Supply, Backshop, and so forth. After your next night off, we'll split you into separate shifts and start this long generation with the B-43 crews. Each career field will be on a separate shift and tag-team each other, with a few exceptions. Ward brothers, we'll keep you two together based on how you work as a weapons team. You'll start on the first shift, but this may be modified depending on when we'll load bombs. Finally, I know we have a situation with avionics. Specialist Johannes?"

"Right here, boss man," answered Justus.

"You are in a unique position. In fact, I think we need to speak after this. Everyone else, please go with Sergeant Malone; he'll get you squared away and in-processed."

Everyone left except the Seniors and Justus. They all sat down at the table.

The First Sergeant, Smith started. "Let's slow things down here. How are you doing with all this, Johannes? Just get it all out. No repercussions. What is going through your mind?"

"Let's see," Justus answered. "I was in a frozen coma, taken a few trillion miles from my home, almost died on a space transport, worked my ass off for three straight days, saw my friend die, was accosted by a chief, spent time in a makeshift jail, was sent to a floating city in space, my girlfriend and I aren't talking, I'm still awaiting a court appearance or whatever for the assault thing, and now since I'm the only Avionics troop, I think I'm being asked to work a double shift to keep this Bully dream alive."

Lt. Michaelson said, "Yep, that sounds about right."

"Your girlfriend?" Senior Ection asked.

"Really, all that stuff and you ask about a girl! Sorry, sir, I didn't mean to..."

"Hey, we're all cool here. Out of all those things you mentioned, it was the only thing I thought I could help with."

Senior Wrangler said, "Listen, Justus—it is Justus, right?"

"Yeah."

"You are in a unique situation. LT, you may want to put some earmuffs on. Justus, you're carrying all the cards. They need you right now. They can't afford to let their only B-43 Avionics troop slip away. My suggestion, if the LT agrees, is to put you on a modified schedule. You'll only work when the flight crews need you. Yeah, you'll bounce between shifts. I'm not gonna lie, your sleep schedule will be all out of whack. You'll probably be called upon in the middle of your sleep and you might work more hours than the others. In the long run if anyone has a problem with you or your schedule, let them answer to me. You can fold and give up or prove to everyone that you can do this. What else have you got to do on this space station?"

Lt. Michaelson nodded in agreement.

Justus agreed, too. "Alright, I'm in."

CHAPTER 10

Who Made Who

Two weeks had gone by. Justus was in his own little zone. He and Pepper were still on uncertain terms. Most of the Dirty Dozen would meet up at the Shack or Green Beans every few days, and Justus would bounce back and forth between the two shifts and would meet occasionally.

They had all received B-43 tech data on their tablets, which was a huge help on the Flightline. It was sent digitally through the Kirkland Bridge. Justus still felt lost, and there were a few times he was called to diagnose an avionics problem, yet he just didn't have the knowledge. The flight crews just stared at him as he felt defeated. He knew he could change parts, he could do that all night long, however it was the troubleshooting that baffled him.

His solution for now was to change random parts in the system until it worked. He always got it eventually. One time he changed four radar parts until the system started working.

The next day, after roll call, Senior Wrangler called for Justus in the Production office. He stood in front of the Pro-Super's desk.

Wrangler spoke harshly. "Specialist Johannes, I know you are new out there, but this crap needs to stop. Every avionics fail, you seem to just go through the motions throwing parts at it without any real troubleshooting. Have you ever heard of the Parts Cannon?"

"No."

"The Parts Cannon is when you stuff every damn part in your system down its barrel. Then you aim this thing at your problem, stand back, ignite the fuse and let it rip. Whichever random part happens to get closest to your target, you then say, 'I guess I'll change that part and hope for the best.' Do us all a favor—no more Parts Cannon! Learn your shit."

"I'm trying."

"One more thing. I need you to report to room D501."

"What's there?"

"An investigation team. They have questions about the DV unit. This is very high profile, so please don't disappoint them."

Justus arrived at room D501. Major Warfield greeted him.

Justus looked around the room. It was full of officers, senior sergeants, and one young cute brunette specialist.

Major Warfield addressed the room. "Now we can begin. This is Specialist Johannes, our Avionics Tech. Over there is Specialist Parker from the Part Supply. Next to me is Colonel Zardin, in charge of the Spaceship Hazard Investigation Team along with the rest of his crew. Colonel Zardin, it is a pleasure to have you."

Colonel Zardin was a short man with thin, graying hair. He addressed the room. "We recovered some of the wreckage from Ship 5050. Our team figures that the majority of that ship broke off and disintegrated in the Viridis atmosphere, along with all those crates. Turns out the maintenance tablets that contained all the B-43s tech data were on those—talk about all your eggs in one basket, am I right? The ass-end of the bomber snapped apart and drifted into space. Our team was able to recover most of that debris. That's where they discovered the black box or Digital Verifier unit, which should be arriving here shortly."

Justus suppressed his emotions as this colonel talked about Ship 5050. He thought to himself, *How could he talk about that ship like it was just an asset? He totally ignored the issue of all those that died on it.* He looked over at Major Warfield, who had his arms crossed and the same rotten expression on his face.

The colonel continued. "We need that black box downloaded. We need to see everything that happened from its last mission. That's where you come in, Specialist Johannes."

Just then, two sergeants carried DV5050 into the room. They set it down in front of Justus. The two-foot-tall component looked like an old trash can. There was large dent on its right side, the forward screen was cracked, and the left side was completely black as it had been charred over its faded orange paint.

Justus could feel the intense pressure as everyone in the room stared at him.

"What do think?" asked the colonel.

Justus took a long look at the DV. On a whim, he hit the "on" button, but wasn't surprised when nothing happened. Then he answered, "Sir, I need to replace its forward screen. Let me open the rest to see if anything else is broken."

The colonel turned to the Parts Supply specialist. "Specialist Parker, order a screen. Johannes, give her the stock number for the screen."

Justus opened his tablet and gave her the number. Parker quickly verified they had one on station.

Justus then used his tiny screwdriver from his pocket and took off the front panel. "Fuses, I'll need more fuses." Then he removed the entire back panel to see the insides. He looked at Colonel Zardin. "Hopefully the memory is intact. This memory circuit card looks good; however, the application card looks burnt."

"Just let Specialist Parker know what you need."

"I think the power supply is shot. You know, these wheels look worn, and the panels are pretty beaten up. Some new paint, pin stripes, a coat of wax."

Major Warfield laughed.

The colonel said to Justus, "Now you're pushing it. All we need is a clean download."

"Yes, sir. I gotta try."

"Once you have all the info you need," Zardin said, "Go with

Parker to Parts Supply to get what you need and verify it's correct before heading back here."

Justus was double checking the stock numbers on his tablet for what he thought he needed. Then he walked with Specialist Parker down the long corridors of the space station.

He told her as they walked, "Thanks. I didn't realize how much this thing was a priority to those guys."

"That's how it is around here," she answered. "Apparently everything is a priority. However, the more stripes or brass makes their priority go to the top the list."

"How far is the parts warehouse?"

"Way at the other end of the station. But we'll take the tram."

"Tram?"

"Yes, we are almost to it. It'll zoom us across fast."

They boarded the automated tram and sped off. Specialist Parker asked, "So you were on that space transport that broke apart, right?"

"I was. I'll have to tell you about it sometime. The name's Justus. How long have you been here?"

"**Virginia.** I've only been here about five months. Still trying to find where everything is around this station."

"Well, once you do, let me know. I'm so lost."

"It takes some time. I usually just bring up the map on my tablet to get around."

"You get around a lot? I mean...do you do much on your off time?"

"Not too much. Just hang with some friends."

The tram stopped and Virginia led Justus down a couple floors and across the way. As they passed by one office, Virginia pointed it out.

"That's the Personnel Office," she said. "Not much going on there. A bunch of lazy office workers, if you ask me."

They arrived at the huge Parts Supply warehouse. Another specialist brought out the parts he needed and Justus took a look at them all and verified them. He was surprised the boxes were so much larger than the parts.

He looked at Virginia. "Yep, this all looks correct."

"You think you can make your way back to your team by yourself?"

"I can manage. Hey, a bunch of us are meeting up tomorrow at the place called The Shack. If want to bring your friends, I'll be there around 2100."

"Well...maybe. See you around," she said, and smiled.

Justus grabbed his parts. He stashed the fuses in his pants pocket and the circuit card on the inside pocket of coveralls, then held the other two boxes under his left arm as he had his tablet in his right hand. The place was a maze of identical looking offices on either side of stale gray and white hallways. He was trying to make sense of it all on his map on the tablet. He passed the Personnel Office and thought, *I must be on the right track—a bunch of losers sitting around with their feet on their desks.*

He heard one yell out to him, laughing. "Looks like you're struggling. You want to get there quicker?"

Justus stopped at their doorway. "Excuse me? Do I look like I need help?"

The young Personnel Specialist said, "I was going to say, you could get there quicker if you walked faster."

Justus set his boxes down right in their doorway. "You know what? I do think I need help with these. Why don't you carry it the rest of the way for me?"

"Hey, you can't leave that in the doorway."

"I'm gonna have to; my arm is tired." He looked around at the three specialists staring at Justus like meercats that just heard a loud noise. They all sat at big fancy desks that had an assortment of toys and other nick-knacks cluttering them.

Justus said, "It's not like this door is a high traffic area. I'm waiting for one of you nonners to carry these parts."

Just then a Personnel Sergeant came out of his back office. "What is going on here?" he asked.

"He won't move his boxes out of the doorway," the desk specialist whined. "He's calling us names, and disrupting the office environment."

Justus responded, "Hey, I'm just trying to do my job here and that one wants to heckle me. All I ask is that one of them get out from behind their lazy desks and give me hand."

The sergeant had a look of disbelief. "You have no right coming in here. It is *not* their job to move boxes. You are out of line."

The specialist said, "Yeah, and he was playing on his tablet when he walked by."

"I was checking my map, you lazy nonner!" Justus snapped back.

The sergeant responded, "That term is not allowed here. You need to step into my office."

"They are non-mission essential, and if they won't help me with this mission, they are by definition 'non' or 'nonner.'"

"Office, now!"

"No can do. My chain of command wants these parts and I answer only to them. My arm is rested now. Since they won't help, I'll take them the rest of the way." Justus made his way for the door fast.

"Oh, no you don't!" demanded the sergeant, yelling across the room.

Justus ignored the sergeant and continued to the other side of the station with the parts. He took the tram, then checked out a toolbox from the Tool Counter. He finally arrived at room D501. To his surprise, most of the Spaceship Hazard Investigation Team were still there. He could tell they wanted this to be downloaded fast.

Now the pressure was really on. Justus replaced fuses with ease. The circuit card took a bit, but he managed, as well as replacing the screen. It was the power supply that really frustrated him. Justus was trying to follow the instructions on the tablet. He had to take out a few other components just to slide this thing in. Eventually he got it. With the whole room watching, he pressed the "on" button.

Everyone expected something to happen. DV5050 remained like

a rock, standing still without displaying anything. Justus double checked everything again. Sweat was beading across his forehead. He was trying to think. Trying to remember the VR training...

"What about your tablet?" Major Warfield asked. "Can't you pull something up in the tech data?"

"Yes sir, I have the info, but it just doesn't tell me. Besides my tablet's battery is almost dead...Wait, that's it!"

"What?"

"Low battery! These DVs charge up from the aircraft power and can run for days. I need an extension cord and adapter."

Justus quickly got what he needed and plugged DV5050 into the nearest power outlet. Within seconds, the lights on the forward screen came on. Justus cycled through the programs. Then he hooked up the DV to the stand-alone computer. Sure enough, they could see the data from the last few flights being transferred. The tech at the computer confirmed the data was correct and started making copies. They ensured they had everything they needed before having Justus erase the flight data from the DV unit.

Warfield smiled and said, "Great job, Johannes. Real good."

"Thank you, sir. What will become of this DV unit?"

"Well, I already spoke to your Production team. Since this unit has no assigned ship, they'll keep it around for spare parts in case another DV needs something off it."

"I see."

"Let's see if we can get someone to help you move this thing to the Production Office."

"No need sir, I got this," said Justus. He had already started walking with his DV remote, toolbox, and defective parts. The beat up DV5050 followed close behind him.

Justus led DV5050 into the Production Office.

Senior Sergeant Wrangler addressed him. "Thanks, Specialist Johannes. I heard the download was a success." He pointed to the corner of the room. "Over there is fine."

"It was. I think they got everything they needed," Justus said as he plugged DV5050 into an electrical outlet near the corner. "What about that one? Are we going to keep it around just in case we need it?"

"I believe so. You never know if another will go bad."

Dosed

The next night, most of the Dirtbag Dozen meet up at The Shack around 2030. Justus showed up around 2045. Pepper just looked at him after he got a drink. She continued to stare at him from across the table.

Then she finally asked in a serious voice, "Are we still together?"

"Truthfully, I don't know."

"What am I supposed to make of that?"

"I need a break. Not from you, but from life. Everything is happening too fast. I just need a moment."

"Do you ever think what I need?"

"See? Why are you making this more difficult?"

"Me? You're the one making it impossible."

"I'm just tired of it all."

"Tired of what?"

Justus didn't answer; instead, he got up to use the washroom. He then got another drink and sat at the far end of the table. Pete was going on about the C.R.A.T.E.S. downloads. Manny talked about diagnosing the engine issue on Viridis and even Wilhelm reminisced about an alien fuel truck driver and helping with the refuels despite the language barrier.

Then three girls came by and stopped next to Justus.

The Parts Supply specialist, Virginia, spoke. "Hey Justus, this is Missy and Caroline."

"Great to see you. Have a seat. I'll signal the waitress for drinks."

Just then Pepper approached Justus and stood beside him. "What's this?" she asked.

"What's what?"

"Did you invite them?"

"Yeah, so?"

At this point the bar went silent. Everyone in the group's attention was on Justus and Pepper.

"I thought tonight was about our group, the Dozen," Pepper said.

"So I wanted to branch out, make some new friends. What of it?"

"Are you done with all of us? Ready to move on?"

"Move on?! I would *love* to move on! We *all* need to move on, but every time I'm with this group, they won't stop talking about fucking Viridis! Let's talk about every Redball, every time you fixed something, how hard it was waking up and escaping on a dying transport. I'm just done. I'm done with all that! All I want is some normal with my life, is that too much to ask for?"

The room was very quiet; one could hear a cannon plug pin drop. Everyone looked at each other.

Pepper broke the silence. "Fine. You want normal, then I guess I'm just too much girlfriend for you and you need to look for others to replace me?"

Virginia stood up fast. "Is that what this is about?! Are you *using* me to get to her?"

Justus was defeated. "No, that wasn't the intent. I just want to live! I what to be normal, to just...you know, it doesn't matter. Do what you want. I'm just done."

Seth stood up. "Hey gang, I'm going to Green Beans, who's with me?"

Soon after, Justus found himself alone at the tables. He ordered a couple more beers, then a couple shots, then another beer, or two, or three. He got up to stretch his legs and look at a few pictures around this '80s bar. Some of the pictures on the walls seemed completely out of place.

He focused his eyes on one in particular. He found himself face to face with an old black and white photo of a gentleman with an epic mustache. Justus then read the plaque underneath the picture:

America inventor Charles Taylor, the world's first aircraft mechanic. He defied the odds by building and maintaining the first lightweight engine for flight. He was quoted as saying, 'I always wanted to learn to fly, but I never did. The Wrights refused to teach me and tried to discourage the idea. They said they needed me in the shop and to service their machines, and if I learned to fly, I'd be gadding about the country and maybe become an exhibition pilot, and then they'd never see me again.'"

Justus thought at that moment that he may have had an epiphany, yet after a little thought, he realized he didn't understand what that word meant. After even more thought, he realized he didn't care, yet he needed to press on and be the best at his job and prove everyone wrong.

With this heighted sense of ambition, Justus approached the bar and ordered another beer, only to find out they had cut him off. Instead of walking back to the barracks, he wandered the space station for nearly two hours, seeing many different offices and functions they provided. He finally made it back to his room and passed out on his bed.

The next day, there was a pause in their generation and Justus approached the Production office.

"Sir," he said to Senior Wrangler, "I want to train on the DV unit and examine more of its capabilities. Mind if I check this one out?"

"That piece of junk? Knock yourself out. Hey Johannes, are you attending the vigil? It's starting soon."

"Probably not…"

"They're having the funeral service on the Flightline for all those on the space transport. The entire Flightline's shutting down. Quiet hours, no ships coming in or out."

"We'll see."

Justus turned on DV5050 and guided it out. He then said to it, "Let's figure you out."

He found an empty office room that had windows that overlooked the Flightline. He planned on spending most of the night cleaning up the orange and black box. He had even acquired some new wheels and started to replace them.

Outside the enormous window of the dark office, he could see the entire Flightline, including the giant dome covering it and the stars and bleakness of space beyond it. He watched the funeral ceremony unfold across the Flightline. He saw rows of people sitting on folding chairs across a few empty ship parking spaces. Various speakers approached a podium. Justus brought up the vigil on his tablet, as it was live streamed throughout all the Stella space stations.

He could now hear the audio as they went on and on about the hundred and sixty-two heroes on the space transport that didn't lose their lives in vain. A new speaker then read each name and career field of the deceased members from the space vessel. After each name was called out, a single firework could be seen in space just beyond the dome.

Justus said to DV5050, "Great, now the Fourth of July is ruined for me."

More names were read, and Justus said, "I bet Sam would be sitting here trying to figure out what type of firework they were using that could create color in the vacuum of space. What do think, Fifty-Fifty?"

Justus continued to scrub off the debris, cleaning up the DV while he listened to his tablet.

He then heard a familiar name. "Senior Sergeant Jay Marston, System Engineer, Lead Weapon System Expert."

He watched the firework display its colors. "What do you think

Marston is thinking about now? He went through all that trouble to learn that ship and train us, now he's useless. He said you had A.I. What's that about? You don't seem very smart to me."

The names continued as the speaker read each one. Justus asked, "How do you learn? How do you open up that mind of yours? I guess you learn with every flight, right? How did I learn? That's a good question, Fifty-Fifty. I learned through VR. Marston taught me through VR...maybe that's the key."

The names continued. A new speaker approached the podium as Justus continued to work on the DV. They started to talk about the crews of the B-43s and how they saved all the passengers, including Ship 5050.

"Here we go, they're talking about you."

There was no mention of the maintainers on Viridis, but Justus didn't expect that. They listed off the crew of Ship 5050 and its passengers, including Brigadier General Eastwood.

Then the last name was read as they released the last firework. "Specialist Sam Kirkland, Avionics Technician."

Justus stayed for a while, just thinking. He thought about Sam, wondering how his parents would take his loss. He thought about Pepper, knowing things would never be the same with her. Justus even thought of his family back home, wondering if starting a new career was this hard for his mom. Then he thought about his dad, trying to figure out what made him leave while Justus was still very young. He wondered what his younger brother was up to. He thought maybe it would be best if he just went back to Earth. Then again, when would they see another space transport vessel?

CHAPTER 12

Don't Bring Me Down

The Station Exchange is a store that contains a little bit of everything, yet it always seems the one thing you are looking for isn't in stock. Justus wandered the Exchange. There were a few racks of civilian clothes, a jewelry counter, cooking supplies, a little toy section, and even video games. He laughed when he saw a couple VR sets on the shelf.

He picked up his Military Dress Uniform that was now ready. He'd had his new slacks hemmed and his stripes sewed on. Good timing too, he thought, since tomorrow he'd have meet up with this lawyer again and possibly stand in front the Commander.

Justus hung up his new uniform back at the Texas Barracks then headed to the gym. He felt out of shape since this whole ordeal and was trying to get back on a regular schedule. Prime's gym was small but had most of the standard workout machines, along with treadmills and plenty of free weights for Justus.

He noticed right away Maisie and Merrick were working out with the free weights. Justus found a bench next to them and greeted them with a guilty, "Hey."

"Hey...how's that schedule working out for you, going back and forth?" Merrick replied while doing his reps.

"Not too bad. The seniors in Resource Office never know how much I've worked on the previous shift, so they don't say anything when I come and go. Besides, they seem to care more about the BX-3 maintainers."

Maisie put down her barbells. "Lucky for you. We're shuffled in with the BX-3 maintainers and have to stand through all *their* roll calls."

"Still, you seem to be on our shift a lot," Merrick said to Justus.

Justus answered as he was doing curls. "Actually I've been on both shifts a lot. Something is always coming up. I don't mind; it gets my mind off other things."

"Speaking of other things, what ever happened with you and that chief?"

"I'll find out my fate tomorrow."

Maisie said, "Really? Let us know the results."

"I already met with the legal team on a few occasions," Justus said, "and explained how the situation went down *multiple* times."

"What about the chief?" Merrick asked. "I haven't seen him since Viridis?"

"That's Chief Cogstorm. He's the Maintenance Chief for the BX-3s and now our B-43 chief, as well. I think he's staying away until he's completely healed."

Maisie laughed. "You really nailed him good!"

Merrick asked, "What exactly did he say to you?"

"They say I'm not supposed to talk about it until after," Justus answered. "Let's just say he was really ripping into our way of doing maintenance."

Maisie said, "I just wish I saw it happen."

Justus' tablet dinged. He looked at it. "Crap. I gotta go. They got a radio issue."

Merrick shook his head. "Well, good luck there, Chief Slayer."

Justus quickly changed into his coveralls, grabbed his maintenance bag, and made his way to the Flightline. He entered the entry control point, hooked up his harness assembly to the track system, then exited to the ramp full of BX-3s. He started to walk out to the B-43s with a toolbox. A bread truck stopped next to him.

"Hey, specialist," the Expeditor said. "Get in, I'll give you a lift."

"Thanks," Justus said as he released his harness and stepped into the back of the Expeditor truck. Inside he saw several other maintainers as he sat on the bench.

The Expeditor asked, "You're one of the new B-43 guys, right?"

"Yeah, Johannes."

"Oh, I heard about you. You got quit the right hook. Where you heading?"

"Ship 26."

"Got it."

Justus checked out the nose art of Ship 0026. This one had a picture of President Theodore Roosevelt on a horse, with the words "The Bully" under it. He made his way to the flight deck. To his surprise, Major Warfield was in the pilot's seat.

The major said, "UHF, won't transmit, all positions. What do you think?"

"Let me check the DV first." Justus had been reading through the tech data and found out how to do a failure history. He brought up DV0026 on the co-pilot's screen, input the error and scanned the system.

Based on past errors, the DV displayed:

> INOP RT 62%...ANT LINE 11%...INOP ANT 7%...UNKNOWN WIRING 2%...UNKNOWN 18%.

Justus looked at the major. "I think a receiver-transmitter may fix this."

He walked outside and saw the bread truck sitting there. Justus talked to the driver through the window.

"Whatcha got?" the Expeditor asked.

"I need an RT."

"No problem. Stay here and check over the system, we'll get your part. Just give me the stock number."

"Thanks."

Justus gave the Expeditor the info and headed back to the ship. He approached Major Warfield.

"They're getting the part; I hope it fixes it."

"Good to hear. How's everything else going?"

"Well, we'll see tomorrow. I gotta meet with legal for that whole chief thing."

"Whatever happens, you've got my support."

"I wish you could tell them that."

The major said slowly, "I *have* been telling them. They used me as a character witness."

"Really?"

"I hope everything turns out alright. I'm really pulling for you."

"Thanks. You guys really want to fly, don't you?"

"We are all going crazy not to."

"I may have found a way."

"How's that?"

"Senior Marston...you worked with him, right?"

"Almost every day. He was my right-hand man. He put his heart and soul into learning this ship and developing that Tech School course."

"Yeah, I can see that. That VR course was nothing I'd ever experienced. I felt like the whole thing was being taught through VR. We had a few questions, but not many."

"What are you getting at?"

"Sir, the chief and seniors keep saying they need experienced technicians trained by a professional. They are waiting for experienced maintainers to go through that course at Tech School, but with the transport delays, who knows how long that'll take? Why don't they just take the course here? The experienced BX-3 guys here can take the course and be qualified within a few weeks. Who better to learn from than Senior Sergeant Marston? In the VR we felt like we were trained directly by Marston. It was no different than him being there teaching us everything."

"That may work, but Johannes, we're light years away from Earth. They'll still need that course."

"That's just the thing. The course is digital. They sent us our technical data; shouldn't they be able to send the course?"

"What about the VR sets?"

"I'm no techy, but maybe they can upload the course onto generic VR units. I saw they were selling some at the Exchange. I think they only had a couple left, but I'm sure there are more on station."

"That just may work."

"I'm just trying to think of all the options out there. I don't have all the answers."

"Did you bring this up to your supervision?"

"I thought about that, but with my record, I thought they'd just tell me to pound dirt."

"I see."

"I'm thinking this may be more persuasive coming from someone like you, Major."

After a bit, the Expeditor came back with the RT. Justus quickly replaced it and tested the system. The UHF radio check was smooth, and Justus felt relieved.

While Justus was documenting the fix in the maintenance logs, he asked Major Warfield, "Do we know anything about that attack in space?"

"Your team didn't hear about it?"

"No, sir. They seem to keep us maintainers in the dark for these things."

"You know. I'll try to set up a briefing for all of you and bring you up to speed. I need to see what I'm allowed to tell you at your level of classification."

"Thanks, Major Warfield."

The loud buzzing sound echoed through Justus' room. He woke up in a panic, jumped out of bed, and turned off his tablet's alarm. He then got cleaned up and ready in his Military Dress Uniform, making sure everything was in its place. He had to bring up an instructional video on his tablet to remind him how to knot his tie with his pristine uniform.

He arrived at the legal office and met up with his lawyer, Lt. Goodman, and the First Sergeant, Smith. They reminded him of all the procedures for addressing the Commander, then escorted him down a long hallway to find out his fate. The First Sergent and his lawyer went into the office first. After some waiting, Justus found himself about to stand in front of "The Man."

Justus approached the Commander's desk, stopped in front of it, stood at attention, saluted, and said, "Sir, Specialist Johannes reports as ordered."

The Group Commander, Colonel Groos, sitting at his desk, saluted back. He was expressionless and spoke in a strong, serious voice as he read from his electronic device. "Specialist Justus Johannes, there were several accusations against you concerning the events that transpired on Beachhead Airfield, Flos Island, Viridis moon. These include the following: performing maintenance without technical data, performing maintenance without proper protective equipment, performing maintenance that you were not qualified to perform, failure to document the ships' maintenance logs, being in a Space Military Uniform that was not up to regulations, misuse of tool accountability as they were scattered across your area, disrespecting a ranking member of the service, and physically assaulting the same ranking member."

Justus stood as still as he could, staring straight ahead of him. He was reminding himself not to lock his knees. He could feal sweat dripping down the center of his back.

The Group Commander continued. "When your team first landed on Viridis you were instructed by the acting Commander, Major Warfield, to do whatever you could to launch those ships. You did not have access to technical data, PPE, nor proper uniforms. You were all asked to perform maintenance that you were not qualified to do. Based on the eyewitness accounts of the flight crews, time was definitely a factor. Considering the nature of the emergency at hand, the lack of maintenance documentation *may* have been excused. Therefore, the accusations I just mentioned will *not* be held against you. However, you have been taught at Technical School the importance of tool accountability, and that *will* stand."

Colonel Groos continued, saying, "Concerning the matter of the disrespect and assault, based on calculations, you worked for almost fifty-two hours straight. You had just discovered the deaths of many on the vessel and that of an entire flight crew, its passengers and your close co-worker. I have a testimony from several members of the medical team here on station that agree no reasonable person would be in the right state of mind to make rational decisions after those events had transpired."

The Group Commander summed up. "You are hereby *relieved* of all accusations, except for the tool accountability. For that one, you will receive a Letter of Counseling from your unit. You are dismissed."

Justus could feel tears in his eyes. He did all he could to hold them back as he saluted the Commander and said, "Thank you, sir," then did an about-face and exited the office.

Outside the office, Justus shook the hands of Lt. Goodman and his First Sergeant, thanking them both.

Senior Smith looked at his tablet. "You are popular today, Johannes. We are both wanted in the Production Office."

With no time to change clothes, the First Sergeant and Justus walked to the work center.

Justus asked the First Sergeant as they walked, "I hate to even ask this but, do you know about Specialist Kirkland? I mean, do you know if his parents were notified?"

Senior Smith's face changed. He looked down and said slowly, "Yes, I was in the office when the Commander radioed Sam's father. It was...it was devastating...heart wrenching. It was by far the worst thing I've experienced in all my time in the service."

"I can see that. I'm sorry. What about Sam's mom?"

"Mom? Sam's mom passed away two years ago."

"Oh, that's strange. I didn't know. Sam talked about her a lot, but never about her death."

"Some things are too hard to talk about."

The two of them went past multiple maintainer's offices to the Production Office. Everyone had eyes fixed on Justus, since they all knew if you ever saw the First Sergeant walking with a maintainer in their Service Dress it could only mean trouble for them. Then some recognized him as the *Chief Slayer* and started to repeat the rumors.

Justus' face dropped fast when he entered the Production Office and saw Chief Cogstorm. He tried to avoid eye contact as he looked around the rest of the room. Major Warfield, Lt. Michaelson, and Senior Wrangler were there as well.

Major Warfield spoke first. "Specialist Johannes, put that on and tell me what you see." He pointed to a brand-new VR set that was on the table.

Justus walked over to it, grabbed the hand controls, and put the device over his face. He quickly scrolled through the various menus, then took it off. "Sir, it's the Tech School course. All of it. How did you do it?"

The major answered, "It still amazes me. Whenever I don't know where to go, I can always count on the Production team to figure things out. They worked hard to coordinate the data transfer from Earth and figured out how to load it on this VR unit. It took them all night."

Senior Wrangler responded. "With a city full of resources, it's all about knowing who and where to go."

"It took some convincing," the major said, "but we got the green light to proceed with training the experienced maintainers here on our B-43s. Chief, anything to add?"

Chief Cogstorm added, "We will take a few BX-3 sergeants and specialists from each career field. Only those that the Resource Office and I handpick. We *may* have your team of Tech Schools grads assist with the training, but *only* if they can't find the answers. Quality Control will be there as well to assist with any questions. I want to start the training as soon as possible, but we only have one of those VR thingies that they found at the Exchange. Any suggestions?"

Justus said, "We can ask the schools on station and offer to buy them off the kids."

The chief, ignoring Justus, looked around the room to the rest of them. "Anyone else…with experience?"

Lt. Michaelson jumped in. "I'll handle it, Chief. We'll find more sets."

Major Warfield said, "Thank you all. I will look forward to seeing this progress. Let me know what you need." They all stood at attention as he left the room. "At ease," he said as he departed.

Chief Cogstorm then turned to Justus. "Walk with me."

Justus fearfully walked next to the chief as he was escorted out of the office and down a long hallway.

The chief spoke in calm and creepy voice. "You may have escaped the situation on Viridis, but you better watch yourself. You need to learn your place here. These sergeants and officers above you have decades more experience than you. They've seen a little bit of everything and deal with insane problems every day. I have even more experience than them. Don't you dare try to cross me again."

They arrived at the chief's office. He pointed to the floor in front of his desk and said, "Stand there."

Justus stood at attention while the chief sat at his desk and read the Letter of Counseling for the misuse of tools on Viridis. Then he had Justus sign the digital form.

"When's your next day off, Specialist Johannes?" the chief asked.

"It was supposed to be today. My next day off is in six days."

"In six days, you will report to the Tool Counter at 0600, where Sergeant Gravel will give you tasks that involve inventorying tools and cleaning them. Your shift will end at 1800. Do you have any additional comments or questions?"

"No, Chief."

"You are dismissed."

Justus turned and was about to exit when the chief said, "Wait, my bad. There's another matter to discuss. I'll need you to stand here again, at attention."

Justus' mind raced. All he wanted to do was leave.

Chief Cogstorm brought up another document on his screen. "This one's for your attempt to start a fight in the Personnel Office."

"No, that wasn't my faul—"

The chief pounded his fist on his desk. "Don't speak, Specialist! If you want to rebuke it later, there is a process! There seems to be a pattern with you, and with patterns, I follow the process of progression. This one is a Letter of Reprimand."

The chief read through the document stating how Justus blocked an exit, called the Personnel specialists names, and disrespected their sergeant. Justus signed the new form.

The chief concluded, "Each time, the paperwork will get more severe. This is all your choice. On your next, next day off, I'll come up with something for you to do that fits this reprimand. You are dismissed."

Justus left the office fuming, wondering how he was able to keep his mouth shut for the most part. All he wanted to do was rip into that chief. He was also very ready to get out of his Service Dress.

He finally approached the barracks, about to head up the stairs when he saw Pepper step out of her room in coveralls, carrying her maintenance bag.

She half-smiled and asked, "How'd it go? Today was the big day, right?"

"Are you heading to work?"

"Yeah."

"I'll walk with you a bit. Today was good *and* bad. I'll explain..."

Justus told Pepper all about the events of the day. They stopped in the hallway just before the work center. "Listen I need to tell you something..." Justus said.

She stopped him. "Hold on, let me go first. We all experienced things on that moon in different ways. I knew you were close to Sam. We all were, but you went through Boot Camp with him and never left his side in Tech School, well...except when we were together. I should have given you more space, been more comforting. I don't know. I'm new at this. I didn't know what I was doing. I guess I'm trying to say sorry."

While he and Pepper were talking, several maintainers walked by, confused by Johannes wearing his Service Dress.

Justus seemed relieved. "You know, that's pretty much the same thing I was going to tell you. I was thinking about myself trying to find answers...and there were none. I treated you like crap by ignoring you. I'm sorry. Since we are being truthful...I don't know if things will ever be the same between us...and I don't think we should try to be together right now. I do miss you and the group. I need this support. Hell, we're the Dirtbag Dozen, right?"

"Thanks." Pepper gave Justus a big hug. "You're right, I think it's best we stay friends for now. I hate that cliché, but I think it's right."

"Same here."

"I better get to roll call, but you know...you look pretty good in that uniform."

"Good enough to sleep with?"

She smiled. "See you around, J.J."

"J.J.? I hate that name!"

CHAPTER 13

Eye of the Tiger

The lack of sleep was getting to Justus, but he had too much on his mind. He stayed up late studying his technical data, concentrating primarily on the DV units. He had an idea that just might work.

Justus put on his coveralls and headed to work. He checked out DV5050 and brought him to the debrief office.

Manny was in the debrief office with DV86. He had just finished downloading it to the main system as Debrief Specialist Brie helped him out.

Manny asked Justus, "Hey, how's it going?"

"Not bad. You got a lot of work out there?"

"Yeah, they just ran up the engines and got some weird fails. I gotta download all the info."

As they were finishing up, Justus asked Specialist Brie, "When you get a moment, could you help me with this thing?"

"Sure, I can do a download. Is that the one from the blown-up ship?"

"Yeah."

"I thought they already got all its info. What now?"

"I wanna try something. These things can transmit and *receive*."

Manny stared at Justus with a confused look on face. Justus hooked up DV5050 to the main system.

Justus looked at the screen and told Brie, "See, right there, there is a copy command." Brie saw it too. Justus told Brie, "Here, try to copy the info from 86 to Fifty-Fifty."

Brie went through the motions, and it seemed to work. Justus checked Fifty-Fifty, and sure enough, it contained the flight info and fails from Ship 0086. Brie verified 86's info was still in the main system.

Manny asked, "So what good is that?"

"Just a theory. I'll let you know if it plays through."

Manny guided DV86 back to the Flightline. Brie had other work to attend to, while Justus played around with the main system connected to Fifty-Fifty for some time.

Justus was wrapping up when he received a message on his tablet. Pete needed help with something on Spot B-2. Justus disconnected Fifty-Fifty, input Parking Spot B-2 on its controls, and ran out to the Flightline, securing himself on the track system. Ship 0721 had a jammer next to it as Pete and Simon were looking at a munition in the bomb-bay. Justus looked up and admired the nose art, which depicted a woman blackjack dealer holding up a king and ace of clubs.

Simon greeted Justus. "Bomb integration isn't linking up. Like the system doesn't know there is a bomb loaded."

"Did you check all your connections?"

"Yeah, like three times," Pete answered.

Justus went up to talk to the flight crew.

The bombardier showed him the system and what it was doing. Justus was clueless how this whole integration worked. He sat in the navigator's seat and brought up DV721, inputting the failure.

DV721 displayed:

CHECK CONNECTIONS ... UNKNOWN ... UNKNOWN.

He stepped out of the ship and waited for his Fifty-Fifty to finally arrive, thinking, *Damn, these things are slow.* He watched the DV unit trail along connected to the track system. He then guided it near the front hatch and plugged its wire into the port on the side of the Bully.

From the navigator's station. Justus brought up Fifty-Fifty. DV5050 displayed:

> RELAY G867 64%…UNKNOWN
> WIRING 13%…UNKNOWN 23%.

Justus came back to the Wards. "I think relay G-867 is bad. Let's see where it's at," he said as he started looking at his tech data.

They called the Expeditor truck and told them which part they needed. Justus and Wilhelm located the suspected relay, which was high up in the rear of bomb-bay. Justus set up a ladder and climbed to the top, using his light rod to search for the right relay. He finally found the panel just above his head.

Justus looked down and said, "Hey, Pete, I need a quarter inch socket."

The first bolt was off when Justus exclaimed, "Shit."

"What's wrong?"

Justus climbed down the ladder and said, "Man, I'm already on thin ice. I just remembered; I need to wear a safety mask."

"Oh yeah."

"Then I remembered we need to write up this panel and the part being removed. Man, maintenance sucks."

Justus found the mask and was annotating the maintenance log when a Quality Control drone flew by very slowly, scanning their work. Then it zoomed off to the next bomber.

They all looked at each other with a sigh of relief as Simon said, "I think you just saved us all."

"With that chief, I can't take any chances."

They wrote up the items in the maintenance log. Then the panel was removed, and the new part arrived. Justus removed the relay and let Simon install the new one, all while doing it by-the-book they best they knew how. They ran through the system operations check crossing their fingers. To their surprise, everything checked good.

"Tell me how you just did that?" Pete asked.

"I will, but later."

Simon said, "Hey Justus, we're all meeting at The Shack after work. Any chance you can join us? The whole team will be there."

"I though the others have to work?"

"No, after tonight we're all going to be on the same shift for bit. They're starting the VR training tomorrow."

———————

Justus arrived at the Shack as the music was in the air.

"This is the B-52s, *Planet Claire*," Pepper told them.

"B-52, like the bomber?" Seth asked.

"Not even close."

Justus, standing by the table, asked, "Got room for one more?"

Pepper smiled and responded, "Is it *only* for one more?"

"Yeah, yeah."

"Good to have you back," Manny said, passing him a beer.

Once the rest of the Dirtbag Dozen arrived, Simon addressed everyone. "So we have this bomb integration problem not reading one of the bombs. The DV wasn't telling us shit, then Justus shows up with his busted Fifty-Fifty. He plugs it in, then tells me to change an obscure relay that no one's ever heard of. How *did* you pull that fix out of your butt today, Justus?"

All eyes were on him. "Alright, I've been doing some tinkering," Justus said. "These DV units record every mission, every flight path, and every fail that pops up. Not only the problems in flight, but they record every break the flight crew encounters on the ground. They also record what fixed it each time. It's all based on statistics. The more info they have, the more of an educated guess they can conjure up. The problem is that each DV unit only has info from the Bully they are assigned to."

Pete asked, "So why not load them all with everything?"

"I read in the tech data that crossing data between two DV units can be an extreme danger to flight. Something about the flight info contradicting the other ship's flight info. However, if a DV unit *isn't* flying..."

Manny asked, "Is that what you were doing in the Debrief office?"

"I was. I copied all of DV86's information into Fifty-Fifty."

"*All* of it?" Seth asked.

"Yeah."

"Okay, when you say *all* of it from the main system," Seth said, "those go back to the history of these bombers, even during the maintenance and test phases from Marston and his team...God rest their souls."

"Yep, I loaded every problem and every fix from the history of Ship 0086. Not only that, I loaded the entire history of *all* our B-43 bombers into its little complex brain. He's got every problem every B-43 has ever encountered and what fixed it. We can now use it to calculate almost any issue. Fifty-Fifty is one bad-ass, troubleshooting, know-it-all on wheels."

The night went well. Justus was feeling better about the group, and everyone seemed to get along. Even Pepper seemed relaxed and happy. They were all excited to start teaching other maintainers the B-43s, and possibly start flying again.

———————

Twenty-five former BX-3 sergeants and specialists stood in formation in the roll call area along with the Dirtbag Dozen. Senior Wrangler and Lt. Michaelson stood up front, along with some others from the Production staff.

The Pro-Super addressed them. "Today, as you know, we'll start the training on the B-43s. We have been told these VR units will give you a very good understanding of your systems. You'll each take the lessons that correspond to your career fields. After we finish this course, we will apply it all to the real bombers. Our team of specialists here that are familiar with the program will assist you. LT, do you have more to add?"

Lt. Michaelson looked over his new team. "I have a good feeling about this. It took the others about a month to get through this course. With our longer shifts and your heightened experience, I think we can do it in half that time. I'll be around as well, since myself and some of the Production team will be going through this course, too. I'm sure it'll take us longer, since we'll be looking at *all* the career fields. Good luck, B-43 team."

They started bringing out the VR masks and hand devices.

"Where did they get all these?" Maisie asked.

The Lt. responded for all to hear, "These are just on loan, until we get a shipment from Earth. We are renting them, so to speak, at a price."

Seth asked, "Renting from whom?"

"We received them from all the kids on station here. We put out a mass message to all the families with children and the response was overwhelming. I think the parents just wanted an excuse to get rid of these things. Since we need to give them back, don't break them, and don't change their...colorful *markings*."

Maisie held up one that had *Five Nights at Freddy*'s pictures all over it. Some VR kits were plain, but not many. Some were painted different colors and most had experienced an "etching." The new trend among kids, they found out, was to use a computerized color etching machine to tag one's personal items.

Maisie started handing out the kits to the new B-43 maintainers and recording which one belonged to whom for accountability.

She described each one, "We got a camouflaged one, a tiger-striped one, Minecraft decals, this one looks like Sabine's Mandalorian helmet, I like that one."

The maintainers lined up and picked out the ones they wanted.

One specialist approached and pointed. "I'll take that one with Zelda holding a sword."

Maisie was taken back. "Zelda? That's Link! Be gone, back of the line for you!"

Everyone laughed.

There were only three left as Maisie called them out. "I got a Barbie, Paw Patrol, and Elmo."

TRAINING MONTAGE, *cue the Rocky music...*
VR users running into walls
The view of the digital cockpit
A specialist vomiting on the floor
The view of various part removals
Crew Chiefs doing virtual pre-flights
Weapon Loaders sitting in rolling chairs
Crew Chiefs refueling and transferring fuel
VR users swinging their harms hitting each other
Chief Cogstorm walking by, shaking his head in disapproval
More Inspections
More part removals
More loading bombs
More operational checks

Moving to the Flightline:
Changing parts
Fueling the ships
Operational checks
Changing the generator unit
Testing bomb-door integrations
Loading with bombs with jammers
Hydro running the landing gear thru
Performing pre-flights and post flights
Engine troops in the seats running it to power
Chief Cogstorm walking by with his rotten glare
Justus imagining himself punching the Chief... and freeze

CHAPTER 14

Message in a Bottle

The new B-43 maintainers and the Dirtbag Dozen were told to leave their tablets outside the auditorium due to classified security protocol.

Major Warfield addressed everyone. "First of all, I don't believe in keeping secrets, and I don't think we can achieve success unless every member understands what we are up against. That is why I have included all the B-43 maintainers, even the new ones. We must be aware of our mission and the severity of it."

"Some of you witnessed first-hand the attack on that space transport," he continued, "and the rest have heard about the situation. Our intelligence has pieced together the events. When the space transport vessel entered the Stella System, it was fired upon by at least four fighter class spaceships with a barrage of munitions. For now, we are calling them alien ships, because at this point, they are alien to us. They don't look or move like anything we have ever encountered. We still don't know where they are from."

"A distress call to the space stations was made from our transport vessel immediately and the evacuation process started. We believe those alien fighters may have left to reload. During this time, the space stations deployed the C-345s as well as the XF-94s over the three-day journey. The XF-94s were brought via the space carriers...just think of an aircraft carrier in space."

"While the last set of B-43s from Viridis went to rescue the shuttle passengers," the Major continued, "a group of four alien fighters entered the zone they were in. Two went for Ship 1895, and two were all over Ship 5050. Ship 1895 was able to evade them for some time due to their impressive defensive countermeasures and eventually our XF-94 fighters engaged and took one out, while the other one escaped. Ship 5050 was able to destroy one of these alien ships with its tail gun, however one of these alien fighters took out their ship, God rest their souls… At this time another couple of our fighters came and pursued the last alien ship and managed to destroy it."

Major Warfield took a moment to compose himself, then continued. "If you know anything about the history of bombers, our tail gunners have never been the best. The fact that this new Bully bomber, with all its technology, took down one of these things give me hope that we have a good chance against them. Do we have any questions so far?"

Seth asked, "Sir, do we know what happened to that dying space transport vessel?"

"Yes, very good question. After our fighters found no additional threat, some of them checked on the space transport. To their surprise, there were a couple more alien ships circling around it. Our fighters were instructed to engage those ships. While our fighters guarded the transport vessel, a few BX-3s arrived to destroy the remaining space transport so it wouldn't fall into the enemies' hands."

One of the former BX-3 maintainers asked, "Sir, do we have any guess as to who theses aliens are?"

"Thanks, Sergeant…Willis. We know what the Viridis are capable of and we've been closely monitoring the Nix airspace. We don't believe it could be either of those moons."

"Sir, what about the Calidums?" Seth asked.

Warfield stopped, shook his head, and answered, "No, we pretty much destroyed any space capabilities the Calidums had. They haven't been a threat since we were abruptly ordered to foolishly and dangerously pull our troops off that moon amidst the chaos. Please, don't get me started on that incredibly stupid decision."

Maisie asked, "Major, why did we even need to use our bombers to retrieve the shuttle passengers? Couldn't the Viridis people do it with their ships? We were right over their moon."

"I was hoping no one would question that, but I'm not about to lie to you. Recently the Viridis haven't been cooperating with us. For some reason, they still believe this new alien threat came from Earth. They also keep reminding us that keeping peace in their system is our responsibility, not theirs. It took a lot to convince them to even let us use their airfield on Flos island on Viridis. In short, yes, we asked for help, but they declined."

Warfield concluded, "That is all for *this* briefing. We still have some time before our next briefing that will include our B-43 flight crews. The chief would like to see all the old B-X3 Maintainers in the roll call area."

Most of the room left.

The major addressed those that remained. "That leaves us with the eleven of you original Bully maintainers. While you wait for them, I'll put this on the screen. It's the next topic we'll discuss. This was the transmission we picked up from Viridis two weeks ago. I already know what it says, but I'll let you have some fun with it. I'll be back in a half hour...Carry on!"

On the screen was written:

```
... --- ... / - . ... .-.. .- / .-.. .. ...- . ... / ... --- ...
```

"That looks like Morse Code," Seth said. "This may be difficult without our tablets."

Justus agreed. "Well I know 'S' and 'O'; my mom says they're really the only ones you need to know."

Lenny asked, "What are they?"

"Dot, dot, dot and dash, dash, dash."

Seth went up the smart screen, picked up the digital pen and filled in the letters.

```
S O S / - . S .-.. .- / .-.. .. ...- . S / S O S
```

"So do those slants signify a separate word?" Maisie asked.

Pete replied, "Yeah, and I might be able remember the rest, but it's been a while."

"What do you mean?"

"We had to memorize these one summer in Boy Scouts."

Maisie laughed. "Are you serious? You two in Scouts. Ha! I'd love to see that."

Pete said, "I know, I know. Simon, help me out. I remember the vowels were somewhat simple, and the patterns got more complicated by the rarity of a letter's usage."

"Well this one's only one dot. What are you thinking?" Seth asked.

Simon said, "That's either an A or an E. "

"A is dot dash. So E is just a dot," Pete said.

Seth added the letters:

> S O S / - E S .-.. A / .-.. .. ...- E S / S O S

"I'm pretty sure the two dots is an I," Simon said.

Pete agreed.

> S O S / - E S .-.. A / .-.. I ...- E S / S O S

Seth asked, "What about this first one after the first SOS that's just one dash?" Seth asked. "What's the most common English letter—T, N, R?"

"T," Pete said.

> S O S / T E S .-.. A / .-.. I ...- E S / S O S

Seth looked at it and said, "Ok, looks like we got two letters left. Dot, dash, dot, dot, this one repeats. Then there is three dots and a dash."

The twins couldn't come up with the last letters.
Finally, Pepper stood up and said, "Tesla lives!"

SOS/TESLA/LIVES/SOS

"Who the hell is Tesla?" Merrick asked.

CHAPTER 15

Breakaway

(In this next section, read Tesla's voice as an older gentleman with a slight Serbian accent. The narration should sound like the actor Jon Lovitz).

The year is 1929. The place is New York City. The man is Nikola Tesla. He was in his early seventies as he sat in his hotel room workstation and stared at the set of numbers he had just written down. He turned off his transmit and receive radio and got up. His head was pulled back suddenly when he realized he was still wearing his headset. He took it off and found an atlas among his many stacks of books all over the room. He grabbed the atlas from the middle of the stack. The other books fell, but it didn't faze Tesla. He flipped through it fast. Using the numbers from his slip of paper, he found the latitude, then the longitude. He marked the specific location with an 'X' and tore out that page. It was in the Atlantic Ocean about twenty miles off the coast of Long Island.

He looked around his rented room. It had everything he owned.

"This is insane!" he said out loud. "What am I doing?"

He found his suitcase, put it on the bed, and opened it. He looked around. "What to bring?!" He opened the closet and stared at his collection of suits then looked back at his desk that had his radio equipment and volumes of drawings, information and schematics.

"I need the research. No! I already have that. *Earth* needs the research, I gotta leave it." He looked back at his closet and grabbed a couple of coats, an extra pair of shoes, and a handful of clothes from his dresser. He then grabbed several books on history and books on science, lots of books on science. He tried to shove them into his suitcase, but there were too many.

Tesla said, "No, too much!" and started pulling out clothes to make the books fit.

He then took out a pen and paper. "Time to write a little note."

Tesla finished, held it up, and looked it over and smiled. Once he was satisfied, he addressed it, put his spare hotel key in it and sealed the envelope. He then grabbed his suitcase.

He looked over his hotel room one more time, seeing all the research still sitting on his desk and said, "Yes. I do believe...time to fake away."

Tesla made his way to the lobby and met with the hotel manager. "I wish to give you specific instructions. I am departing on a trip, so to speak. If I do not return within three days, I ask that you mail this letter to the *New York Times*. This letter is already addressed. Here is some money for your troubles."

The manager questioned him. "If you don't return? Whatever do you mean, sir?"

"This is not the time nor the place. I must be off. Goodbye, my good man."

Tesla went outside and hailed a taxi with suitcase in hand and headed for the harbor. It was late in the night. Rain and wind came. Telsa kept looking at his pocket watch, urging the taxi driver to go faster.

Once at the harbor, Tesla approached several sailors in the nearby eating establishments and pubs...but most refused his offer. He finally convinced an old sea dog to take him out, for a very hefty fee. The small boat set sail with only the captain and Tesla on it. Tesla gave the captain the coordinates.

The old boat captain asked Nikola, "Tell me again what this is about?"

The wind and rain continued and only got worse; they were getting soaked and it was hard to hear each other.

Tesla yelled, "I'm meeting someone out here!"

"At this time of night? In this weather? Are you the insane one, or are they?"

"I am only insane if they don't show up."

"Either way, you won't get your money back!"

"Don't worry. If they show, I'll give you even more money. I won't need it!"

When they finally approached the coordinates, the captain yelled, "I don't see any other boats!"

"Just wait."

Half an hour went by. The rain was coming down harder, and the waves grew bigger.

The captain said, "Five more minutes and I'm heading back!"

"Give it more time!" said Tesla, and he gave the captain more cash, doubling the original price.

The noise was incredible and they both looked up into the blinding light. To their surprise, an enormous structure flew over them, then hovered over the water next to the boat. They shielded their eyes and just made out a door opening. Then a grapple line flew from the structure and attached to the boat and started to yank them closer. The captain tried his controls, but his boat was being pulled toward the enormous thing until it was adjacent to an open door. A man appeared in the doorway wearing a purple jump suit that was completely foreign to them.

The man spoke one word, "Tesla!"

Nikola Tesla, without looking back, took his suitcase in his hand and climbed aboard the spaceship through the doorway. The grapple released the boat, the door closed, and the spaceship lifted high into the sky.

The old sea captain stared up for as long as he could see this impossibility. He then opened a compartment, grabbed a bottle of whiskey, and took a few swings. He knew this was one fish story no one would believe.

Major Warfield addressed everyone including the Dirtbag Dozen, the new B-43 maintainers, and all his bomber flight crews. "Most of us have heard the story of Nikola Tesla, the brilliant scientist who made first contact with aliens outside of Earth over his radio. He's the one that mysteriously disappeared in 1929, and the one that left all his Viridis alien knowledge and research as a gift to the world. His work included the space bridge wormhole, advance ship capabilities, a Viridis language guide and how the cryo-sleep system works, to name a few."

The major displayed the morse code message on the screen:

> ... --- ... / - . .... .-.. .- / .-.. .. ...- . ... / ... --- ...
> S.O.S., Tesla Lives, S.O.S.

"About a month ago we received this repeating message from Viridis. I won't go into much detail, but our Special Forces were able to extract Nikola Tesla from a remote island on Viridis and bring him to Space Station Delta for questioning. Keep in mind this is over a *hundred* years after he disappeared from Earth, and, might I add, he was in his early seventies at that point. I have a video of the initial questioning once he arrived on Delta a couple weeks ago. Here we go..."

The video played on the forward screen. The man looked to be in his late seventies and sat at a table in an empty room, looked at the camera, and spoke in a calm voice.

"My name is Nikola Tesla. I speak to you with a sound mind. I was born in 1856 in Smiljan, the Austrian Empire. That's on Earth. I won't bore you with my life. I have been told you have extensive records readily available for all to study it. What is important is what happened in 1929. I had already been in communication with them for almost thirty years. The Viridis, they were studying Earth, as I was studying them. They told me the news...they were in the area, so to speak. They agreed to take me with them, and I agreed to go willingly. Who wouldn't? This was my life's work. I would be able see it all first-hand. I know, I was old...It was what I needed. That final affirmation."

Major Marston stopped the video and said, "He goes on to explain being given exact coordinates and being picked up by a Viridis spaceship in the middle of the night from the Atlantic Ocean. They froze him in cryo and thawed him out when they got to Viridis. There he went on and on about his time learning more from them, and they did the same. They even brought him a few scientific problems and had him solve them, such as radio jamming and wireless energy transfer. They even showed him their space-ship engines and he gave recommendations on how to improve them. I'll play some more of the footage."

Tesla spoke. "I am a student of learning, always wanting, need-ing, to see more. Yet progression is slow. I know I am old. I want to see it all. I want to see the science evolve. I know I can't live forever, *but I can get close to it.* I made them a deal. Every ten years or so I would take a look at their research and discoveries and make suggestions to improve them. During the *in-betweens,* they'd keep me in a frozen state. It's been decades upon decades, but I've only been awake for a couple years. Each time I wake up, I am astounded by the technological advancements. I can't wait to sleep again and discover what's next."

He continued, "When I am awake, I live in luxury, with all the amenities, a beach house, servants, and a wide collection of exotic birds. Who would pass on this? I learned about Earth and its space stations. I thought about contacting you, but at the same time, I didn't want to give up my wonderful house overlooking the ocean... You understand. To put this in perspective, imagine if you will that the last film I saw in a theater was *Steamboat Willie* at the Colony Theater in New York. Last night I watched the latest *Spiderman* film. Whoa! You can see how this is fun."

Justus looked around the room. The flight crews and maintainers alike were glued to the screen. Major Warfield was trying to find the next recording. He pressed play.

Tesla was holding an object as he spoke. "This thing is absolutely fascinating. They have this puzzle toy all over Viridis; a cube, of all things, that has nine squares on each side, six total colors. I calculated over a quintillion combinations of this Davy Cube..."

The Major stopped the video. "Sorry. Wrong video. Here we go..."

Tesla continued, "This last wake-up was different. I was not greeted with praise, but with accusations. I didn't recognize the scientists questioning me. They said there was a threat— accused you, in fact, of causing the problems. They believe this new threat of advanced saucer spaceships could only come from Earth. I refused to help this time. I told them I needed more information. I can't make conclusions with no facts; that's preposterous."

"This time my accommodations were not so good," Tesla continued. "I was put in a prison cell. I thought I would die in that cell. Every few days, they'd take me out and question me. However, I was sneaky. When they weren't looking, I set up their radio to send out a code on repeat. A code they would never recognize, yet you on the space stations might. The old Morse codes. Then my only worry would be that it would not be recognized by you, my future Earth friends."

The Major summed it up, saying, "From his transmission, we pinpointed Tesla's location and had him extracted. We got him up to speed on all that's been happening. You might ask why we are even talking about this? Well, over these two weeks, Tesla has been studying our Stonehenge, as well as the one on Nix that is a close resemblance. Let me play this last video..."

Tesla came on the screen. "See, by looking at the photos and videos from Earth's Stonehenge, it is not possible to ascertain a conclusion or even a hypothesis, since it not fully intact. You see, pieces have been lost to history. Now, the second example from the Nix structure, although not identical to ours, it is incomplete as well. But when you combine these two, you start to see the whole image! Now we are getting somewhere. Stonehenge is a compass combined with a calendar! At the right moment of our Earth's revolution and rotation, it points directly to the wormhole that connects to the Stella System. I have proven the same is true on Nix, which points to the same wormhole that allows travel to Earth's system. Now, of course, the Virdis had never figured this out. They found the wormhole by dumb luck."

Major Warfield paused the tape. "Okay, now is where this gets really interesting."

"Stonehenge is a circle that can be divided by two," Tesla said on screen. "I found if you reverse your thinking and look at it from the other angle, they both have another pointer. You see, the one on Nix points to Earth, yet it also points to another direction, which I believe is a second wormhole."

Warfield stopped the video. "Within the Stella System, we recently scanned the exact spot where Tesla predicted this second wormhole would be located. The results came back positive. We believe he is correct. This is where many of the alien ships were spotted. We are predicting this is the direction our new alien threat came from."

The Major continued, "Our plan is to investigate this new wormhole and figure out more about this threat. Also, based on the information obtained from the black box from Ship 5050, we know we are dealing with something far beyond our technology. I can't say much, but these new ships don't move the same as ours and have systems unlike ours. The more we know about the enemy, the better position we'll be in. I'll keep you posted."

CHAPTER 16

Boys are Back

Weeks flew by. The new crews were trained, and the old BX-3 maintainers learned the B-43s quickly. With the technical data at hand and the course available for reference, they seemed to have most of the information available. Justus was finally on a set schedule and was paired up with the new B-43 Avionics **Sergeant Baudouin**. Justus rarely checked out Fifty-Fifty, but would on occasion, if there was a hard fix he couldn't figure out. Sometimes if another member of the Dirtbag Dozen was stuck, they'd ask Fifty-Fifty for advice. Not many of the other maintainers knew what that DV was capable of.

They were to have one last generation before given the green light to fly. This was the big one. The generation of generations, loading all the bombers to the max with munitions. Other agencies on station were involved, as well as a whole team effort to simulate a major deployment.

Justus sat in the back of the Expeditor truck with other maintainers, waiting. Sitting on the benches of the truck with him were Avionics' Sergeant Baudouin, Hydro's Flange, Engine's Maisie, E&E's Lenny, and his supervisor Sergeant Richard William. In the driver's seat sat Expeditor Sergeant Malone, who was listening intently on his radio in case they were needed. On the Flightline they watched as Simon, Pete, and a few other Weapons troops acted as a solid team and orchestrated the movement of jammers loading the munitions on every Bully out there.

Each ship had a couple of MPs guarding it to simulate an outside threat. In the meantime, the various career fields just waited in the trucks with their toolboxes ready, hoping they wouldn't be called upon for a Redball. Waiting all night leads to way too much idle time...

Sergeants William and Baudouin challenged each other to arm wrestling. A board was set up on top of a couple toolboxes and it was on. Maisie was sitting close to the table acting as a referee.

She held both their interlocked hands and said, "Okay, it's the best two out three. On the count of three, I'll release, and you start. One, two, go!"

Everyone was cheering as the two went at it. Sergeant William had the upper hand and powered through, bringing Baudouin down quickly.

William said, "See? I still got it. Ain't no one gonna beat me."

Baudouin rubbed his forearm. "We'll see. Still two more rounds."

"Don't you mean one more? Whenever you're ready. Or do you need to take a month off and hit the gym, big guy?"

"Yeah, yeah, I'm ready now."

The two got into position as Maisie gave the count again.

Initially William was on track to win. His arm was within inches to end it. Then Baudouin was able to pull through, over the top, almost to the win. The struggle went on with both men battling back and forth. You could see it in their eyes: William wanted to finish him, while Baudouin couldn't accept defeat twice. The tides turned. Sergeant William powered through and slammed the hand down, winning two in a row.

William let out a roar as he stood up. "Ha! See? Unstoppable!"

"I've seen better," muttered Justus, who was sitting in the dark back corner of the truck.

"What did you say?" asked William.

"I'm just saying, big deal, you won a match."

Maisie laughed. "Ha! Looks like new challenger has entered the game."

William looked surprised. "This little shit? No way."

Lenny said, "Well, he was the one that knocked out the chief."

"Who cares! Anyone could knock him out. That doesn't take strength; that takes stupidity."

Maisie asked, "So you gonna arm wrestle or not?"

"Oh, we're doing this," William said as he put his arm on the makeshift table.

Justus got up, pulled his neck from side to side, stretched his right arm, and sat down across from William.

Maisie held their hands and counted down. "One, two, go!"

Justus grabbed William's hand tight and slammed it down fast. The match was over.

William looked surprised. "Hey now! He went too fast. We didn't even start yet."

Maisie answered, "Nope, I think you just lost." She waited a few seconds as they repositioned, then said, "Okay, round two. One, two, go!"

This round lasted longer, and most of the truck was rooting for Justus. The advantage went back and forth as they both struggled. Eventually William took over and powered down, winning the round.

As they were getting ready for the final round, Sergeant Malone turned around from the driver's seat. "Hey, guys, Redball!"

Everyone was silent listening to the Expeditor.

"Ship 310, Code Loader inop."

Justus grabbed a toolbox and followed Sergeant Baudouin as they raced to the ship. Ship 0310's nose art showed the front of an old train. The female engineer was hanging out the window pulling down on a whistle chain, and a plume of smoke trailed above the smokestack.

Justus could see a familiar MP guarding the ship. "Hey, what's up, T-Rex?"

T-Rex gave him a nod and a smile. Baudouin and Justus entered and approached the bombardier.

The Lt. showed them the problem. "See, in order to activate the bombs, I need to input the code here. Right now, I am just using the test code, but this thing should still respond. There should be an activation light here, but I'm not getting anything."

Sergeant Baudouin quickly turned off the system and reset the circuit breaker. Once back on, the fail still persisted. Justus looked at the DV's fail page and it seemed like everything pointed to a bad C.L.U., Code Loader Unit. Baudouin checked the wires going to it and nothing seemed off. They both agreed to get a new C.L.U. from Parts Supply. It took some time for Justus to order the part, go to Parts Supply to get it, ignore the Personnel Office, and make his way back to the Flightline.

Justus and Baudouin documented the part removal, pulled the circuit breakers, and proceeded with the actual maintenance. The actual maintenance consisted of flipping a couple handles down, pulling out the old part, sliding in the new, and securing the handles. It still amazed Justus how much other work went into a twenty-second part change. They had the bombardier run through his procedure, and everything worked as it was intended. After finishing the maintenance logs, they headed back to the truck.

Maisie said, "Good job with the Redball, but I think we have one more round."

"Yeah, right," Sergeant William said. "This smart-ass punk has nothing on me."

Justus and William squared off again. Maisie counted down and it was on. This round was similar to the first. Justus had enough of William and forced his arm down fast. It was over, and Justus had won.

Justus asked, "So you were saying...?"

William smiled. "Big deal! I betcha you couldn't handle yourself in a real fight."

Maisie yelled, "Launch truck fight!"

"Nah, I'm good," Justus said, sitting back.

William smiled again. "Yep, that's what I thought."

Just then Sergeant Malone turned around from the driver seat. "Hey, don't fight back there! If you do, just make sure I don't see it."

"So how's the generation going?" Maisie asked him.

Expeditor Malone answered, "Well, they got half the bombers loaded, so we got a long night ahead of us. Anyone got a story?"

Justus turned to Lenny. "Hey, tell them about Tom Phineas."

"Who?" Sergeant Malone asked.

"You'll see. Lenny tells a good story."

Lenny started. "Most of you probably hadn't heard about Tom Phineas since this story emerged only a few months before our group left Earth. Phineas was the self-proclaimed leader of a group called the *Flat Earthers*. Over time, more and more fanatics joined his club. Despite all the research and evidence, they still believe the Earth is flat. Mr. Phineas had organized and expanded his group by the hundreds of thousands. They had sects all over the world. Not only did they believe the Earth was flat, they refused to believe we ever encountered aliens or a wormhole. These conspiracy theorists were convinced."

Lenny went on, "It's believed that the majority of their members knew the truth about Earth but find trying to convince anyone to join their farce entertaining. This is similar to the *Church of the Flying Spaghetti Monster*, which was a made-up religion for those that wanted to mock real religions. Of course, even this one obtained thousands of people who actually believed in it."

"Then one day," Lenny continued, "Charles LaMarche got involved. He was the son of former Texas Governor Sam LaMarche, the trillionaire oil tycoon who has his hand in almost everything. Maybe it was out of compassion, or perhaps truth, but I believe it was out of spite that Charles invited Mr. Phineas to accompany him on one of his fleet of private spaceships. He wanted to show him the spherical world as it is...with his own eyes."

Lenny stopped, then said, "Here, let me pull this up on my tablet. It's LaMarche, describing the event in his own words."

The recording of Charles LaMarche started. "Phineas was terrified to go to space, but knew he wanted to press through. After the initial shock of leaving the Earth's atmosphere, he was in extreme awe in space. I watched as he gazed out the window and witnessed the marvel of it all. We weren't in space long, but long enough to see the orb of Earth and all its glory. Phineas even took pictures of it all as he marveled at the sight. I have never seen someone so ecstatic about the whole thing. He was crying, he was so happy and emotional. He thanked me for this eye opener, thanked me for this experience. He said he always knew the world was round, deep inside, and felt a sense of wonder taking it all in firsthand."

Lenny stopped the video and continued speaking. "Once the ship landed, media from every news channel were there. Reporters from everywhere had the stage set as the crew departed the ship. Phineas walked down the red carpet, approached the podium, looked straight at all the cameras...and *lied*."

Malone asked, "He lied?"

"Yes," Lenny answered. "Phineas said, 'Ladies and gentlemen, I have been to space! I have seen its wonder! I have confirmed the truth...the Earth is indeed flat!'"

"Those that knew the truth were confused by his actions," Lenny continued. "The Flat Earthers, in their mind, now had conclusive evidence to their claim. There would be no denying it now. If their leader witnessed it firsthand, it had to be true. All in all, the trillionaire's plan backfired...bad. Now even more people joined the Flat Earthers."

Most of the truck seemed impressed. Sergeant William started a slow clap, saying, "Wow, I feel dumber after hearing that lame story."

Justus responded, "Hard to imagine that would be possible."

"Hard to imagine what?"

Justus ignored him.

"Listen kid, you still haven't answered. Could you beat me in real fight?"

"Hey, not now!" Sergeant Malone said. "E&E, we got a problem on Ship 3034, AC unit acting weird."

After Malone drove to the spot, Sergeant William and Lenny ran up to it. After some time, they came back saying they adjusted a valve, but thought the entire assembly might have to be changed out soon. Sergeant Malone agreed to write this one up and have it replaced after the generation.

The Expeditor then drove over to the end of the Flightline, away from most of the ships and trucks. He even placed a rag over his windshield rearview mirror. William kept talking about how great a maintainer he was, diagnosing the bad AC assembly, saying he could beat anyone in maintenance or a fight. Lenny looked around and caught eyes with Justus. Maisie even looked at Justus and gave him a quick nod.

After about a minute, Justus stood up. He went to William and said, "Let's do this."

Lenny and Maisie moved the toolboxes to the side, leaving a small area between the benches open. Very quickly, Justus and William were locked up, their arms grabbing each other in a wrestling stance. William swept his right leg out and brought Justus to the floor of the launch truck. They both struggled as William was on top of Justus and both men tried to get in as many cheap punches as they could. Then Justus overpowered William and got back on his feet. The truck was shaking back and forth, still attached to the track system.

Squared up on each other, Justus grabbed William's arms and used his right leg across William's legs to bring him down fast. With William on the ground, Justus slammed his knee into his neck and pressed down hard, still holding onto his arms. William was pinned. It was obvious to everyone that Justus came out on top. After a moment of William being unable to move, Justus released his grip and let him go.

There were cheers as Justus sat back down. William shook his head, knowing he was beaten. His neck showed a dark bruise. Once the commotion calmed down, Sergeant Malone, without commenting on the situation, took down the rag from the mirror and drove back near the ships to wait for any more Redballs.

———————

The B-43s got the green light to fly. Months flew by. Every shift, B-43s were being launched and recovered. The new B-43 Maintainers enjoyed working these bombers since they had far less problems than their old B-X3s, which was both a blessing and a curse. They learned fast that fewer problems equaled less time having to fix them, which equaled less experience knowing what to do.

———————

Time to hit the gym, thought Justus as he made his way across the station to it. It was his day off, so he had lots of time. He approached the weights and saw Maisie working out with Simon. There were another couple guys with them.

Simon said, "Hey Justus, meet our newest Weapon's troops, Matt and Nate."

Justus nodded. "What's up?"

"I think the chief realized we need more Weapon troops for the B-43 and added a few more," Simon added.

The five of them continued to lift weights.

"So, I take it you're on the second shift with Simon and Maisie?" Justus asked Matt and Nate.

Matt replied, "Yep, both been there for about a week and half now. Learning all about your new bombers."

"Cool."

"Yeah, they don't seem too hard," Nate said.

"Weapon's maintenance doesn't change much," Matt said. "Once you learn the bombs, the loading is similar. Learning the connection points and integration takes a bit. But the integration is more your job, right? Aren't you Avionics?"

"I am. However, the integration is totally a Weapons problem. They just always seem to call Avionics out to fix your stuff."

"Oh, really?" Matt said with a smile. He continued his reps, then asked Justus, "Hey, what do you know about that Crew Chief on my shift, Pepper?"

"Why do you want to know?"

"Just curious. Are you two still together?"

"Not right now."

"Good!"

"I don't like where this is going."

"Well, as long as it doesn't go anywhere, I'll be fine with that. I'm just saying, I know she can do much better than you."

"Listen, man, I'll date who I want and I'm sure she wouldn't be interested in you," Justus said.

"You think you're so tough beating up the chief and getting into fights. You need to watch yourself. It'd be best if you stay away from Pepper."

"Watch myself? Who do you think you are, coming in with all that?!"

Maisie jumped in. "Hey guys, keep your voices down. People are starting to look."

Nate then said, "You know...there is that little sparring room over there with the boxing gloves...I'm just saying..."

"No, I'd be too afraid," Justus said.

Matt laughed. "That's what I thought."

"Too afraid to damage you."

The five of them put their weights up and headed to the small sparring room. Maisie helped Justus get the gloves, helmet, and mouthguard on as Nate did the same with Matt.

"Ding, ding," said Merrick.

The two of them danced around the ring for a bit. Justus could see Matt was about a foot taller, which meant he had a longer reach on him. Justus could also see Matt was in a southpaw stance, which was a good sign that he was left-handed.

Justus swung twice at Matt's head but missed both times as Matt dodged fast. His third swing hit Matt hard in the stomach. He tried another gut punch, but was taken back by a blow to the head as Matt hit hard, knocking Justus back.

They went back and forth. Justus got a few hits in, but they were nothing compared to those jabs from Matt. Justus could tell right away he was out of his league. He figured he needed to change his style as he thought, *stay back, watch for the hits, dodge, and only swing when I know I'll connect.*

Justus could see Matt coming for him. Justus stepped back, dodging each swing, trying to find an opportunity. He continued to step back and found himself trapped in the corner. Matt went for his stomach, and Justus blocked but left his head wide open. Then Matt gave a barrage of hits to the head. Justus was delirious as he tried to block, but couldn't get to it fast enough. The next hit jarred Justus bad. He dropped to the ground in a daze. Merrick jumped in fast, declaring Matt the winner.

Matt helped Justus up and said, "Hey man, great fight."

Justus tried to stand, but his legs gave out.

"Whoa, I got you," Matt said as he helped Justus along. "Let's get cleaned up and hit The Shack. My treat."

The five of them started walking toward the barracks in good spirits, laughing at the situation.

Justus said to Matt, "Hey man, you definitely have a strong left hook."

"Thanks. You had some nice gut punches."

"So, are you two in *our* barracks?"

Matt stopped walking. "Actually, my quarters are the other way. I think we need to properly introduce ourselves to Justus. This is Sergeant Nate Clover and I'm Sergeant Matthew York, Pepper's brother."

The 80s music was pumping. Justus sat with Manny, Lenny, Merrick and Maisie. Matt and Nate joined as well. Matt bought them all a round of drinks.

Lenny said, "Hey, listen to the music. *Dead Man's Party*. That reminds me, we've been hearing some strange things on Ship 0086."

"What do you mean, strange?" Manny asked.

"I forgot, which one is Ship 86?" Maisie said.

Lenny answered. "That's that chick that looks like the Grim Reaper...with the sickle."

Justus asked, "I thought the Grim Reaper was on Ship 0341?"

"No, 341 has the schoolgirl in the dunce cap," Lenny said. "Ship 86 has the Grim Reaper and is definitely haunted. Seth and I were fixing a wire when we heard a creepy noise in the back, like someone was moving things around in the bomb bay. We looked out there and there was no one. Another time, I swear we heard a voice call down from the gunner's station."

"A voice?" asked Manny with a worried face.

"Yeah, it was like a whisper that we couldn't make out."

Matt took a drink, put his mug down and said, "You know there is usually one in a fleet of ships."

"One what?" asked Manny

"One haunted ship. A ship that may have a bad past or someone died on." Matt then gave Justus a quick wink.

Pepper had walked in and stood behind them listening in, trying to figure out why Matt was with them.

Justus added, "Yep, there's always one. I heard Marston talk about an engineer that died on that one during the production phase. I think that's why they choose that specific nose art."

Manny was looking pale. He got up to use the washroom. Matt and Justus started laughing.

Lenny asked, "What, guys? That ship really is haunted."

Matt shook his head. "Yeah right. You sure freaked out Manny."

"What was all that about the dead guy?"

Justus laughed. "Come on. You believe all that?"

Maisie was laughing, too, as Matt gave Justus a high five and they tipped their beer mugs together. Then Matt noticed Pepper behind him.

Matt got up and gave her a hug. "How's it going, sis?"

She looked confused. "You two...know each other? ...And are getting along?"

"Oh yeah, we go way back."

"Way back?"

"Yeah, about two hours ago. I'll tell you about it sometime."

Manny came back to the table, still looking freaked out.

Matt asked his sister, "So you know about Ship 86 being haunted, don't you?"

"Well yeah, everyone knows that."

"Yeah, Justus said an engineer died on during the production phase," Manny said. "Justus...how'd he die?"

Pepper blurted out, "You mean *her*?"

Justus looked at Pepper. "Oh, so know all about this. Do tell."

"She was crushed...in the landing gear," Pepper said.

Manny asked, "What was her name?"

Justus and Matt looked at Pepper.

Matt said, "Yeah, Pepper, what was her name?"

Pepper scratched her chin. "The engineer's name was...Jamie... Curtis."

"That sounds really scary," Manny said.

Matt added, "Very scary. Don't piss her off or Jamie will start breaking stuff on the ship."

Everyone got another round of drinks.

Maisie asked Matt, "So we've been wondering, and Pepper won't tell us, how did she get the nickname Pepper?"

Pepper cut in, "Hey, now!"

Matt answered, "It's really not that hard. Her name is Patricia York, or Patty York. I used to call her *York Peppermint Patty*. Then it just got shorted into *Pepper* and stuck."

Just then Wilhelm showed up.

Lenny asked, "What up, Wilhelm?!"

"Oh, man. I've been talking with the some of the other Crew Chiefs, who heard it from the Production staff. There's a lot that's been going on out there."

They all looked at him intently.

Maisie asked, "Out there, as in...?"

"Out there, out there, in space," Wilhelm explained. "So, you know all that stuff about the other wormhole? Over these last few months, we've been sending ships through there. Turns out it only takes twelve days to get though it to the other side."

Pepper asked, "Really?"

"Yeah, at first they sent a couple drones, and once those returned safe, they started sending more ships. They've been doing all sorts of recon and found the enemies' home base!"

"No way," said Manny.

"Yeah, there is a planet that can sustain life. They even located where a bunch of their spaceships were coming from."

Justus asked, "Is this for real or are you just messing with us?"

"It's real, I swear."

Even Matt looked skeptical.

"They're going to announce it tomorrow," Wilhelm said. "We're going to war!"

ACT IV

CHAPTER 17

Battle Symphony

The auditorium was full of maintainers all chatting amongst themselves. Justus was sitting next to Lenny and Wilhelm.

"Room ten-hut!" spoke the First Sergeant in a loud voice. Everyone stood up as the Squadron Commander walked in.

"At ease," she said as everyone sat down and remained quiet.

Colonel Bucket turned to the First Sergeant. "Senior Smith, have all their tablets been checked at the door?"

"Yes, ma'am. The room is secure."

The Commander addressed the audience of maintainers. "I'm sure most of you have heard some rumors. I am here to give you the facts. The threats against our ships in the Stella System have increased. A dozen of Viridis and Nix spaceships have been destroyed by this alien force, including many of their fighters and a few assault carriers. The largest attack still remains our space vessel and Ship 5050. Even in the last couple months, our ships have been threatened, yet we have been able to evade them so far. However, they did manage to destroy a few of our satellites. The Nix and Viridis continue to amass casualties."

The Commander continued. "Our reconnaissance teams have found the enemy's location. As most of you have heard, this is beyond the newly discovered space bridge on a planet that has yet to be named. In two weeks, we will depart for this new system. We will take a few space carriers that will carry a squadron of XF-94 fighters, a number of C-345s, and a handful of B-43s. Since this trip should only take twelve days, we will not be putting anyone in cryo-sleep."

"Once over their planet, we plan on sending ground troops in a C-345 along with fighter support to take over a remote airfield. This airfield does not appear to be currently in use. Once that location is secure, we'll land the remaining cargos, set up a base of operation, and then send the bombers."

Colonel Bucket finished up. "After that, it'll be business as usual, going after the enemy's capabilities as we always have. There are a lot more details, but at this level I won't go too much into them. I ask you what I always have: perform maintenance safe and effective. I have confidence in everyone. If there are any questions, your Production team and Resource Office can answer them. That is all for now."

The First Sergeant called out, "Room, ten-hut!"

"At ease," the Commander said as she left.

The next several days, the Weapons troops were busy loading four Bullies to the max with munitions. The rest of the maintainers were getting the bombers prepared as well as themselves. The specialists had no idea what to expect, but they got with the veteran sergeants as to what should be packed for this unknown adventure.

They found out fast that all of the Dirtbag Dozen would be on this trip, as well as most of the new B-43 maintainers.

Justus asked Sergeant Matt York, "I heard you're deploying, as well?"

"Hell, yeah. I won't let you have all the fun."

"I thought you just got back from Nix?"

"I did, but I volunteered for this. I'd rather be deployed anywhere then stuck on this space station."

It was the night before their deployment. The Dirtbag Dozen was sitting at The Shack in anticipation of the trip. The mood of the room was inconsistent as some were worried about the trip and others were celebrating one last night there.

Seth noticed the song that was playing was coming to an end as a news report started on the display. "Hey guys, check it out! News from Earth."

The Shack's screens displayed a reporter as he spoke. "Charles LaMarche, the son of the former governor of Texas and trillionaire oil tycoon, has done the unthinkable! Not only that, but he also convinced hundreds of thousands to join him. Hello everyone, my name is Larry the Llama and this...is MTV News."

The newscaster continued. "Earth's second wormhole has been verified. They found out the secret to Stonehenge and it points to a second space bridge within our solar system. The new system has been evaluated by our scientists. They are 94 percent sure they have found a planet in the Goldilocks zone. The eccentric trillion-aire LaMarche took volunteers, and boy did he get some. Almost a million people raised their hands for this. In a few months, they will launch to the new system and new planet named *LaMarche*. Hey, highest bidder gets to name it, right?"

"Due to past problems with the interstellar threats, this barrage of space carriers will also be taking an entire force of military-like ships to support them. Protect them, I think is a better word. Here is a recent interview with Charles LaMarche himself."

The next video played with LaMarche standing behind a podium with a crowd of reporters around. "In my 'Great Planet Acquisition Plan,' we will be taking people from all walks of life and professions. Everything has been examined and thought out carefully. We have enough equipment and supplies to last for many years. That will get us started to create this new civilization. We will be also taking the latest technology of advanced weapon systems. Most of these ships were purchased from various militaries and we have the most qualified men and women at their helms. Not only that, but we also have the latest in A.I. technology on our side. We are not taking any chances out there. I will be taking a few questions now."

One reporter asked, "How confident are you with this jump through the new space bridge? You have no idea how long it will take."

"Full confidence! We have the latest technology of engines. We can go almost three times faster than the current military transport vessels are going through those wormholes. With the rest of us in cryo-sleep, I'm sure our crews will have no issues."

"What if the new planet is unlivable or there are hostiles?" another reporter asked.

"I don't predict that'll be an issue. Just to put everyone's mind at ease, if we foresee any issues or we don't think we can handle it, we can easily turn around and head back through the space bridge. It'll be like we just went on a long cruise."

Another questioned, "You mentioned this advanced A.I. Where did you acquire this and are you afraid of its overpowering implications?"

"As many of you know, I buy and sell various things through many different channels. Yes, some of these are from military stock. I won't go more into that. The second part was about being afraid of A.I.? Did you watch too many movies? Were people afraid of robotics in factories, nuclear power, or driverless cars?"

"Actually, yes!" a reporter blurted out. "To all of those!"

"What we have here is utilizing our tech for the good of all."

Another asked, "What do you expect to find out there?"

"We expect a new beginning. We may start off as farmers living in huts, but this will be our chance to make a fresh start. We have something our ancestors never had. That is 'knowledge,' my friends. We know what we are capable of and are ready to hit the reset button on life. That is all. I bid you all a hearty farewell!"

Reporter Larry then wrapped it up. "There you go, my listeners. Soon those carriers will embark on this unknown journey. Stay tuned as we'll keep you updated on the latest news and stories from around the galaxy. *The Llama* is out...This has been an MTV News update."

The music resumed and Simon commented, "What a bunch of losers. Why take that risk?"

Seth answered, "Who knows? Some would do anything to start over."

"Hey, think of it this way," Pepper said. "At least Earth doesn't have to deal with all those people ever again."

The next day, the Dirtbag Dozen, as well as most of the new B-43 maintainers, were loaded into C-345's and made the short trip to Delta. Space Station Delta was a hodgepodge of people coming and going. The next several hours consisted of standing in lines upon lines. They were issued their battle suits. These jump suits had built in armor plating as well as a helmet. The rest of the suit was specialized to withstand a chemical warfare attack. The gear included the jumpsuit, outer boots, gloves, gas mask and voice emitters to talk through the mask.

Pepper's brother, Sergeant York, told the maintainers, "Hey, make sure all your voice emitters work. There is *one* rule that shall not be broken, a very specific phrase must be spoken to test these voice emitters. I will demonstrate." He put on his mask and spoke through the emitter that changed his voice to a deep baritone robotic sound. "No...I am your father."

They all donned their masks and repeated the phrase, ensuring their equipment worked. Pepper rolled her eyes and shook her head.

Lenny asked Matt York, "How often do we use these battle suits?"

"Every deployment."

"Really?"

"Every deployment we take them. Then we store them under our cots the first day where they remain throughout the whole deployment. On the last day, we retrieve them and pack them up."

On the new space station Delta, they were issued temporary sleeping spaces. They'd be departing for the new space bridge the next day in one of the large space carriers.

Matt was standing next to Nate as he told the told the Dirty Dozen, "After you get your cots and get cleaned up, meet us at the Bra."

"The Bra?" asked Wilhelm.

"It's called 'The Pavilion' on your map. You'll see."

Wilhelm and Justus secured their gear and made their way to the pavilion on this new station.

Wilhelm asked, "Why did he call this the Bra?"

Justus said, "Beats me." Justus looked around the large pavilion within the station and could see various food places surrounding it, including Green Beans and one that looked like a sports bar. Then he told Wilhelm, "Hey, man, look up."

Above the tables in the middle of the courtyard were two enormous white domes.

It finally hit Wilhelm. "Oh, the Bra."

The night was fun as they sat around and talked. They tried to speculate what this new planet would look like. Justus and Merrick tried to get a fourth beer and found out on Delta they were only allowed to have three a day.

———

The next day, the maintainers boarded another C-345 along with their new gear. They made a very short flight to an enormous space carrier. These monstrous carriers contained the bombers, cargos, and/or fighter ships in their various enclosed hangars. They found out there was a whole city's worth of career fields that worked on these carriers to ensure everything went smoothly as they traversed space.

The specialists were led through tight hallways, then down numerus stairs to be put in the bowels of this ship. They were all shown their new living quarters, which contained rows and rows of bunks, three beds high, each one within inches of the next one. They found it difficult to walk through the crowded, narrow sleeping quarters without tripping over others. There was an atrocious smell of dirty, wet socks. They tried to sleep in this overly cramped room.

———————

Justus woke up fast; someone was trying to wake him.

"Hey, get up," the specialist said. "You're in my bunk."

"What?"

"My bunk...this one."

"I thought I was issued this one?"

"Oh, you were, but it's time to swap out. It's mine now."

"Oh, what the hell? Alright, alright, just give me a minute."

Justus got up and could see the others crowding around the other end of the corridor. There was a sergeant yelling for all of Team 'B' to gather around. They were waiting to hear from their new guide, Sergeant Hanson.

Wilhelm asked Justus, "Did you get much sleep?"

"Nah, man. All the people coming and going and making noise. Lights coming on and off. How 'bout you?"

"Nope, not much. So, we're stuck on this carrier for twelve days?"

"That's what I hear."

"What are we supposed to do with our time, stare at our tablets?"

Once Sergeant Hanson saw everyone there, he addressed them. "Hey Team 'B,' I'm going to show you around this carrier and address where you'll be working."

"Working?" asked Justus.

"Well, yeah, you all have additional duties here."

Everyone looked at each other with confusion and disgust.

Hanson continued and gave out everyone's carrier assignments. Some were on laundry details, others had to clean up various areas of the carrier. Justus and Manny got KP duty and would have to spend hours upon hours in the back of the tiny kitchen cleaning whatever the cooks threw at them.

They all experienced horrible sleeping conditions, subpar food, and wandered endless hallways with the feeling of being trapped. This twelve-day luxury cruise carrier seemed more like a prison ship. They were all relieved to finally get to the new solar system.

CHAPTER 18

Don't Tread on Me

The stale, hot, murky, humid air hit them first as they departed the cargo ship onto this new soil of the unnamed planet. It was dark, yet not completely night. The dark clouds lingered, and the sky behind them had a green tint. There was a glow in the sky as if it was mid-twilight. They couldn't see much vegetation except for a scattering of small trees, void of leaves. There was an odor that they just couldn't place, almost a sulfur smell that left a bad taste in their mouths.

The group was led into a large, decrepit hangar. It didn't look like anyone had used it in decades. Justus found out he'd be on a shift with Sergeant Baudouin as well as their new Avionics troop, **Specialist Luke 'Shorty' Patrickson**, who was by far the tallest maintainer. They waited after Chief Cogstorm and Lt. Michaelson had them form up. The Seniors from the Resource Office stood up front, as well as Senior Sergeant Ection and Senior Mendoza. Soon after, the two Pro-Supers approached, Wrangler and Hunter.

Senior Mendoza spoke first. "I sent you all your work rosters on your tablets; check which twelve-hour shift you are on now. I need everyone on the *day* shift to follow me to the luggage yard to retrieve our gear. Then I'll show you which tents we'll be staying in. You'll relieve this night shift in about nine hours."

After the day shift departed, Senior Wrangler greeted their night shift. "They are downloading the rest of the cargo now and will be bringing our tools, spare parts, and all your gear into this hangar. Sergeant York, you'll be leading the Weapons team in getting all the bombs off the cargos and secured. We are setting up a munitions yard next to the hangar. Sergeant Baudouin, you and your pointy-heads need to locate your defensive system components from the CONEXs and secure them. I'll show you the small room where we'll be locking up the classified equipment, to include your IFF kits."

He continued. "The rest of you need to help sort through the rest of the cargo. The LT will point out where we are setting up the Tool Counter, Debrief, and Parts Supply. The B-43's will be landing in a few hours. Knuckle Draggers, I'll show you which spots we'll be marshaling them to."

Baudouin, Justus, and Shorty set up their classified equipment in the tiny room. Justus even found DV5050 on one of the pallets and brought him to the room outside the door. He had convinced Wrangler to bring the DV before they left. They spent lots of time moving things around and helping others get set up. The entire hangar was sectionalized, with each specialty having their own area to stage from. Even the Production team had set up a table and computer equipment to work from, along with generator units to supply the power. The Weapons team was busy setting up a yard next to the hangar with rows and rows of bombs in it.

Halfway through the night, Justus could see the LT talking with Chief Cogstorm. They were working twelves, as well, but off-shift as the rest. Justus was uneasy at the fact that the chief would be here through half his shift.

The rest of the night was busy. The Parts Supply personnel were trying to organize their boxes. The Tool Counter team was working fast getting the tools and equipment sorted next to the new Debrief area. The Pro-Super and chief were getting their new workstation setup.

They all stood outside the hangar waiting for the bombers to land. At times, when the clouds allowed it, they could see two moons trying to shine through the green haze. Looking over the expanse of their new Flightline, they saw rows of XF-94 fighters parked, as well as a handful of C-345s. They watched as their Bullies landed and taxied in. Pepper, Wilhelm, and the other Crew Chiefs marshalled in the four B-43s to their new spots. Afterward, they started their post-flight inspections.

The flight crews talked to Debrief as the downloads from the DVs were examined.

Senior Wrangler addressed the maintainers. "I need E&E to look at 341's transformers; there were multiple faults. MFE, we got indications of low engine oil on Ship 86."

Manny had a concerned look on his face when he heard it was Ship 86, the *Grim Reaper*.

Lenny told him, "Careful, Manny. Don't upset Jamie."

The Pro-Super continued, "Hydro, look at 310's landing gear. We may have to run it through. Lastly, Avionics come with me. Major Warfield has some questions."

Sergeant Baudouin, Justus, and Shorty approached the flight crews in their tent. Major Warfield, Senior Wrangler, and a handful of other pilots and navigators stood around.

Major Warfield started. "So we have a bit of a navigational challenge. I was hoping your maintenance team could help us with it. I know they are still working on deploying some satellites from the carrier. Until those are operational, GPS is out. The next issue is our compass system. Most planets have a magnetic north, but this one is acting strange. I verified it with the other crews; all our compasses just spin as they can't get a definite reading."

"Perhaps there is too much metal in the ground...or air," Baudouin answered.

"That's what we thought, as well. Our traditional map systems are worthless since this terrain hasn't been mapped out yet. We do have troops on the ground that would typically send us a signal and ping it on our map system, but even that isn't possible until the maps are updated."

"So what's left?" Wrangler asked.

"Well, we do have imagery, photos taken from the recon missions that contain our first set of primary targets in relation to this airfield. With the dark cloud coverage, that'll be a hinderance. There is also dead reckoning...it's doable...but could be dangerous. Any suggestions?"

Baudouin asked, "Do you have a sextant?"

"Celestial navigation...I didn't think of that. Sure, just tell us where we are in comparison to the stars in this unknown system."

"Oh, I see."

"Yeah, unless you got some crackpot astronomers with you, sorry."

Justus was thinking, then said, "Radios."

"Radios?" questioned Warfield.

"Yeah, there is a system, a really old system that I was forced to learn. I'll have to look it up, but I know it's on these Bullies. If those ground troops could transmit a strong enough radio signal, these bombers can pick it up. Their instruments will point out where it is."

One navigator asked, "Are you talking about ADF?"

"Yeah, that sounds right."

Shorty asked, "ADF?"

Justus told him as he brought it up on his tablet, "Automatic Direction Finding."

The Major said, "Just picking out a signal won't tell us how far it is. We need distance."

Justus was trying to think, then asked, "What's that called, when have like three signals and use like a triangle and math or something?"

"Triangulation. You might be on to something. Do we have radios?"

One of the pilots responded, "I know we have ones on the space carrier, and the ground troops have comm devices. We just need to know how strong the signals are."

Major Warfield looked at his team and started giving orders to coordinate with the carrier and the group troops to see what they could find about any radio capabilities. He thanked them as they headed out.

Senior Mendoza came back as the day shift was straggling in. Sergeant Baudouin gave turnover to the Avionics counterparts. Sergeant Van Mobb and his two specialists listened in. He showed them all the secure room and let them know their first launch would be in a couple hours.

The night shift of maintainers grabbed their clothing bags, gear, battle suits, water bottles and a couple food rations. They all walked towards their new living quarters. Justus looked up as the main star was trying to make its way up past the horizon. Looked like morning was coming.

Walking outside the hangar, Justus looked across the Flightline and said to Baudouin, "Wow they really brought everything: fuel trucks, Expeditor trucks, weapon jammers, forklifts, maintenance stands…"

"Yep, they thought of everything."

Just off the Flightline were huge tents. Each one had about fifty cots set up. They found a couple of empty cots and put their bags and gear down next to them as they sat and opened their ration packs.

Justus asked Baudouin, "How does this compare to your other deployments?"

"All I can say is, wow! I hope we're not here long. Living in a tent, eating ration packs. I don't see any showers around. This is nothing like my other deployments. I can't believe I'm saying this, but I'd rather be on Nix."

"I guess we just treat it like we're camping, right?"

"Camping? If I wanted to camp, I'd join the Army."

Walking outside after a decent sleep, Justus looked out towards the hangar. He could see many more large tents set up, as well as a tall radio tower being constructed. He relieved himself far behind the tents, and washed and shaved his face with his water bottle and razor. Then he made his way to the hangar while brushing his teeth. He could see Pepper walking with Matt and Nate. She was smiling. He was glad she seemed happy and felt good knowing her brother was here to support her. They were all on the same shift as they stood for roll call.

Senior Sergeant Ection addressed them. "We are working on better living conditions and the washroom situation. They should be setting up a few porta potties soon, as well as some combat showers. They are also getting the kitchen set up so we don't have to rely on rations for every meal. Everything is going to take time. All I ask is that you have patience and be flexible. Help out when we ask you to. Senior Wrangler, it's all you."

The Pro-Super stepped up. "Our test launches during the day shift were a success. Tonight's launch is the real deal. Our first launch is in three hours. Get your tools ready and remember to slow down and take your time. Slow is fast, everyone...slow is fast. Sergeant Malone is your Expeditor. Let's roll!"

Shorty checked out tools from the makeshift Tool Counter as Baudouin was getting the IFF equipment ready.

Justus asked Baudouin, "What did Wrangler mean by 'slow is fast'?"

"That's just what he says. It means if we rush through something, we'll end up messing it up so bad it may take longer to un-screw it. So, if we go slow and get it right the first time, we are saving time."

They sat in the launch truck watching. Justus and Shorty had already tested each ship's IFF codes on each of the four ships to ensure everything matched. Now was the waiting.

Warfield was piloting the lead ship, 0026. It was ready, munitions loaded and engines running. Pepper stood outside it, headset on, marshaling wands ready. On the next spot over was Ship 0086. Wilhelm was in the same position, ready and waiting. The crew gave the signal as Pepper guided it out. Once out of its turn, the second ship started, as well. Soon after, the next two Bullies followed, which were Ships 0341 and 0310.

The four bombers lined up in their elephant walk taxing towards the runway. One by one they launched into the night sky of the musty green planet. They could see all four bombers make their way toward the enemy. Soon after, eight XF-94 fighters, one at a time, ripped down the runway in a monstrous roar as they caught up to the bombers as escorts. Their section of the Flightline was empty.

Justus turned to Baudouin. "Now what?"

"Now we wait."

———

Baudouin approached Justus, who was sitting on the floor of the hangar next to DV5050 and asked, "What are you up to, Justus?"

"I have my tablet hooked up to Fifty-Fifty here. I found out from Parts Supply that they keep records of every single part ordered. It has the history of these parts. I'm downloading that list of parts now."

"So why will that help us? You said you already downloaded every fix, which includes our parts."

"Yes, the B-43 fixes, but not every part change. Our bombers use many of the same parts from your B-X3s, as well as some from the C-345s."

"Should you really be doing all this?"

"Fifty-Fifty isn't flying, for now he's just used for troubleshooting. I figure if he can see the fail history of all these parts, he'll have a better understanding of our ships."

"Just be careful."

———

Looking up, the maintainers could see the set of bombers and fighters returning with the twin moons shining behind them. As they landed, the crew of maintainers instantly pointed out the empty bomb bays. The flight crews were all smiles as it seemed the mission was a success. One crew member brought out a bottle of champaign and opened it with an explosion of foam. The flight crews all high-fived each other and patted each other's backs, as pilots do.

Justus was standing near the Debrief desk in the corner of the hangar listening to the discrepancies. He saw the navigator from Ship 310.

Justus asked him, "Any issues with navigation?"

"No. It took a bit to get used to, but we were able to pinpoint our targets and where the ground troops were using ADF. We could even return easily, thanks to that new antenna." He pointed at the giant radio tower.

All the maintainers received their list of discrepancies as their Expeditor Sergeant Malone directed them. First for the Avionics' team was to look at the satellite radio on Ship 341. Baudouin, Justus, and Shorty were in the navigator's section.

"How'd this work?" Justus asked. "We don't have satellites yet, right?"

Baudouin answered, "We don't, but they use this to bounce transmissions off the space carriers up there. What's the write-up again?"

Justus pulled up his tablet and read the crew's discrepancy. "SATCOM inop."

"That's it?"

"Yeah."

"I really wished they'd be more descriptive."

They started to run through the system. They could see the system powered up but was continually locking up.

"Do you need me to get Fifty-Fifty?" Justus asked.

"Nah. If this was having trouble transmitting and receiving, it may be a bad antenna, but this won't even let us get to that. I'm betting it's a bad SATCOM RT."

"Got it."

"Hey, Shorty, get with the Expeditor and order a new one. I'll stay with this one and we'll change out the part. Justus, why don't you get started on Ship 26? That's got the infrared scanner problems. I don't know much about that system. You may need Fifty-Fifty for that one."

Justus walked across the Flightline. The humid air surrounded him. He looked over at Ship 310, the *Engineer*. Simon was driving the jammer as Pete was directing him to load the bombs. On the other side was the *Grim Reaper*, and he saw Matt loading a bomb with Nate spotting.

He approached the lead ship, 0026, the *Roosevelt*. Justus saw Pepper walking across the top of the ship with a light rod and tablet in hand. She came down through the hatch, looked at Justus, and gave him an exhausted smile.

He greeted her. "How you holding up?"

"Not bad. Just finishing up the thru-flight inspection."

"What were you looking at up there?"

"Just your regular look over, making sure all the panels are secure, checking the surfaces, looking at *your* antennas."

"After every flight?"

"Every one. Not just that, but we look at everything, inside and out. You should see this checklist."

"Nah, I'm good."

"Whatcha looking at?"

"The infrared scanner. Apparently the image is all skewed and only works in some modes."

"Looks like your friend is here." She pointed to DV5050 as it slowly rolled up to the ship.

"Yep, I called him out here to help with the system."

"Is that DV really any different than the ones installed on these ships?"

"With all my downloads, you'd be surprised. This thing is finding all sorts of stuff and points out the parts to change."

"The correct parts?"

"Most of the time...Okay, some of the time."

Pepper kept staring at him.

"Okay, he's right about fifty percent of the time," Justus said, "but still points me in the right direction."

"I guess its name fits then, Fifty-Fifty."

"Yep."

"Well, enjoy. I gotta finish these maintenance logs then help with a re-fuel next door."

"Thanks, Pepper. Good luck."

Justus ran up the scanner system and could instantly see what the crew was talking about. This system had a number of parts to it, and the last thing he wanted to do was unleash the parts cannon. He plugged Fifty-Fifty into the ship and looked at the faults.

DV5050 displayed:

> INFRARED: ERROR...VDU 62%...SCANNER 23%...UNKNOWN 15%.

Looks like I'll change out the Video Display Unit, thought Justus.

He was about to shut off the system when another error popped up on the screen.

> ADF: ADF RCVR ERROR 74% - NXT MSN.

Justus asked, "What the hell is this, Fifty? Does that mean next mission?"

He ran up the ADF System. The system had no errors. Everything worked normally. He inputted the radio frequency for their airfield tower and the digital needle pointed right away. Just to make sure, he went outside the ship to see where the tower was, and sure enough, the indicator pointed right to it. Justus sat back down and looked at 5050's message again. He then disconnected the DV and looked at DV26's messages. There were no error codes except for the one concerning the infrared; however, this one couldn't decide what part was causing it.

After shutting off the ship, Justus typed the command for Fifty-Fifty to report back to his spot next to the secure room in the hangar. Then he called for the Expeditor. He got on the truck with his tools. There were a few other maintainers on the truck.

Expeditor Sergeant Malone asked, "What have you got?"

"I need an infrared VDU."

"Is that one of those complex parts, or a simple one?"

"Extremely easy. Just slide it in."

Lenny called out, "That's what she said!"

Everyone laughed.

Justus told Malone, "Also, I think we need to change out the ADF receiver."

Malone was looking over the write-ups. "ADF? I don't see it on here. What's wrong with it?"

"Well, nothing. Works good now. The DV thought it may become a potential problem."

"What?"

"I got an error code for a future issue."

"I'll ask the Pro-Super. I don't think he'll go for it. We got a policy around here."

"What's that?"

"If it ain't broke, don't fix it."

The VDU fixed the infrared, and Justus was told not to touch the ADF. The next night, the ships were launched again. This time Ship 26 landed with no fails. *So much for Fifty-Fifty's predictive insight,* thought Justus. However, before its next launch, Justus was sent up on a Redball to find that very same ADF inoperative. Replacing the receiver fixed that ship, and Justus' confidence in that little black box increased. Senior Wrangler was a bit surprised and wanted to know more.

———————————

Simon and Pete approached Justus, Wilhelm, and Pepper.

Pete said, "Hey, we gotta show you something."

The five of them walked outside the hangar to see the munitions yard. It was guarded by a couple of MPs. The cops were both armed with the X-J4M machine guns and wearing their battle gear with their gas masks secured in a pouch on their sides.

Justus stepped aside and approached T-Rex. "I didn't know you were here?"

T-Rex replied, "Yep, they got me all over the place. They said I'll start here, then soon be monitoring the perimeter."

"You think we'll see any action?"

"Who knows?"

"How's your living conditions?"

"Shitty. You?"

"Same."

They both laughed and Justus then met up with the others. Pete and Simon led them around the munitions yard.

Simon said, "Here you go," as he handed them all some white chalk sticks. "Feel like sending the enemy a message?"

At this point they could see various slogans or names written on the bombs: "Death from above," "Speak into the mic," "From Hannah with love," "Larry Loves Llamas," and "Yossarian was right."

Wilhelm said, "I don't even understand what half of these mean. The enemy won't be able to read English, and even if they could, they won't have time to read a bomb landing on their head."

Pete said, "You're missing the point. It's all for morale. Most of these are inside jokes. We write on it, take a picture, then always remember this moment in time. The time we when we sent a message of *huge* impact right into the enemy's lap."

Justus turned to the twins. "What'd you guys write?"

Simon pointed one out. "This one's mine. The message on the bomb says, 'If you can read this, you're dead.'"

Pete pointed to his. "Speak softly and carry a big stick."

Justus took some time thinking, then wrote out a short message: "For Sam."

Wilhelm was staring. "I don't know what to write."

Pete responded, "It doesn't matter. There are no lame sayings."

Wilhelm scribbled something. They all took a look. "Hi Mom!"

Simon asked, "What in the world?"

Justus and Pepper looked confused.

Pete shook his head. "Really man, I don't even know what to say. That's totally lame."

Pepper wrote out her message and stared down at the bomb. "Don't Tread on Me."

CHAPTER 19

For Whom the Bell Tolls

Weeks went by. The living conditions improved, but not by much. They were able to get a hot meal from the kitchen once a day, so that was a plus. The combat showers weren't too bad, and they were getting new supplies via the C-345s every few days. Bombs were loaded and the Bullies came back empty most of the time. They had a slew of write-ups as they continued to toil through it all. Justus could see it on the other maintainers' faces—the stale look of tiredness and acceptance as they pushed through each shift.

They were all called into the hangar and formed up as Colonel Bucket addressed them. "I just landed, as I have been on the space carrier for most of this. Thank you for your outstanding job! These missions continue to be a success, and they couldn't have happened without your maintenance support. I have a few updates. First off, we are calling this planet *Ignotus*. That is a Latin term for the *unknown*."

The Commander continued. "That brings us to another point. Our enemy is still very unknown. We have taken out several of their airfields and maintenance facilities. I'm sure some of you have heard their ships are very different from ours. They have a flying saucer look to them. We were able to obtain a few of their broken ships. We have our experts studying them as we speak. Each time, we have discovered the same thing. Remote controlled. So far, every ship we have found has been a drone, pilotless. This may be hard to believe, but we have yet to discover what this species looks like."

There were confused looks from everyone in the crowd.

The colonel concluded, "Over and over we have tried to communicate with whoever is out there. Yet we are still baffled by the lack of anyone on this planet. Even their production plants are all automatized. There are many speculations—maybe they live underground, maybe they are controlling this army from somewhere afar. I have confidence we'll know soon. Until then, each facility we take out is a win for both Earth and the Stella System."

———————

The constant turnaround week after week was getting to everyone. It's not so bad when you can see an end in sight or even count the days until you're done, but not knowing how long something will last puts a stress on someone that is like nothing else.

The next set of bombers had all sorts of avionics problems. Ship 86 had bomb door integration problems. Ships 26 and 341 both had radar issues and Ship 310's interphone was intermittent as the crew complained about how bad it was.

Justus approached the *Grim Reaper* with Fifty-Fifty trailing behind him. Wilhelm was on the top of the ship doing his in-depth post-flight inspections. Justus looked up fast when he heard the whirl coming from the opposite direction. He couldn't believe it. In a split second it happened—a rocket, launched from the unknown! A rocket struck the side of the fuselage near the top of the ship. Justus hit the ground fast to avoid shrapnel, which only nearly missed him. From the ground he looked up as he saw Wilhelm being projected off the top the of ship and falling fast to his fate.

Wilhelm let out a scream, "AaaaAaah!"

Justus saw him land hard, just a few paces away from him. He could smell fuel and a putrid gaseous odor. He tried to get to Wilhelm. Everything was in a daze. Wilhelm was convulsing. Justus crawled towards him, then sat there and held him up. He looked over across the Flightline. He could see the Expeditor truck's headlights beyond the cloudy haze of smoke. *Why weren't they coming?* He looked at Wilhelm's eyes. They looked puffy and red. Burrt Wilhelm's breathing was slowing down, almost as if he was gasping for air. Justus had no idea what to do; he just held on to him tight. *Why wasn't anyone helping?!* He looked down. *Why are there blisters forming on Wilhelm's hands? ... And on mine?*

Justus felt helpless and nauseous. He closed his eyes. *Only for a second,* he thought. Then he woke up fast. Someone in a battle suit was helping him. He looked up to see a gas mask in front of him. Two people in battle suits and masks attended to him and Wilhelm. Justus was given a shot in the leg and passed out...

Justus woke up in a cot in a tent, but not his tent. *Where was he?*

He took off his medical oxygen mask and called out, "Anyone there?"

Someone approached him wearing a gas mask. "I'm here. Just take it easy. You're going to be fine."

"What happened? Where am I?" It was hard to speak as his lungs felt extremely weak.

Through their gas mask, she said, "You're in a medical tent. Everything is going to be okay."

Justus could feel the person holding his hand through their gloves.

"What happened? Who are you?"

"You got hit. The rocket contained a biohazard. We are still trying to figure it out. My name is **Lieutenant Beth Knightly**. I'm your nurse."

"How is Wilhelm? Burrt, did Burrt...make it?"

She said, "He did. He's...I think...I think he'll pull through."

"Now what?"

"Now you rest. We've got you on an IV with antitoxins to counter the effects. I'm here for you. You just need to rest and get better."

"Thank you, so much…"

She put his O2 mask back on as Justus dozed off again.

———

Justus could finally sit up. His blisters had finally subsided, and he felt much better. Medics came and went, yet it was Nurse Knightly that seemed to stay extra-long to talk to Justus. Although Beth continued to wear her gas mask, Justus knew it was her. She would give him updates on Wilhelm, who was in pretty bad shape. His arm was broken in a couple places, as well as two broken ribs. However, that wasn't the main concern. The chemicals did some real damage as he was still on oxygen.

Justus' tiny room had dark tent walls that surrounded his bed and area. He could hear others to the sides of him at random times but couldn't see past his area. Bored out of his mind, he asked for his tablet. Beth came back with it, then left.

Twenty minutes later, she entered his area again and asked, "Do you know anything about this? There is this dirty orange box trying to enter the tent."

"Yes, let him in. I called him from my tablet."

"Him?"

"It's a DV unit, basically the black box of the ships…He's my…well, it's a maintenance thing. Don't worry, he can't get contaminated, if that's what you're worried about."

"I'm not worried about that. I'm worried about you, referring to boxes like they are alive."

"Just let him in. I'll introduce you."

DV5050 made its way to Justus, who plugged it into his tablet and started to scroll through some pages.

Beth asked him, "What are you doing?"

"Just going through all the maintenance logs. I'm seeing what our bombers have been doing out there. I am also uploading all that info to Fifty-Fifty here."

"Oh, now it has a name?"

"Yep. So how long do you all need to wear your masks around me? Am I still infected or whatever?"

"It's probably safe now. Just a precaution."

"How is Wilhelm?"

"Not so good, but we're all hoping. When he gets better, I'll bring him here, so then you can annoy him."

"Really? Am I annoying you?"

"Nothing I can't handle."

"Right."

———

A few days later, Lt. Knightly checked in on Justus. Her demeaner seemed off as she was taking his vitals and going through the motions.

Justus asked, "What's wrong?"

"Nothing..."

"No, really, I can tell...What's wrong?"

She stood for a second, then sat in a chair next to Justus. "Everything. I don't know how much more of this I can take."

"Go on."

"You're in the easy tent. You should see the tent next door. They have me bouncing back and forth. The cargos ships keep bringing in ground troops. It never ends. The battle wounds from the rocket attacks...missing limbs...I don't, I can't do this. Today we lost another one..."

"That's hard."

"It's too much. I wanted to be a nurse. I've seen so many medical shows where they help the elderly and kids. They work in a pristine hospital with doctors. Put a smile on someone's face."

"You and I watch very different shows."

"I don't even know why I'm telling you this. I'm sorry. I just needed a break."

"I know...I know...You'll get through this. We all will. Believe me, what you're doing matters. Everyone needs to stop now and then and let it out. I don't mind if you vent to me."

A week went by. Lenny, Pepper, Manny, and Flange came in to surprise Justus as he was sitting up in his bed. Or course they were all in their battle suits and masks. He could recognize most of them easily, but confirmed it with their name tags.

Pepper asked, "How are you feeling?"

"I'm fine now. I'm still having a little trouble breathing, but it gets better each day. I never want to go through that again."

Manny said, "Great to hear. You gave us all a scare."

"How about Wilhelm?" Lenny asked.

Justus answered, "They say he'll get better, but they won't let anyone see him yet."

"Pete and Simon wanted to come," Flange told him, "but they are way too busy out there with all the bomb loading. The others will try to make it when they're awake."

"How's it going out there?"

"It's insane. Once Ship 86 got hit, it was mass chaos. We saw various rockets coming down. Our airfield defense system took out most of them."

"Any more attacks? I've been hearing the alarms."

"Yeah, there's been about a dozen close ones. There were a few hurt bad from other sections, some still in critical condition. A few of our maintainers may have had contact with the bio. They had to go medical for testing and recovery."

Justus asked, "Do all the rockets have the bio?"

"No, they are finding that less than half of these rockets contain chemicals," Lenny said. "When you were attacked, we all had to grab our gear fast, in case. You should see it out there. Checkpoints everywhere. Decontamination stations. Everyone is in the gear. Not just with the Bullies, but across the Flightline. Fighters and cargos are going through the same thing."

"Are you in that gear all night?"

Lenny said, "Pretty much. You can take it off in our sleeping tents, but that's only after you go through the whole decon process. Once the alarms go off, you need to put it on fast. Many of us end up sleeping in most of our gear."

"Working in this crap really sucks," Manny said. "There is only so much we can do with these bulky gloves."

Pepper asked Justus, "How much longer do you have in here?"

"They said I got about a week and a half left. Then I can join your fun."

"Well, you really do know how to get out of work, don't you?"

"How is the work?" Justus asked.

"Steady. I've been helping with the Grim Reaper. That ship is a mess. After the initial hit, that fuel's maintainer was a real trooper getting that leak stopped. Poor kid was drenched in JP-88 as he did all he could to stop it. He even went to medical after to get checked over. The Sheet Metal team is still working on replacing panels."

"Yeah, and we had to replace two engines," Manny added. "There was so much shrapnel throughout those things."

"With that ship down," Pepper said, "we've been launching the others like crazy. You can even see the exhaustion in the flight crews' faces. Mission after mission without end."

"All coming back safe, right?"

"Ours have. However, the fighter unit lost eight of theirs. Three pilots safely parachuted the to the ground, but the others didn't make it."

Manny said, "Don't forget that cargo ship that was hit while taxiing. A bunch of people were hurt. A few died."

"That's horrible."

"I know."

"How are my Avionics guys?"

"Baudouin said he'd try to stop by tomorrow. I'll tell you, he's been working hard since you've been gone. Him and that tall kid. What's his name?"

"Shorty."

"Yeah, their work hasn't seemed to stop."

Lenny added, "I even showed them how to call Fifty-Fifty out there. They used his knowledge for a bunch of problems."

The gang stayed for a bit, then said their goodbyes.

Lt. Knightly came in to check on Justus. "Guess what? I was told I can be in here without a mask on now." She took off her mask. Her blonde hair was tied up in the back. "Well, now you can finally see who's been talking to you."

"I must say, I am relieved."

"What do you mean by that?"

"I am on a foreign planet. Nothing here makes sense. My mom made me watch every episode of that old black and white *Twilight Zone* show. I half expected to see an ugly alien face."

"Sorry, all you get is me."

"Don't be sorry. This is way better than I expected. In fact, I am stunned."

"Stunned?"

"Stunned they forced *you* to put on mask. I do believe that is a crime."

She smiled and blushed. "Take your medicine so I can check on the others."

For the next week, Justus continued to tell Beth Knightly all about his Dirtbag Dozen crew. He told her about Tech School, the time on Virdis, and on Station Prime. She told him about Officer Training and everything they went through, including landing on Station Delta about a year before he did.

It was finally Justus' last day. He was standing up and ready to go.

He asked his nurse, "Beth..."

"We should probably stick to Lt. Knightly."

"Okay. So...what are doing after the war?"

"What do you mean?"

"I don't know. You've helped me out so much. Least I can do is take you to dinner...buy you a drink."

"You're cute and all, but I think I need to remind you, I'm an officer."

"Do you really think I care about that?"

She just shook her head and smiled.

Justus continued, "So, hypothetically...if I was an LT, would you consider it?"

She smiled. "You, an officer? *Right.*"

"So, you're saying I have a chance?"

"Alright, what the heck. If you were a lieutenant and I was still single, I would go on *one* date, and it better be good. No taking me to Green Beans or something."

"Okay. I've just got to take a bunch of classes, get a degree, go to officer school, no problem."

"Right."

"So, we have a deal?" Justus said, extending his hand for a shake.

She shook his hand. He hesitated, then pulled her closer and gave her a quick kiss on the lips. Beth was shocked as she stood there motionless.

Justus backed off fast and said, "Sorry...I just...I just..."

"Don't be...sorry..."

Beth approached Justus, put her hands on the back of neck, and gave him an even longer, more passionate kiss.

CHAPTER 20

Seek and Destroy

It was game on. Justus felt like he had a lot of catching up to do. He'd been away for almost five weeks. He saw a real change in this Avionics team. However, it was hard to see much through their gas masks. Shorty was all over the IFF checks and troubleshooting. He was even in the habit of involving DV5050 on many of the fixes. Baudouin was quieter now, more focused. He was all business as he got the priority write-ups from the Expeditor and was just trying to get through each fix quickly and accurately.

Manny was right; it was a challenge working in these suits. Some part changes that could easily be done with hands sometimes took extra tools like plyers. Everything took twice as long in the chem suits.

Justus realized the psychological effects of gas masks. Without seeing anyone's face, he felt more isolated. There was no emotion. There was no joy of seeing one smile or look of confusion. He even saw this on the Expeditor trucks. There was less talking. Everyone was in their little zone. How much longer could he handle this? How much longer could anyone handle this? Nothing about wearing a mask seemed right and it never would.

Justus was called out to the Roosevelt for a Redball. He approached the pilot. It was Major Warfield, as usual.

Justus said, "Hello, sir. Radar issue?"

"Yeah, radar won't display. It works at the nav's and pilot's station, but not here."

Justus looked over Warfield's co-pilot's display that only showed the standard spaceship configuration. Justus looked over at the pilot position and discovered the problem.

Justus was pretending to look at his tablet. "So, how are these missions going, sir? Any end in sight?"

"You know, I think we're close. We still haven't found their headquarters, or whatever is controlling these drones, but it's just a matter of time. You know we got the satellites up and running now and we uploaded a better map system, so the GPS has been a help. However, the ADF is still working well. Very reliable system."

"Good to hear. What's the target today?"

"A production plant, a big one. The three of us bombers are going to hit it. We believe they are constructing more saucer ships there. However, it's heavily guarded by SAMs, Surface to Air Missiles."

"Sounds scary."

"So, what are you thinking about this radar? I really need it today."

"Not thinking anything, but let's see what happens if you turn your mode select switch there to *radar*."

The major rotated the switch as the radar was displayed on his screen. He let out a deep breath, shook his head and said, "Johannes, good to have you back."

"Thanks, Major. Good luck. Come back safe."

———————

Another week had passed. Justus woke up and made his way to the hangar. He looked across to the other side of the Flightline at all the medical tents, wondering how he'd be able to see Beth again. He'd seen her a couple times last week for some quality time, but that took some coordination with her work schedule and a precise time for him to develop a 'cough.'

On the Flightline, the rocket attacks had lessened. They could now work without their gas masks and gloves, but had to be ready to don them if the alarms sounded. Sergeant Baudouin arrived at work and was getting turnover from Van Mobb. Justus overheard something about DV5050.

"What's that about a DV?" he asked.

Van Mobb said, "Ship 26. It's DV unit was totally glitching out. I think we can fix it, but that ship had to go back up in a hurry. With little time, the Expeditor said to just swap it with 5050."

"So, you gave it Fifty-Fifty?"

"Senior Hunter agreed to it."

"No, no! This is bad. I need to talk to Senior Wrangler."

Baudouin asked, "How is this so bad?"

Justus started running to the Production area. "The Technical Manuals specifically state it is unsafe to fly with multiple ship's flight information on the DVs."

Baudouin said, "Yet, you still loaded it on Fifty-Fifty?"

"He wasn't flying!"

"How bad is this?"

"Let's just say this wasn't a note, or even a caution, this was a *warning*! That thing has flight info from everything. I even loaded all the XF-94 fighters info into him. All their breaks, all their maneuvers, even the dogfights with the aliens. I have no idea what he'll do!"

Justus and Sergeant Baudouin told the Pro-Super the same information.

Senior Wrangler had a concerned look on his face, then calmly said, "That's it. I'll just call the ship back. Wait here."

He ran off to make the radio call. Justus and Baudouin just stood there, unsure what to say. Justus figured it would be the end for him.

Wrangler came back and addressed the two of them. "I talked to Major Warfield. I told him everything you told me. He said this mission is too important to turn back due to a hunch. He said they haven't seen any problems yet and if they suspect anything out of the ordinary, they'll turn around and head back."

Shorty came back with his tools and IFF checker, then he and Baudouin went out the launch truck. Justus asked to stay behind for a bit.

He told the Senior, "I'm sorry about this. I didn't mean for…"

"Hey, you thought what you were doing was right, loading all that info into that DV. I knew what you were doing. Look at the ships you fixed with it."

"I know, but I'm just worried about the unknown."

"You were smart and brave to call this to my attention. All we can do is wait. Why don't you have a seat?"

Justus sat in a chair across from the Pro-Super's desk.

Senior Wrangler continued, "Have you heard of the Skywalker Principle?"

"I can't say that I have."

"Let me start this way. How much trouble would a person in the US get into if they shot a firearm in the air?"

"Does it hit anyone?"

"That's exactly the point. Let's say it didn't."

"I guess it depends on which state they're from. Maybe disturbing the peace or reckless endangerment."

"Okay, now, what if that same person fired it and the bullet struck a random person and killed them?"

"Well, now we're talking involuntary manslaughter. Unless of course you're a Hollywood producer and actor."

"Ha! Even if you take that same scenario with the drunk driver, the punishment for the action is entirely dependent on the result. Not a fair system."

"I agree."

"You can respond to a Redball fast, skip a few steps to fix the ship to make an on-time launch, and everyone will treat you as a hero. However, if something unexpectedly breaks in flight that was tied to your missed operational checks, now you're in a world of trouble."

"So, what's this got to do with Skywalker?"

"That was the biggie. We're all familiar with the scene. Luke is on his final attack run against that technological terror. He only has one more proton torpedo and there are no other ships left in the area to pull this off. Time is of the essence. If Luke misses this tiny window, the moon being targeted by that monstrous station will be destroyed, killing nearly four million people. So, what does Luke do?"

"Well, we all know he blows up the station."

"Before that...Luke *apparently* hears a voice from beyond the grave telling him to turn off his targeting computer. Of course, no one can prove this. Then he does just that. During this Hail Mary effort, he just shuts it all off. Here is when it gets worse. Then the Control Tower sees this and gives this rookie pilot a *direct order* to turn that thing back on before he kills them all! What does Luke do? He completely disobeys orders and relies on dumb luck, or the 'Force,' if you believe in that sort of thing. He hits his mark, the threat is eliminated, and there is much rejoicing."

"So as long as the outcome is good...no one cares."

"That's the point, but we should care. The story gets better. Instead of being reprimanded or even jailed for disobeying orders, they give Luke the Congressional Medal of Honor, or whatever."

"I see."

"The Skywalker Principle will never change. DV5050 should have never gone on that flight, we both know that. However, things have been put in motion. A motion that we cannot stop. Now all we can do is wait. If the flight is a success, we'll have a party and I'll even buy the beer. If it fails, then maybe we'll be cellmates. That's how life is."

———

DV5050 was synced up to Ship 0026. It scanned every system, every component, every computer, data bus, relay, circuit card, power supply, transistor, transceiver, transponder and transformer. DV5050 could detect no current errors. It scanned over the crew's flight plan and calculated the targeted area. These coordinates had been targeted prior to this mission from a few other XF-94s and other B-43s. DV5050 calculated each of these missions. 92.1 percent of munitions delivered to these coordinates failed to hit their designated target. Most of the bombs were targeted and struck down by the surrounding Surface to Air Missiles. DV could see the issue and calculated the correct course that should be taken. A low-level approach below the radar signature had the highest success rate. However, it also had the highest rate of being shot down.

The systems continued to be monitored as the ship drew closer to the target. The DV could see two XF-94 fighters on the radar in proximity. Scanning the IFF, it knew they were on his side. Ship 0026 then went into a slight dive, reaching a lower altitude. This was caused by the flight crews' manual commands. Autopilot was then engaged, as well as the terrain-following function. DV5050 was now in control. It could sense all the systems working together to keep the ship at the desired altitude while maintaining speed and direction. Every change of elevation, the ship continued to rise and lower, keeping the exact altitude across the range of hills.

DV5050 concurred with this approach. With the SAMs constantly targeting the other ships and munitions, approaching from low level was indeed the logical decision. The DV was making calculations from every system. It was sensing the radar scans, the flight controls, the engines, and even the defensive systems. Everything was lined up for a perfect approach. The only factor that could hinder success was that of unknown ships in the area. DV scanned the area.

Ship 0026 was approaching the drop zone. With each second, the ship grew closer to the targets. The SAMs were visible within the infrared system. The bomb doors were opened. The countdown was approaching zero as several targets were pre-selected. Within an instant, the munitions fell and rocketed toward the SAMs. Ship 0026's autopilot disengaged as the bomber went into a steep climb. Fifty-Fifty scanned the area again to see two of the SAM's were not selected. It sensed an 89 percent probability these Surface to Air missiles would target their ship. Bypassing the manual inputs, Fifty-Fifty hacked into the targeting computer and launched two bombs on his own.

The ship continued to climb as the XF-94 fighters were close by. The radar system picked up a squad of six Ignotus alien saucers coming in from the left. The fighters scrabbled left as the bomber continued gaining more altitude. DV5050 continued to check the ship's system for any errors as it simultaneously scanned the current dogfight.

Three of the Ignotus ships were destroyed by the XF-94s' air-to-air missiles. The fourth was being targeted by one of the fighters. The last two aliens were approaching Ship 26 fast as the second XF-94 was in pursuit behind them. The saucers were getting closer. Just then, one swerved right, came to a near stop, then targeted the XF-94 with a barrage of munitions. There was little time to react. The XF-94 tried to evade but was struck. DV5050 calculated a near zero percent chance the lifeform on the XF-94 would have survived.

Two saucers were targeting Ship 0026 as its munitions were launched. The defensive system was engaged by the flight crew as it took out every approaching missile. Fifty-Fifty could sense the tail gun attempting to shoot one of the Ignotus drones. DV calculated the flight trajectory of both 0026 and the alien, as well as the path of the tail gun. It could see that at their current altitude, the shots would miss. Once again, hacking into the ship, DV5050 engaged the autopilot and took control. It then put 0026 into a slight descent to ensure the tail gun would hit precisely. Its calculation was correct as the alien ship took a direct hit, disabling its flying capability.

Fifty-Fifty could sense the pilot's commands as they were trying to disengage the autopilot. DV5050 overrode each command as it could see the last alien ship in a close pursuit. DV also detected multiple errors in 0026's defensive system, making it inactive. A barrage of munitions were launched toward them. DV calculated each one and shifted the ship right, then left, then into a steep drop, each time dodging the threats. The alien saucer did everything it could to avoid the tail gun as it danced around 0026. This game of cat and mouse continued for some time.

Then the Ignotus ship flew high above 0026, almost out of sight. The alien went into a fast dive toward them. DV5050 calculated at this speed and direction, there would be a direct hit—not by munitions, but by the drone itself. It was on a suicide run. DV could not calculate any possible scenario to avoid this attack. DV disengaged the autopilot, giving their doomed ship's manual control back to its flight crew.

Out of nowhere, the last XF-94 approached fast and destroyed the saucer moments before it would have struck 0026. DV5050 continued to monitor the ship's systems as the flight crew flew back to the airfield. DV did not comprehend why the crew flew the entire distance manually without turning on the autopilot.

CHAPTER 21

Racks on Racks

Pepper waved her marshalling wands as the Roosevelt slowly approached its parking spot. Justus watched as Pepper guided it in, then she made an 'x' telling the pilot when to stop. Justus was the first to approach the flight crew as they were shutting down and gathering their gear.

Major Warfield came down the ladder and gave Justus a harsh look and said, "Not here. Meet me in the pilot's tent, the first one near the hangar. Get the LT and the Pro-Super."

"Yes, sir," said Justus as he headed back to the hangar.

Major Warfield and his flight crew stood in the tent along with Lt. Michaelson, Senior Wrangler, Sergeant Baudouin, and Justus.

Major Warfield addressed them. He had a look of concern as he spoke with sharp authority. "First off, we lost another fighter out there. The pilot did not survive. Secondly, we have a serious issue with 26! We had two un-commanded munitions launched. There was also an intense situation where the autopilot took complete control of the ship for over twelve minutes. Nothing could override it. Our crew was completely helpless as we were being targeted by the enemy. I have never been more scared for the safety of my team."

Everyone had the same look of concern. Justus knew this had to be the work of Fifty-Fifty. All he wanted to do was look at the download and see the results.

The LT asked, "How were you able to escape? How did you override it?"

The Major answered, "First off, it's been confirmed that the bombs that launched on their own hit something."

"What?"

"Not just anything; they hit two SAMs that we weren't tracking. Also, during the locked autopilot, our Bully took out one of theirs with the tail gun. We were being tracked hard by the other drone. During this time, our ship was swerving left and right. Somehow this ship was able to evade them long enough for our XF-94 to take them out. I'm thinking this has something to do with that DV. Saving the mission or not, this can't be trusted until we understand more."

Senior Wrangler responded, "First things first." He radioed Sergeant Malone. "Ship 26 needs to be impounded. Lock it down. I'll give you details soon." Wrangler continued, "Yes, Major, I agree. I think DV5050 may be behind this. This is incredible, yet dangerous. We need to elevate this. LT, we need to get the chief involved as well as our Commander, and even the general."

Baudouin and Justus looked at each other in concern.

Senior Wrangler turned to the Avionics troops. "Until we know more, keep quiet about this one. No one is to work on Ship 26 until we know more. I've got to make some phone calls."

Major Warfield addressed the maintainers. "You know, all in all, I do believe that A.I. saved our lives out there. Still, I don't like not being in control."

Work continued for a few days as Justus looked at the Roosevelt sitting there. Being impounded, no one was allowed to work on it. Fifty-Fifty was trapped in its hold awaiting his fate. Justus felt as he did after striking the chief. He didn't know how far this was going to escalate and he was unsure if he'd be blamed for it all. He even told Beth all about the situation. She seemed concerned, but also surprised and happy that it seemed to have saved the mission.

Senior Wrangler approached Justus and Baudouin. "We got word, you are to retrieve the DV5050 and bring it here. When I say bring it here, you need to physically carry it. Do not turn it on! Is that understood, Johannes?"

Justus responded, "Yes, sir. What's going to happen to him?"

"It will be sent off to the Spaceship Hazard Investigation Team. They will have experts figure it out. It may even be sent back to Earth."

Sergeant Malone drove Justus out to the impounded ship. He was directed to retrieve the unit and touch nothing else. Justus lowered the DV. He looked at the Expeditor truck. He could see Malone was looking down at his tablet. While Malone was distracted, Justus secretly connected Fifty-Fifty to his tablet and copied the last mission. He then secured the panel, picked up Fifty-Fifty, and carried it to the truck.

The days went by, and more and more ships landed with full loads of bombs. There were just no more targets out there. Even better, there were no more rocket attacks. They could store their battle chem suits back at their tents. The morale of the maintainers was up. Well, not exactly, since morale doesn't exist on the Flightline, but still, they were in good spirits.

Roll call the next day was great as Senior Ection addressed them. "Please, will everyone give a round of applause as we greet this specialist returning to work."

Everyone clapped as Wilhelm walked out. He had a big smile on his face as he approached the formation with his left arm in a sling. After roll call, members of the Dirtbag Dozen approached Wilhelm.

Pepper said, "You look good. How you feeling?"

"I'm just happy to be back. I'm still a bit sore, but I'll be alright."

"You still able to Crew Chief?" Manny asked.

"Not just yet. Ribs and arm are still healing. They said I'll be in Debrief for now."

"That sucks, but at least it'll be easy. The flying schedule eased up with only one or two launches each day."

"Cool."

Justus took Wilhelm aside. "Hey, how was the recovery? What'd you think of Nurse Knightly?"

Wilhelm gave Justus a look with a smirk. "You sly dog. I know about you two."

Justus looked around, then said quietly, "What? How'd you know?"

"She talks in her sleep."

"What?!"

"No man, I'm kidding. Come on. My room was next to yours. I may have been on oxygen, but I could still hear some of what was going on."

"You can't let the others know."

"I know, I know. She is pretty hot, though."

"Yes, yes, she is."

Justus and the others rode in the Expeditor truck, enjoying the last couple weeks. The Crew Chiefs were having fun as they marshalled the ships in and out. Sergeant Kurtz came out with two enormous foam hands as he directed the ship in. Specialist Jackson would go into a full breakdance as he maintained control of his marshaling wands, giving the correct directions. Another, Specialist Ralphie, went out there with nothing on but a thong to guide the ship out.

Even Sergeant York got in on the action. He convinced his sister to style her hair with buns on each side of her head. Then with two toy lightsabers, blue and green, Pepper brought in the Bully. The pilots loved it all as they didn't know what to expect next.

Pete and Simon finally had extra time since the bomb loading was minimal. They started recording their own music video and included most of the maintainers in it. They'd go from ship to ship, set up the music, and record everyone. The maintainers all joined in without hesitation as they went through whatever dance moves and motions the twins asked them to do to make the perfect music video for some song concerning *racks*.

The Bully maintainers were finally told there were no missions. Both shifts of maintainers were formed up in large formation in the hangar. Everyone was there, even Chief Cogstorm. Justus was confused, yet relieved, as to why he barely saw the chief this whole deployment.

Colonel Bucket stood in the front as she addressed the maintainers standing in formation. "Well done, everyone. Well done. The threat has been eliminated. That last site with all the SAMs was eliminated by our bombers a few weeks ago. Then the ground troops went in and found the source of our troubles, taking out their central planetary defense system."

There were lots of smiles around the formation. Yet, many were still confused as to who the real enemy was.

The Commander continued, "We have a few medals to give out. Senior Sergeant Ection, proceed."

Senior Ection called various members to stand up front as he read each citation and the Commander presented them with medals. The first set included every single Weapons troop, as everyone was reminded how many bombs were dropped on the enemy. Pete and Simon looked professional and happy as they each received their medal. Matt and Nate looked indifferent as they received yet another medal to add to their racks. The Production staff was next to receive medals, as well as the LT. Even the chief received a medal, though no one had a clue what he did this deployment. Lastly Specialist Wilhelm was called up and received a Purple Heart for his injuries.

After the ceremony, everyone was blessed with a hot meal. Makeshift tables were set up as lots of food was brought out to the hangar. Senior Wrangler stepped out in front of everyone. He looked over his shoulder, watching one of the C-345s take off heading to the space carrier. It had both Commander Bucket and Chief Cogstorm aboard.

The Pro-Super made sure it was off the ground before he addressed his maintainers. "LT, open that crate! Great job everyone. I have something for you all." The LT opened the crate as others helped him bring out several kegs of beer. He started handling out cups to everyone as the kegs were tapped. Senior Wrangler continued, "It took a lot of coordination on the LT's part, but I'm so glad we were able to deliver. Enjoy your last meal here!"

Lt. Michaelson responded as he continued to give the maintainers cups, "I may have coordinated this, but it was all Senior Wrangler! Make sure you thank him! He footed the bill for all this, and I know it wasn't cheap."

The Dirtbag Dozen sat together, along with Matt and Nate. They all reminisced about the events of this deployment. Simon and Pete even displayed the final edited music video of 'Racks' for all to see. It was all smiles and laughs. Justus got up at one point and noticed that Pepper and Nate were sitting very close to each other. He glanced down to see Nate's hand on her inner thigh under the table. Although surprised, he had mixed emotions. He liked seeing her happy, yet he wasn't sure how he felt about Nate.

At one point, Matt stood up, raised his beer, and declared, "Happy Franksgiving!"

———

They arrived back on the space carrier and shuffled in, finally ready to embark off that ugly planet. The specialists were assigned bunks again in the bowels of the carrier. Justus was thinking how unfair it was since the Seniors and Officers all got their own rooms. The Dirtbag Dozen and the other tired specialists then learned their extra duties for this trip back.

Sergeant Hanson read through the names and finally said,

"Specialist Johannes, report to Medical."

Simon said, "Well, at least you're not cleaning the poop deck."

Hanson smiled. "Medical usually means you'll be assisting an orderly. So, there is good chance you *will* be cleaning the poop deck."

Justus shouted out, "Hey, thanks a lot, Hanson!"

"Don't thank me. I don't pick these jobs."

Justus made his way up a few levels and found the Medical Bay.

He walked in and approached the nurse at the front. "Hello, I'm Specialist Johannes, supposed to report here for extra duty."

The nurse said, "One second...let me check."

As she was checking the list, another nurse came around the corner. "Don't worry, Nurse Duckett, this one is mine. Come with me, specialist."

Justus stood still for a second as a slight smile formed at the side of his mouth. He quickly joined Nurse Beth Knightly.

Lt. Knightly continued to look forward and walk fast through the corridor past a crowd of others as she spoke with authority. "You have been assigned to me personally. Which means for the duration of this voyage, you will be tasked with various jobs in and around this medical facility. In other words, whatever I tell you to do, you must comply with fully and without question."

"Yes *ma'am!*"

ACT V

CHAPTER 22

Skills to Pay the Bills

Two and half years had passed since the Dirtbag Dozen returned from Ignotus. Justus sat in the courtyard outside of the Texas barracks with his tablet opened to the 'mesmerizing' world of Business Law. He couldn't take much more of it. *Why is it that every single college textbook contains this blasted Maslow's Hierarchy of needs?* He turned off the screen.

Justus thought about the last couple of years. He didn't see much of Beth since she was working in the medical bay on Space Station Delta. But every few months she would have to come to Station Prime for training, and they were able to sneak away during her visits. However, her schedule hadn't allowed her to see him for over six months now. He would message her from time to time and send her provocative stories. In the last letter she warned him about messaging, expressing concern that someone would find out. That was three months ago. He figured their relationship was probably over.

Pepper was doing great things on the Flightline and really excelling at her job. She earned the position of Flying Crew Chief, which meant she could go with the bombers in case they needed maintenance support off-station. She continued to date the Weapon's troop Nate, and had also recently been promoted to the rank of sergeant. Her only goal, it seemed, was to outrank her brother Matt at some point. Matt continued to be the center of laughs at The Shack or Green Beans, and was now in the position of leading all the Weapons troops for the Bullies.

Manny and Maisie kept up with their engine maintenance. Maisie seemed to be the most experienced Bully engine troop. Even though she was still a specialist, she was granted a waiver to be engine run qualified early. Justus was a bit suspicious since he saw Maisie and Merrick together quite a bit. Merrick was still excelling in Hydro work. Flange was Flange, the unknown Hydro troop that seemed to just blend in.

Pete and Simon both made sergeant and were still making music videos when they weren't out there loading bombs and asking Avionics to troubleshoot their systems. Lenny even took an interest in their videos as he worked as their unofficial manager trying to get their vids out on the space station channels. Seth Harvard was the fourth Dirtbag Dozen to make sergeant, and he was also taking college classes—a lot of college classes. It seemed he was on the officer track, as well.

Wilhelm was the one Justus was concerned about the most. Ever since his accident, Burrt was quieter. He'd healed fine physically, but he seemed distant at times. Justus would ask how he was doing, and his response was always the same as he shrugged it off and said everything was good.

Work on Flightline was constant. Every few months, the seniors in the Resource Office decided to switch up everyone's shift. Each time, the maintainers would have to readjust their sleep schedules and who they worked with. That was a constant hassle.

Justus was still convinced that Chief Cogstorm was out to get him and he felt that the Quality Control drones were always targeting him. He received a Letter of Counseling for not looking directly at his technical manual while working. Then within two weeks, he got a Letter of Reprimand for not documenting the maintenance logs correctly. The chief assured him the next problem would result in an Article 15, a serious offense in military terms.

The chief kept making up new rules each week. First, he banned backpacks on the Flightline, saying they caused FOD. No one could figure out why they were banned. Your backpack had everything you needed: gloves, extra ear plugs, extra T-shirts, rags, safety wire, copper wire, warning tags, and the almighty scrounge. Scrounge is any piece of small hardware that has the potential to fix anything. All the *no backpacks* rule did was slow down maintenance for everyone. A week later, Chief Cogstorm banned water bottles on the Flightline, saying they could get their water from the Expeditor trucks.

Warfield hardly flew ever since he was promoted to colonel. He was still in charge of the B-43's flight crews, but it was rare to see him. The now *Captain* Michaelson continued to lead the way as their main Maintenance Officer as they flew the bombers every day. Six more ships were scheduled to arrive in the next couple weeks and everyone was waiting for their arrival. There was even a new maintenance officer, Lt. Handelman, who was trying to learn the ropes.

DV5050 was gone. Justus never saw nor heard anything about him since his last flight in the Roosevelt. This forced Justus to learn his systems better. He'd get with Lenny or Seth to have them teach him how to read the wiring diagrams. He also found out he could access the same statistics and history as Fifty-Fifty did to see which parts were most likely to fix each situation. Although it took much longer, it proved to be effective. The last thing he wanted to do was unleash the parts cannon.

Ever since returning from the deployment, the transport vessels were back up and running as they brought new supplies from Earth every four months. They even slowly received new B-43 troops. Justus enjoyed meeting the new specialists but hated training them. To him, it was so much easier and faster to do the tasks himself.

Specialist O'Reilly was one of the new Avionic troops and was also Justus' new roommate—and the reason Justus liked to hang out in the courtyard or anywhere else outside his room. He turned on this tablet again, looked at his course material for half a minute, then turned it off. He just couldn't concentrate. School was hard enough by itself, but adding full-time work to that made it nearly impossible. He wondered if he'd ever get his degree at this rate. Justus then got up to see if anyone was hanging out at The Shack.

———————

Strolling through the doors of the 80s bar, Justus caught sight of Simon and Pete right away. They were sitting with a few girls.

Simon spotted Justus. "Hey, man, over here. Have a seat. I want you to meet Missy, Caroline, and Virginia."

Justus sat and said, "I know you. Virginia from Parts Supply."

She smiled "That's right. Justin, is it?"

"Justus. I know last time was a bit awkward for all of us. How about a do-over?"

"Sure. Caroline here works in Supply with me and Missy's a dental assistant. Missy is also my roommate."

"Cool. Let me buy the next round."

Pete said, "In that case, make mine a double!"

Missy put her hand on his arm. "Slow down. You know what happened last time."

Justus smiled. "Last time? I gotta hear this."

Simon laughed. "Lightweight."

"Last week, he was stumbling so bad I had to guide him down the corridors," Missy said. "Then he threw up all over when we got near my barracks."

Justus inquired, "Near *your* barracks?"

Missy blushed. "That's all I'm going to say about that."

They all smiled, exchanged looks and took another drink.

Caroline stood up. "You'll have to excuse me."

The other girls got up as well.

"We'll be right back," Missy said.

The three headed to the washroom.

Simon leaned in and said, "So Pete's last visit to the dentist went better than anyone can expect. He hit it off with Missy. Next thing you know, we were all hanging out. Sorry, Justus, but I have a good feeling about Caroline."

"Don't be sorry. Do your thing."

"I'm just putting it out there that I've already got my eye on her.

I know you got some skills."

"Skills?"

"Hey, we all know about you and that nurse."

"Alright, alright, let's just keep that one on the downlow. I don't think we're together anymore."

"You don't *think* you're together?"

"It's complicated. No, we're pretty much done...Yeah, we're done. Besides, you have nothing to worry about. I'm more interested in Virginia."

Pete whispered, "Shh...they're coming back."

Simon asked, "So what were we talking about before Justus came?"

Caroline answered, "You were trying to describe your Flightline jammies."

Justus laughed. "Jammies, I love it."

Simon corrected, "No, *jammers*...weapons loaders. It's a vehicle with a lift on the front, low to ground, it's..."

Justus jumped in. "It's a short forklift."

"It's nothing like that."

Missy asked, "So when you get out of the Space Military, what job would that transfer over to?"

Justus snickered. "Forklift driver."

Pete shook his head and smiled. "There's more it and you know it."

"Alright, alright."

Simon asked Justus, "So what brought you up here tonight? I thought you might be studying your classes or messaging your girlfriend from the Delta Station."

"No, we're no longer together."

"Dude...I'm so sorry to hear that."

"No problem. It's for the better. I was trying to study for my college classes but couldn't concentrate. Thought I'd jump in here for a bit."

Virginia's face lit up. "What classes are you taking?"

"I'm trying for my bachelor's. Going for a Business degree."

"Wow, you trying to become an officer?"

"Maybe. We'll see."

Justus exchanged a quick glance with Simon, then smiled and blinked, as if to say *thanks for that push.* They had some more laughs and more drinks as they continued to talk about college and future goals. Pete then noticed a newsreel starting on the displays in the bar. He got up and turned up the volume as they all watched.

The reporter said, "No one has heard from LaMarche or his crew. The near million-passenger transports are still missing in action. Hello everyone, my name is Larry the Llama and this…is MTV News. The lead ship named the *Galaxy Commander* 6980 and its other transports have seemed to vanish from existence. Their ground control on Earth said their trackers went off-line at some point, most likely while they were in the new space bridge. Radio calls continued with no answer. Meanwhile, everyone else is too afraid to enter that doomed wormhole."

The reporter continued, "They were able to send a drone through. After over a month, it returned. It was able to scan the planet, narcissistically named LaMarche, and found no signs of life. Where is the Galaxy Commander transport? Possibly destroyed. Maybe rerouted to another system. We may never know. Stay tuned as we keep you updated on the latest news and stories from around the galaxy. *The Llama* is out; this has been an MTV News update."

They all discussed that crazy lost voyage and wondered what had become of it, then talked some more about what they may do after their enlistments. The maintainers talked about the Ignotus deployment and the horrors of being in chem suits. By the end of the night, Pete and Missy were getting close and holding hands. Simon and Caroline were also exchanging looks. They all started walking back to the barracks. The twins and the two girls went far ahead.

Justus told Virginia, "Okay, I'll walk you back."

She smiled. "I didn't ask you to."

"I know, but I bet you were thinking it."

"I am perfectly able to walk back on my own."

"No problem. I'll just head the other way."

"I said I'm capable, but I wouldn't mind the company."

"Sounds good to me."

They walked through the white and gray corridors, talking the whole way. Getting to her barracks courtyard, they found a bench to sit on while continuing their conversation. Justus learned she was taking classes, as well. She wasn't looking to become an officer but didn't want to be empty-handed once she got out. She was going for an education degree to possibly become a teacher. It was times like these he almost forgot he was trapped in a space station, nowhere near Earth.

They continued to have deep conversations. She invited him to come study with her in a couple days, which of course he accepted.

Justus asked, "So do you always sit out here?"

"Not really, but Missy's my roommate."

"Oh...ohh!"

Justus then realized where Pete must be.

CHAPTER 23

Meet Virginia

Virginia and Justus were at the education center in the evening after both of their shifts. It was their second study session, and she was really helping him see his course work clearly.

After reading through his chapter, he asked her, "So, what about tonight? Could I take out you for a drink?"

She looked at him, "Are you asking me out?"

"Well, yeah."

"There is something you should know."

"What's that?"

"Don't take this the hard way. I'm great friends with Missy and Caroline, but I'm not like them...I...I'm not willing to go as far they are. I'm just not ready for all that."

"You know, I don't care. I mean I care, but I completely understand."

"Sorry."

"Are you still interested in dating? Holding hands, the occasional kiss?"

"Well, yeah. I just wanted to be upfront with you. I've had *boy-friends* before."

"Is that what you want to call me?"

"Sure...if you're good with it."

"You know what? I am. I really am. I'm enjoying this. Don't worry, I won't push you into anything you don't want."

"Thanks, and if you're still up to it, I would I love to go sit somewhere and have a coffee with you."

"That, we can do."

––––––––––

At roll call the next day, Justus stood in the formation wondering what new hell the Flightline would bring for him today.

Chief Cogstorm addressed them. "There has been a recent problem with the lack of professionalism here. I see many of you choose to wear coveralls, and not our camo uniforms. I need to remind you that coveralls are only to be used for spaceship maintenance. You may only wear these while on the Flightline. Roll call is *not* on the Flightline. I expect to see everyone at roll call in their camos! Even if you're going off station, you need to be in camo. You can change into the coveralls only prior to stepping foot on the Flightline. The only exception to this is if you are an FCC flying with the crew. Is this understood?"

"Yes, Chief," said about half the formation.

There was a hand up.

The chief asked, "Yes, Sergeant Harvard?"

Seth asked, "Chief, what about if we are on the Flightline in coveralls and need to go to Supply to get a part?"

"Then you better hurry up and put on your camo. There will be no walking down those corridors in your coveralls. One more thing: if you are caught 'out of uniform,' paperwork will be given."

Chief Cogstorm looked right at Justus as he said that last part.

––––––––––

The guys on the Flightline started wondering why Justus kept volunteering to pick up everyone else's part from Supply. Justus felt a new emotion for Virginia that he couldn't explain. He couldn't wait to see her again. He felt a renewed interest in his classes as his grades were improving.

They met at the Education Center during their usual time. Virginia gave Justus a gift bag.

He asked, "What's this for?"

"Just open it. I got you something."

Justus opened the gift and took out a nice new set of music headphones. He looked at Virginia. "Wow, it's not my birthday or anything. Why would you…?"

"Hey, can't I just get you something for no reason? You said you had trouble concentrating while studying for your classes or writing research papers. I'm telling you, put these on with some music. You'll see a difference. It'll get rid of all the other distractions."

Justus gave her a hug. "This is outstanding, really. I'm just taken aback. I'm not used to getting gifts at random times."

"No problem. I wanted to. Please, don't feel you need to get me anything."

"I'll think of something."

"No, really, don't just go buy something for no reason. Gifts are special, they need to just jump out at you."

"Did you get lots of gifts at Christmas?"

"Nothing big. My family wasn't too rich growing up."

"No problem. What's your favorite holiday?"

"Halloween, by far."

"Why's that?"

"We couldn't go all out on decorations, but my siblings and I would find all sorts of ways to freak each other out."

"*Really?*"

"Whatcha thinking about?"

Justus smiled. "Do you have any suggestions? I have someone in mind that is already scared of a particular bomber."

Manny, Maisie, and Pepper approached Ship 0086, the Grim Reaper. They needed to run the engines through after the previous shift made some adjustments. Maisie and Manny sat in the pilots' seats to start through the pre-engine run procedures as Pepper was out in front of the ship with her harness hooked up, monitoring ground.

Maisie tried her interphone, then asked Manny, "Can you hear me?"

"Yeah, I got you."

Pepper said, "Yep, we can hear you."

Maisie said, "Nope, I can't hear anything. This stupid headset's always giving me trouble. I'll leave this broke thing here. Stay here and go through the pre-run procedures. I'm gonna run to the Tool Counter and get a new headset."

Manny, alone on the ship, started getting the controls in the right configuration. The lights in the flight deck flickered. He didn't think much of it. Then the interior lights turned off again, this time for longer.

He looked around, then tried his interphone. "Hey Pepper, these lights keep flickering."

He saw Pepper in front of the ship as she said, "What are you talking about? I can see the cockpit from here. It looks normal to me."

Just then Manny heard a loud moaning noise coming from the nav's station. He quickly ran to the ladder, climbed down and looked around. No one was there.

He approached the flight deck again and looked at Pepper. "Hey, there is something going on!"

She responded, "You're just freaked out about Jamie. None of that is real."

Manny heard another noise from the rear section. He turned to look. Nothing. When he looked out the window again, Pepper was nowhere in sight. He sat still for a while just looking and the lights flickered again a couple times. He stared out the front windows... then there was a tap on his shoulder.

Manny screamed, "Ahhh!" as he almost jumped out of his seat.

Behind him was Pepper. "Dude you gotta calm down," she said. "I'm just here to see what you're talking about."

"It's fine. I'm fine. We're fine. I'll just continue these steps."

Pepper stood there for a while as if nothing strange had happened, then she asked, "Are you good now, or do you need me to hold your hand?"

"I'm good."

Pepper left the ship. Manny saw her again at the front of the bomber. He continued his steps, flipping switches to the run configurations, wondering when Maisie would return. The lights flickered again, off and on, off and on, off and on. Then there was a loud bang. Manny jumped again. He ran towards the ladder and was about to step down when he saw it: the lower crew entry hatch was closed. He tried the handle. It wouldn't budge.

A creepy female voice was heard in his headset. "Are you trying to leave me?"

"Who's there?!" he asked in a panic.

Manny hurried back to the flight deck and looked out. Pepper was talking to the Expeditor, whose truck was parked in front of the ship. Pepper's headset was off and she was holding it by her side.

The voice continued in Manny's headset. "Jamie is here...I am always here."

He instantly threw off his headset.

The voice then echoed across the intercom system on the loudspeakers. "Jamie is here." All the lights in the bomber went out as Jamie said in a deeper voice, "However...today call me the Grim Reaper!"

Manny fumbled around the controls until he found the master intercom switch and shut it off. Yet he continued to hear moaning as the lights flickered off and on. He then ran down to try the hatch again.

Jamie's voice could be heard echoing within the walls of the ship. "Have you had enough? Or are you willing to come to the dark side?"

Manny screamed, "Don't hurt me!"

He went back up the ladder to look out the pilot's window. Then he heard a noise at the hatch. Manny went back down and tried it again and it opened. He climbed down fast, then took off running across the Flightline screaming, headed towards the entry control point. As he ran *Alarm Yellow* started. Manny freaked out, and was trying to connect his harness. The alarm changed to *Red*. Manny had the harness end tangled between his legs. He was on the ground, tangled up, trying to figure it out in a panic. He did all he could to try to secure it with his shaking hands as the pressure changed and the air thinned. Manny finally got it connected and sighed with relief. He looked down to see his O2 mask dangling at his side. Holding his breath, he managed to get the mask on.

The alarms ceased. Manny took a moment to compose himself. He then looked up to see Justus, Lenny, Pepper, and Maisie standing near ship 86. The Expeditor truck pulled up to him as everyone in the truck was laughing, including Matt and Nate.

Manny stood up. "Will someone explain what just happened?!"

Matt said, "I think the Grim Reaper happened."

After work, the maintainers headed to The Shack to give Manny the complete run down. Justus even bought Manny's drinks all night.

Manny said, "I know you guys all got me. I'm sure you enjoyed it, but I gotta know how you did it."

Justus was sitting next to his girlfriend and said, "Most of it was Virginia's idea. We just knew how to implement it. Too bad she couldn't be there to see it."

Nate said, "I got some of it recorded on my tablet, especially the part with him running out of the ship screaming."

Pepper said, "That was the best part."

Manny looked embarrassed.

Maisie said, "Okay, step one was to make up a fake problem on the ship. The Expeditor helped with that. Before we got out there, Justus and Lenny were already on the ship."

"Where?" Manny asked.

Lenny said, "I was in the wine cellar in front of the nav's station and Justus was crouched behind the gunner seat."

Maisie explained, "I made an excuse about my headset being broken, then headed off. I really just went down the hatch then climbed up through the bomb-bay to that narrow trough between the nav's section and the bomb-bay. Justus already had that bulk-head door unlocked and left me an extra headset up in there."

Manny asked, "So you were hiding in that crawl space the whole time?"

"Yep."

"We all had headsets on and could hear everything," Justus said. "I could see where you were from the gunner station. We'd switch to channel two to talk between ourselves for coordination. Lenny was in the wine cellar as he was disconnecting and reconnecting the wire harness that controlled the lights."

Maisie spoke in a creepy Jamie voice. "Do you recognize this voice?"

"That was you?" Manny asked.

"Yep. Justus showed me how to switch between interphone and the overhead intercom. And you heard the echoing of the voice from where I was in the crawl space."

Manny asked, "What about the hatch being locked?"

"Oh that was easy," Matt said. "I just put a pad lock on it. When we thought you had enough, they gave me the signal to unlock it."

They all had a good laugh.

Manny sat there thinking, then asked, "Okay, one last thing. How in the world did you coordinate the launch with alarms and a giant window opening?"

Justus said, "That was *not* planned. Just a happy coincidence."

Matt added, "Actually, we were a bit scared at that point, wondering if you'd be able to hook up in time. Sorry, man."

Nate brought out his tablet and showed his video of the lights in the flight deck flickering and Manny running out screaming, fumbling with his harness.

Justus smiled big and looked at Virginia. "Thanks babe. That was so awesome."

"Anytime, Justus."

CHAPTER 24

Space Trucking

Four maintainers were called into the Production Office.

The brand-new Lieutenant, Handelman, addressed the team. "You have all been selected as a Maintenance Response Team to repair and retrieve Ship 3034. There was that big air show on Viridis for the last few days. Once it was over, Ship 3034 launched into space and headed home, only to have an emergency. They had to land back on the moon fast to resolve it. The only maintainer on it was its Flying Crew Chief."

Maisie asked, "What was the emergency?"

The new LT answered, "I don't have all the details. I just know while they were in the Viridis skies, they opened the bomb-bay doors. Once open, the crew was unable to close them."

Merrick asked, "Opened the bomb doors? Were they bombing Viridis?"

"Well, no. They had no munitions on board. Maybe they were training or had to…"

Maisie blurted, "Training? During an emergency?"

Pro-Super Donnelly said, "Hey! Stop interrupting the LT. Let him finish, will you?"

Lt. Handelman continued, "They don't tell me much. All I know is that Ship 3034 is currently sitting at Beachhead Airfield with its bomb-bay doors stuck open. They obviously can't re-enter space in that configuration. Any more questions?"

Merrick asked again, "I'm just trying to figure out why they opened the doors?"

"Like I said, I don't know!"

Lenny asked, "I was just wondering, is Beachhead that one place where we were, that one time, when we had to…"

The Lt. was getting agitated. "How would I know?" he snapped.

Senior Donnelly said, "Yes! You were all there before. It's the only place on Viridis you have ever been and now you're going back."

The Lt. was looking at his tablet, looking flustered.

Senior Donnelly looked at Lt. Handelman. "You alright?"

"Just a bit stressed. They don't tell new LTs anything. Anyways, we don't have much time. A C-345 will be here shortly to pick up this team and get them there. The trip will take about nine hours."

Justus asked, "Nine hours? How come it took three days when we took the same trip about four years ago?"

The frustrated Lt. threw up his arms and left the room.

Senior Donnelly shook his head and said, "Get your tools, gear, and scrounge, ASAP. That cargo will be here soon."

Justus, Maisie, Merrick, and Lenny boarded the cargo ship in their camo, along with their gear, tools, and ration packs. They also needed a set of coveralls and civilian clothes as the standard MRTs required. The C-345 flight crew also contained its own Crew Chief and Loadmaster. As they were waiting in the cargo bay, a group of eight military police came aboard as passengers with all their gear. One was a Senior Sergeant.

Justus asked T-Rex, "Hey man, why are you guys coming?"

"There was a possible sabotage. We're coming to guard this cargo ship as well as that broke bomber."

"Wow. Hey, I almost didn't notice the rank. Congrats, sergeant!"

"Thanks. I put it on last month."

"Cool. Did you bring your hammock?"

"Hammock? What are you talking about?"

Once the ship took to space, all the maintainers strung up hammocks across the cargo bay to sleep comfortably during the journey.

———————

They landed without incident at Beachhead Airfield, Flos Island, Viridis Moon. It was mid-day when they arrived. They saw Ship 3034, *The Beach Babe*, and sure enough, its bomb bay doors were wide open. The Bully maintainers departed the cargo ship with their tools and gear.

The FCC from 3034 approached them.

"What up, dirtbags!" yelled Pepper.

Justus was visibly confused. "You're here?" he said. "I thought your ship was the Roosevelt? I mean it *literally* has your name on it."

"Oh, that's my Teddy Bear alright, but with a lack of FCCs we get shuffled around sometimes."

One of the crew members of 3034 approached the maintainers. "Hey, team. I'm Captain Nguyen. I'm a pilot."

They all greeted him.

"How much did they tell you about our distress call?" the captain asked.

Maisie answered, "They didn't tell us shit."

The captain looked a bit taken back, then said, "Well then, you've got a story to hear."

The four from the MRT were all ears as Pepper stood by the captain.

"My crew and I had just left Viridis when I heard Sergeant York here on the interphone," Captain Nguyen continued. "She starts freaking out. Go ahead York, tell them what you discovered."

Pepper said, "I was in that seat behind the pilot's when I noticed the crew's food crate. I don't know what I was thinking, but it looked suspicious. I opened it and underneath the food trays was a device. I called the captain and told him the situation. He even came back to look at it. Neither one of us knew what it was, but we were pretty sure it was a bomb of some type."

"This situation sounds somewhat familiar," Justus said.

"I know, right?" Pepper agreed.

Lenny asked, "Did the bomb have blinking lights?"

"Why would it have lights?" Penny answered. "It was supposed to be concealed."

"I don't know. In the movies all the bombs have blinking lights."

"It doesn't matter," Merrick said. "Let's hear the story."

Captain Nguyen resumed. "You should have seen her. She was like, 'We need to throw this thing out! Open a window, toss it out!' I explained that we're in space. I have a strict rule on my ship about not opening windows in space. Then I figured she may be onto something. I had an idea. Getting back in my seat, we started our re-entree procedures back to the moon of Viridis."

The captain continued, "Bursting into the atmosphere, we brought the ship to a good cruising altitude in the sky. I told York over the interphone the plan. She agreed to do it." Nguyen nodded to Pepper.

"So I had the plan in my mind," Pepper said. "I carefully took the suspected bomb out of the food crate and made my way down the ladder. From there I opened the aft bulkhead door behind the Nav's station and crawled through the long, slender trough. I'll tell you guys, that thing was so narrow. I was just inching through it in a slow crawl. I felt like freaking John McClane going through that tiny space. I had this damn bomb in my hands. I was cringing, crying, half expecting it to go off at any time in front of my face."

She continued, "I still had my headset on, so I was listening to the captain. I told him I was at the end, right at the bomb bay, staring at the last bulkhead hatch. It took a minute or so, then he answered, 'Okay, the bomb doors are open now. It's all you.' I opened the last tiny bulkhead door. I could see into the bomb bay. The water was far below. I then pushed the bomb out, closed the bulkhead, and shimmied backwards."

Captain Nguyen summed it up. "She saved us all. Our bombardier then tried to close the doors, but to no avail. We tried everything, including flying high, then dropping fast to force a close in manual. Nothing worked. We can't fly into space like that. We landed here and waited."

Merrick asked, "We can just close them physically. What's the big deal? We don't need to open them until we get to the station."

"You don't think I tried that?" Pepper responded. "I've been messing with this thing all freaking day. Yes, we can close them manually, but everything on this damn ship is automated. Even while closed, it continues to show an 'open' error and disables the other systems."

The captain said, "Well, over there is Ship 3034. The rest of the crew is at Hotel Flos, four blocks that way. Sergeant York knows the way. You can get some rooms there. When you go into town, wear civilian clothes and make sure you get some Viridis cash. The hotel can exchange it for you. Let me know when the ship is fixed. If you need anything, I am in room 104. If I'm not there, check the beach. Until then, I plan on laying out and getting drunk. Good luck, team."

Four of them started to head to the Beach Babe. Justus just stood there.

Lenny called back to him, "You coming?"

"Yeah, I'm just thinking."

"Come on, ain't nobody got time for that."

There were a couple of MPs standing by, making sure the area looked secure. Merrick and Pepper manually closed the doors again to see if they could override the system. Lenny was checking the DV3034 messages, looking for any suspected faults. Justus had his wiring diagram up in his tablet. He looked over to Maisie, who had her t-shirt sleeves rolled up as she laid out across a couple toolboxes with sunglasses on.

Justus called out, "What are you doing, Maisie?"

Without looking towards him, she said, "Just getting some sun. Let me know when you're ready for an engine run."

Justus knew the bomb doors required an engine run to get the hydraulic pressure to the right level to activate the doors. He just shook his head and continued to look through screens and screens of complex schematics.

To no avail, they tried the system repeatedly. Even with the doors closed and locked, the ship's computers showed them as 'open' and would not allow any progression with flight preparations. It was getting late. They all agreed to call it a night, get some food, and resume in the morning.

Lenny asked, "How's this work? We can't walk to the hotel in our uniforms."

"You're right, Pepper said. "I've been changing in the bomber, then heading out in civilian clothes. We can also leave our tools here on the ship."

"Sounds like plan," Justus said. "Let's all change together."

"Not so fast. You guys got the bomber. Maisie and I got the cargo."

As the guys were changing in the cramped bomber, Merrick said, "How did this happen?! We got the raw deal."

"You're telling me," said Lenny, as he almost fell over trying to get his pants off in the small space.

Justus was locking the crew entry hatch as he looked at the couple MPs standing in front of the ship.

T-Rex asked, "You heading out?"

"Yeah man, so you gotta guard this thing all night?"

"Yep."

"Ah man, that sucks. You want me to grab you some food or something?"

"Thanks, Justus. Nah, I'm good. My other guys will swap us out every so often."

"Cool. Where are you all staying?"

"We got some cots set up in that building right there. I think you remember one of those office rooms."

"Don't remind me."

"Yeah, we all gotta stay close in case anything crazy happens."

"Got it. Good luck, man."

"Thanks."

———————

The dirtbags stopped by the hotel first and everyone got their own room. Well, except for Maisie. She said she'd share a room with Pepper. They all knew she'd end up in Merrick's room.

Near the hotel, a couple blocks away, was a local diner. The waitress came by and tried to take their order, but they were having a hard time. Lenny had his tablet out and was trying to translate the menu.

The Viridis waitress said a foreign word and left for a moment.

Lenny looked up the word she said. "Holder or owner. I think she went to get the owner."

The waitress came back with a woman in her mid-sixties.

The owner spoke in English. "Put your menus down. What'll it be? We've got a meal that is like your steak back home. We also have vegetable soup. Then there is a dish like your lasagna. We also have fish cooked every which way. If you're looking for duck or goose, forget about it. You all look like you're the drinking type. We don't have beer, but I can get you a cider if ya want. Can I get you a round while you decide?"

Everyone had the same look of surprise.

Pepper said, "Yes, that'll be great, thank you."

After receiving their drinks and ordering food, Maisie asked, "So Pepper, what were you doing out here again?"

Pepper answered, "Oh my gosh. It's been such a freaking ordeal. I was *selected* to come here for their annual *whatever*. It's basically a big airshow where everyone comes and shows off their spaceships. The Nix brought a bunch of theirs, and the Viridis had all theirs there. Of course, we brought our Bully, a C-345, and a couple of XF-94s."

"Then a bunch of stuffy aristocrats walked around admiring all the ships," Pepper continued. "Hell, even people from Calidum came here. Apparently, it's this whole effort to make peace with all the moons."

Lenny asked, "Really? We let *them* see our systems?"

"Oh no, we kept this Bully locked up," Pepper answered. "They just walked around it. The worst part of this dog and pony show is that I had to stand next to 3034 the *whole* time and answer whatever questions they had about it."

They received their food and dug in.

Maisie asked Pepper, "How bad was it? What were they asking?"

"First off, they don't speak English! Yet most of them have a translator with them. I have learned to hate that 3034."

"Why's that?" Merrick asked.

"Most of them pointed up the nose art to ask about the *Beach Babe*."

"What?" Maisie laughed.

"Yeah, these old men would be like, 'Hey, is that you?' or 'Why aren't you wearing that?' After about the tenth one, I was disgusted. The next man came up and pointed to her, saying something. The translator asked if I modeled for that. I said to the man, 'Oh yeah, that is definitely me. In fact, originally they wanted to use your *mom* for the picture, but there just wasn't enough space on the bomber.'"

Everyone laughed.

"You didn't!" Maisie exclaimed.

"I did. I'm not sure if they even understood the joke, but I felt better."

Justus asked, "Have you had any time to relax since you've been here?"

"Not really. All day at the airshow, then late dinners with the flight crews. I haven't had time for anything. Once it was over, the next morning we refueled, received the food trays, and headed for space—only to turn around fast."

They had a great time and lots of laughs. The owner stayed around to answer any questions about the local area. They left a big tip.

As they were leaving, Pepper asked the owner, "Thank you so much. What is your name?"

"Columbae," she answered.

———————

The next morning, no one saw Justus at breakfast.

There was a knock on his door. Justus opened it to find the whole maintenance team there.

Maisie asked, "Are you ready?"

Justus looked confused.

Pepper said loudly, "Take off your headphones!" She motioned with her hands for him to take them off."

Justus took them off. "Sorry. Forgot they were on. Come in, all of you. See it. See it all!"

He opened the door and let them in. They looked in his small hotel room as their jaws dropped.

Justus continued, talking fast, his eyes wide. "I'm glad you're here. I need you here. I need you here. I want to show you everything."

Every wall in his room had paper pages of wiring schematics taped up, displaying a maze of wires, relays, junctions, diodes, grounds, and more.

Maisie asked, "What in Valhalla is going on here?"

"This is bomb-door integration," Justus said. "I needed to print it all. I got with the hotel lobby girl and convinced her to print it all. We printed it all!"

Pepper asked, "Did you sleep last night?"

"Why? What for?"

"So did you find out anything?" Lenny asked.

Justus spoke rapidly. "Anything and everything. This system connects every system on the ship. So many relays. So many wires. Whoever designed this is insane. A genius, yet insane. I can see it all now! I see it all. I see it all."

Merrick was walking around the room looking all the walls plastered with schematics. "You have a bunch of lines highlighted and other points circled here and there."

"Those are our problem children. I want to check each of them with a meter and make 'em squeal."

Lenny spoke slowly. "Well, Justus, why don't we get you some breakfast, then we'll check these points on the ship? But first I think you need to put on some pants."

———————————

The team walked from their hotel to the airfield.

Lenny asked Justus, "You look better now. Whatcha thinking?"

"I have a list of points to check. I want to start with the relays. Based on what the ship is doing, or not doing, in our case. I predicted which relays would most likely cause this. After that I have a list of wires I want to check."

Merrick asked, "So how do you check the wires? You got that meter thing right?"

"Yeah, we should only need to check for continuity," Justus said. "You check one end of the wire to the other, making sure it makes a loop with ground."

Merrick looked confused.

Lenny added, "It's to make sure there isn't a break in the line. I know your hydro lines will show a leak if there's a break. These just show nothing, unless it's a short."

"Okay, I think I got it. One more thing. What if the line you're checking is longer than those meter leads you got?" Merrick asked.

Lenny and Justus just looked at each other and shook their heads.

Justus said, "We'll show you. I'm sure we'll have plenty of time. There are miles of lines we need to check."

They arrived at the ship.

Justus called the shots. "Alright, the first set of relays we need to check are high up in the bomb-bay. Merrick, can you rig the bomb-doors open so they don't close on us? I need to check the relay as we run the system through. Lenny, I'll get the system ready and show you how to activate it."

Merrick and Pepper worked on rigging the doors. Everything was set up. Justus was up on the ladder checking the relay with his headset on. He thought to himself, *Well, here goes nothing.*

Justus spoke through the interphone, "Okay Lenny, go for it. Activate the doors."

"Got it, here they go…"

"What the hell?"

Pepper and Merrick were looking up at Justus. "What's wrong?"

"The relay's not working."

Merrick said, "Oh, well. I guess you'll check the next one."

"No, I mean the relay is not working! Here, let me check the ones next to this one. Lenny, go ahead and activate it again. Okay, once more. And again."

Justus slid down the ladder. "The relay's not working!"

"And…?" Pepper said.

"I found it. The other ones *are* working, this first one isn't! We found the problem!"

"Are you sure?" Merrick asked.

"Yeah, here, let me try something." Justus banged on the relay with the handle of a screwdriver and had Lenny try it again, then again. He banged on it again then got a signal.

Merrick said, "So is it good now?"

Justus tapped on it a few more times, each time having Lenny run it through.

He came down from the ladder and addressed them all. "The relay is intermittent. It didn't work, then did work for a while, then didn't. It needs to be replaced."

"Why don't you bang on it to get it to work?" Merrick asked. "Then we don't touch it, close the doors, and call it day?"

"No, man. What if that comes back? What you're talking about is a good way to cause it to open in flight or lock up. We need to order a new relay."

Lenny approached. "Do we have another relay on the ship that isn't used that we can swap it with?" he asked.

"I thought about that. These relays are specific to bomb-doors. They're all needed, so we can't risk swapping relays."

Pepper already had her tablet out as she asked for the stock number. She ordered the part then had a concerned look.

"What's wrong?" Justus asked.

"This says the part could take anywhere from two to five days to get here."

Lenny asked, "Can they just send a cargo or bomber with a new one on it?"

"I'm not sure. Let's tell Captain Nguyen and see what he thinks."

———

The team locked the ship and tried to find the captain. Justus and Lenny checked his hotel room. The others searched the beach.

Justus received a message on his tablet and told Lenny, "Pepper says they talked with the pilots on the beach. Nguyen said there is no point in sending a whole other ship here. We are just going to have to wait the few days."

"Alright, now what?" Lenny asked.

"Hold on, I'm getting another message...Okay, the flight crew wants to take us out for dinner tonight. Pepper sent me the location."

"Cool. So should we hang out with the others until then?"

Justus shrugged. "If you want to. I'll meet up with you later. I really gotta get some sleep."

———

Dinner with the flight crew started with a grandiose meal at a local restaurant as the crew gave the maintainers a celebratory toast with shots. One would think the night would end after a nice meal and a walk along the beach. One would be wrong.

The only thing more dangerous than a group of maintainers drinking on a TDY is mixing them with a rambunctious flight crew. This is especially true when this crew isn't scheduled to fly and has near unlimited per diem to spend.

This unforgettable night was truly legendary. It consisted of endless laughs, shenanigans, horseplay, antics, and even some tomfoolery. The concerning and overwhelming problem with this unforgettable night was the fact that most of them were too intoxicated to remember it.

CHAPTER 25

Toes

Justus woke up the next morning and slowly made his way down to the hotel lobby. He saw Pepper sitting alone at a table outside drinking coffee. He got a coffee for himself and approached her and pointed to the seat. She gave a hand motion and he sat down and slowly took a couple sips of his mug. She pointed to the creamer and gave him two fingers. He passed her two. They both sat there for a while with droopy eyes, trying to wake up enough to have a coherent conversation.

After sitting for about fifteen minutes in a mutual silence, Justus asked, "What's your plan for today?"

"I wanted to go check out the shops along the beach, but I know we're not supposed to venture out alone."

Justus took another sip of coffee.

He answered after two minutes. "I checked on Lenny this morning. Apparently, he'd been throwing up all night. I don't think he's up to anything today."

"Maisie and Merrick will probably sleep till mid-day. I don't expect to see them any time soon."

They both sat for a few more minutes, then Justus said, "Oh, alright."

"What's that?"

"I'll walk around with you to all those shops."

"You sound so thrilled."

"Yep, just give me some time. Still trying to process."

"Take *all* the time you need." Pepper drank some more coffee, staring off past the line of palm trees towards the open beach.

Pepper and Justus were feeling better as they were walking near the beach, looking at some of the local stores.

Justus said, "Hey, check it out. Swimsuits. We should get some and head to down to that beach."

"I don't know."

"We have all day. Besides, how often can you brag about going to the beach on a foreign moon?"

"That would be cool to jump in the water."

Pepper was looking around the store at the various swimsuits. She found a couple that she kind of liked and looked for a dressing room.

"Hey, I think they only have girl swimsuits here," Justus said.

Pepper pointed to a rack. "What about these?"

"Yeah, still girls."

She laughed. "Have you looked around? The guys here all wear the Speedo type."

"Oh, hell no!"

She smiled. "When in Rome..."

"I'll think of something."

"Hey, if you want to meet me back here in a while, that'll be cool."

"Why's that?"

"It's going to take me a while to find the right suit. Unless you feel like waiting."

"Got it. I'll go pack a lunch and meet you on the beach. Just head out straight from this shop."

"Cool. I'll pick up a couple of towels here, as well."

Justus carried a cooler with a couple of sandwiches, fruit, and a few drinks as he walked out on the beach. He could see Pepper sitting on a towel in a two-piece, looking out to the water. Justus felt as if he had déjà vu. Pepper looked like the picture Sam had shown him of his mom vacationing here with the waves and the purple sky in front of her.

When Justus sat down next to Pepper, she commented, "Nice shorts."

"Sometimes you gotta improvise."

The shorts in question were of his camo uniform, cut off just above his knees. They sat there for a few minutes, taking it all in. There were others on the beach, all Viridis, some playing in the water, others laying out, some walking along the edge of water and letting the waves come up just above their ankles.

Justus asked her, "So whatcha thinking about?"

"Thinking about that last mission. I had that bomb in my hands, not knowing what would happen. I was scared, afraid that thing would blow up in my face. I knew what I had to do. I keep replaying the event in my mind. It's like it's on repeat. I just want to move on."

"I don't know what to say."

"I know. I just keep looking at those waves like I'm almost in a trance. They don't seem to ever stop coming."

"They don't, yet they look *great* for surfing. Have you ever surfed before?"

"Surf, no. You?"

"I have. My family spent a week in San Diego. My stepdad taught my brother and me."

"Was it hard?"

"It took me some time to get it. Have you ever skateboarded or snowboarded?"

She smiled big. "The hoverboard was my skill."

"Hoverboard? The real one or one of those cheap wannabe exploding ones?"

Pepper shook her head. Her mood seemed to change. "Oh no, mine was the real deal from Mattel. I have to admit, I was pretty darn good. I could even drop-in on the half pipe and do a bunch of tricks. I'll have to show you someday."

"All this time, I never knew you were a skater chick!"

"You never asked! All that time in Tech School, you only had one thing on your mind."

"Not true."

"Come on! You were always asking me what I was wearing under my uniform."

"Okay, okay...so, I can see what you've got under that swimsuit?"

"Hey! At least I have the *courage* to wear it. You with your board shorts!"

Justus sat for a moment staring at the waves. Pepper got out some sun block and started to apply it.

Justus leaned in. "You need to me help you with that?"

"You really gotta stop doing this," Pepper said in serious voice.

"What do you mean?"

"With our past, you applying sun block...or I guess *Stella* block. I know how your mind works. You got Virginia now and I'm with Nate."

Justus paused, then asked, "What if we weren't with them?"

"What are you saying? You *can't* keep doing this."

"I know."

"You need to ask yourself the question."

"What's the question?"

"It's not what makes you happy *today*. It's...what would make you happy for years to come? More importantly, what will make her happy? It has to work for both of you, long term."

Justus sat there thinking.

Pepper continued, "Who would make the best lifelong journey with you? It's gotta work both ways."

"Is this Nate for you?

"Maybe. I don't know yet."

Justus pulled out the food. They ate their lunch and watched the other beachgoers.

Pepper pointed. "Hey, check it out, Justus, that lady is topless."

"Where?" Justus looked around fast. "Ah, come on! She's like seventy."

Pepper laughed. Justus finished his food as he stared out towards the water.

"Whatcha thinking about?" Pepper asked.

"I'm just looking at that sky above the ocean. Thinking the last time we were here, Sam's ship was exploding over it."

"I'm sure he's in a better place now."

"Probably with his mom somewhere. Maybe even sitting on this beach together, or maybe out there past the breaker."

After some time, Justus got up and said, "I'll be right back. I've got an idea."

Pepper called out as he was walking away, "If you don't come back in a Speedo, I'm gonna be disappointed!"

A few minutes later, Justus came back still wearing his camo shorts, but he was also carrying a couple of surf boards.

Pepper smiled. "Really?"

"Yeah, why not? I rented them. Come on, I'll show you how."

They walked towards the water with the boards under their arms.

Justus told her, "First, we need to get past this first set of waves."

They started walking out, wading in the water as the foamy waves continued to come at them in an endless cycle.

Justus yelled, "Hooooly crap!"

"What's wrong?"

"Nothing, I just forgot how cold the water feels when it reaches my shorts level."

"Wimp."

They continued to head out, past the first set of waves. They were out far as they both laid on their boards, watching the waves come in.

Justus said, "Okay, now the trick is to wait for a good wave. These little ones, we can just go over them. If it's too big to go over, you can go under it. Once we see the perfect wave, you take it."

"How do we know?"

"It's all instinct. Once you get that feeling, you need to commit. Paddle with your arms as hard as you can and try to reach the same speed as the wave. After that you'll feel it guide you. Once you're in a comfortable spot, you gotta do the jump. Pull your legs under you in a squat, get your feet in position, then attempt to stand up."

"Easy-peasy, right?"

"I'm just saying, it's way harder than it looks. Don't be discouraged if it takes forever to get it."

They both floated for some time, waiting for a good big wave.

Pepper asked, "How about this one?"

"Go for it!"

Pepper started paddling fast. Justus sat up on his board watching Pepper. The water took her fast and she was cruising along, then she did the jump, got in position, as was up! Justus couldn't believe it. She rode for seven seconds until she went down, crashing into the foam.

Once she got up, Justus yelled, "Way to go!"

Justus took the next wave in. He paddled hard, but as soon as he tried to stand, he was consumed by the wave and fell under it.

He swam, then walked back to the shore to Pepper with his board.

Pepper said, "That was so much fun!"

"I was going to tell you not to worry about falling since no one ever gets up on the first try. However, you once again proved me wrong."

For the next couple of hours, they continued to surf, each getting up a few times and greatly improving with each run. They took a break for a bit, sat and had a drink as the waves washed up to their feet. Soon after, they were back at. They were even to the point of guiding the board back and forth, in control, as they approached the shore. It was all laughs as they almost forgot they were on this foreign moon.

———

They were walking back to their towels, laughing, when they saw the group. Maisie, Merrick, and Lenny stood there clapping.

Maisie said, "You looked great out there!"

"I didn't know you could surf," Merrick said.

"Neither did I," Pepper answered.

"Sorry to spoil your fun, but our part came in early. Looks like we'll be working this evening."

CHAPTER 26

Black Betty

Pepper, Maisie, Merrick, Justus, and Lenny approached the bomber in slow-motion. They walked in a line, all wearing coveralls and sunglasses. Justus had the new relay in hand. There was a foggy haze and one could barely see the water and its horizon across the purplish sky and ocean.

They continued in the slow-motion strut until T-Rex asked, "Why you all walking like that?"

Maisie answered, "Man, you ruined it. It's all for effect."

"Did it look cool?" Merrick asked. "Was it cool?"

T-Rex was standing next to another MP as he said, "Yeah...yeah, it looked cool. Whatcha working on tonight?"

"We got our part," Lenny answered. "A fast relay change, then we gotta run the engines up to power the doors through. Should be a quick fix."

Everyone looked at Lenny and all said at once, their voices overlapping, "Why would you say that? *Quick fix!* What the hell? You jinxed us. Now we're screwed."

Lenny said, "Sorry...my bad."

Maisie asked the MPs, "You guys got earplugs or something?"

"Nope," T-Rex said. "Just my gear and Black Betty."

"Black Betty?"

"That's what I call my weapon."

"Got it. We'll get you some plugs. It will be best if you stay towards the front of the ship with Pepper during the run."

As they were approaching the ship, Maisie said, "I like that name. We should call the ship Beach Babe Betty."

Justus and the others agreed. The relay replacement started smoothly. They already had the old one out, and then it was a matter of installing the new one. Justus was in the bomb-bay high up on a ladder changing the part as Lenny stood on another ladder with a light rod.

Lenny asked, "You need a screwdriver?"

"Yeah. No, wait, I got one. My lucky screwdriver."

Justus pulled out the tiny tool from his coverall's pocket and finished the install.

Pepper yelled up to them, "You two look cute and cozy up there. How about you show us a kiss?"

They both looked at her with a concerned look. The rest of the change went fine, without issues. Justus made sure all the maintenance logs were documented correctly. Everyone was in position: Justus in the bombardier seat bringing up the system, Lenny next to him, Maisie going through the startup procedures with Merrick in the other pilot's seat, and Pepper outside the ship monitoring ground.

Maisie asked, "Ready to start number one. Are we clear?"

Pepper responded, "Clear as a nonner's workload on a Friday."

"Alright, here we go!" Maisie exclaimed.

The ship began to rumble and shake as the other engines engaged. Justus had his system ready to go.

After a bit Maisie said, "Okay, we're good, whenever you're ready, Justus."

Justus asked, "About to run the bomb doors through. Are we clear?"

"Clear as a...yeah, you're clear," Pepper said.

They ran it through multiple times without any problems or fails. The ship was fixed. Maisie kept the engines going, ensuring everything was good. Justus had the infrared scanner up as he was showing Lenny its capabilities, even its 360-degree radius.

"What's that?" Lenny said, spotting a dozen images that looked like people crawling towards them in the far distance behind the ship.

Justus turned off his interphone and signaled Lenny to do the same, then said, "I see it, too. Don't say anything over interphone."

"Aren't the radios secure?"

"The radios are, not the interphone. We don't know their technology."

Justus and Lenny went upstairs to Maisie and Merrick. Justus turned off their interphone, then brought up the infrared on their screens. It was clear on the infrared that about a dozen people were sneaking up on the ship from far behind. They could see them inching forward very slowly.

Merrick asked, "Is that what I think it is?"

"I don't know," Justus answered, "but it doesn't look good."

Lenny asked, "What do we do?"

Maisie's eyes lit up. "I have a plan."

They all listened and agreed. Maisie and Merrick turned on their interphone again and continued to run the engines in a slow idle, giving almost no exhaust. Justus and Lenny met with Pepper and the MPs. They told them the plan, and everyone agreed. The Senior MP and T-Rex added some more elements to the plan, then walked off to the building to tell the other MPs.

T-Rex walked back with a couple extra rifles.

Lenny asked T-Rex, "Why are you only walking?"

"If I run, they might know something is up. Stick to the plan, act casual. Take your headsets off." He handed Lenny and Justus a couple of rifles. "Take these, in case. You'll notice the safety is on and there is one full magazine in each. Just stand here and pretend you're MPs. Take this radio as well. Radio silence until I'll give you the signal, Justus."

Justus and Lenny gave their headsets to Pepper as they put ear plugs in and stood with their guns shouldered. Pepper secured the headsets in the ship. T-Rex went back to the building. Looking towards the building, they could all see all eight MPs sneak out, armed and wearing infrared goggles. Four of them walked out towards the cargo ship, then snuck around the Bully's right side.

The others went left. After that, no could see them through the foggy haze.

Justus waited and waited, staring at his handheld radio. Then he heard it. The radio beeped three times. Justus got Pepper's attention and gave her a slight spinning motion with his hand above his head.

Pepper talked through the interphone, "Good to go, run 'em up."

Just then the noise of the engines was extreme. Justus and Lenny put their hands over their ears and watched the huge bomber in front of them pull hard as it tried to move forward. The engines blasted hard, taking out anything behind them. After a moment they saw a flashing of lights off in the distance, and heard a barrage of gun shots.

The engines went back to an idle. Pepper, Justus, and Lenny ran up to the bomber and secured the hatch behind them. They all went upstairs.

Maisie was ecstatic. "You should have seen it; it was marvelous! We could see it all on the infrared. Those people kept inching closer. We could see the MPs hiding to the left and right of them. Then the enemy stood up and made a run for the airfield towards us. Closer and closer they came. I was doing everything I could not to run up the engines. Then Pepper gave me the signal and it was on. My dream came true! I put Betty into full throttle. We could see them topple. They were rolling from the jet blast."

Merrick added, "Then the MPs came. They were all over them. I saw a few of the unknowns stand up. I'm not sure who shot first, but it was over quick. I hope our guys are all right."

Lenny said, "Justus, your radio!"

"Oh yeah," Justus responded. He clicked transmit. "T-Rex, Chief Slayer here, what's your position?"

"Slayer, all is good! All is good. I'm coming your way to give an update."

There were all sorts of emergency vehicles at the site of the incident.

T-Rex gave the maintainers the recap. "When they got closer, we could clearly see the enemy was armed with guns. Then they charged. After the initial engine blast, they fell hard. A few tried to get up. Once they saw they were surrounded, two of them actually tried to shoot at us. We...killed them fast. The others put down their weapons and surrendered. There were even two knocked unconscious from the blast."

Maisie said, "Nice."

Merrick was shaking his head. "Holy crap, who were they?"

"I don't know. We took all their info: pictures, fingerprints, eye scans..."

"Even the dead ones?" Lenny asked.

"Yes."

"Eww."

"Then we gave them over to the Viridis authorities."

Pepper asked, "What if they *were* the Viridis authorities?"

"That's why we took all their info. I'm sure someone will figure it out. Right now, it's out of our hands."

Captain Nguyen arrived. "We heard the news. Great job. Outstanding! How's 3034?"

They looked at Justus as he answered, "Good to go, sir. You can leave now if you want."

"Better make it in the morning. I'll alert my crew. Actually, with my crew, it may be closer to midday. We'll set up the C-345 to leave at the same time. Thanks again, really."

Merrick, Maisie, Lenny, and Justus watched the *Beach Babe* barrel down the runway and make its way for space with Pepper on board. The MPs would have to stay and sort things out; there would be another transport to take them back. The rest of them boarded the C-345 and launched without issues. The maintainers were out for most of the flight, strung up in their hammocks.

After the long flight, the C-345 Crew Chief let everyone know they were about an hour out until they would arrive back on Space Station Prime. The team started to get the cargo area cleaned up and change into their camo uniforms. The guys even started dry shaving. Justus started to panic.

Lenny asked, "What's wrong?"

Justus held up his camo cut-off shorts. "Do you have an extra set of camo pants?"

"No."

Justus asked the others, with no luck.

"I got a pair," Maisie said.

Justus looked at her and said, "There is no way those will fit me."

Lenny said, "The chief will kill you if he finds out."

"I know, I know. We just got to make sure he doesn't."

Justus put on his maintenance coveralls instead.

"Okay. Here is the plan," he told Lenny. "I'll give you my room card. As soon as we land, you've got to go and get me my camo. Or better yet, see if anyone at work has pants in their locker. I'll stay behind on the ship and act like I'm doing maintenance or something."

They landed and taxied into the spot. Once the engines shut down, the team saw the crew entry door open. Lt. Handelman came on board to greet them all.

"Great job, team! Before you get your gear, come on out here. Everyone wants to thank you. They're standing outside the ship."

Maisie asked, "Who's out there?"

"The Commander, the Chief, the First Sergeant, and a couple of seniors from the Resource Office."

The Lt. caught site of Justus and said, "Specialist Johannes, where's your camo? You know you need to be in camo uniform when traveling."

"I know, I know. There was a situation."

"Well there's no time now. Come on out. The chief won't like this."

The team headed out the door to be greeted by all the higher-ups as each one thanked them and shook their hands. Justus was surprised when he got to someone unfamiliar.

The new maintenance chief greeted them. "Welcome back. I'm Chief Nikmor. Thank you for the mission success!"

Justus said, "Thank you, Chief. And Chief Cogstorm is…?"

"I'm his replacement. He's heading back to Earth."

Once the higher-ups started to disperse, the Lt. approached the chief and Justus and said, "Chief, this specialist is in his coveralls. Everyone is supposed to travel in the camo uniform."

The chief looked disappointed. "I'm sure he has a reason."

"Yes, sir, my camo pants were ripped," Justus explained. "I thought it would be more appropriate to wear clean coveralls than ripped camo."

"See LT, no issue. Thanks, Specialist Johannes. Good job."

The Lt. looked confused, trying to process what had happened.

CHAPTER 27

Back to The Shack

Months went by, another day, another roll call. Senior Sergeant Malone addressed the maintainers concerning the regular notes, including volunteer opportunities, upcoming appointments, and those that needed to see him regarding their APRs.

Towards the end of roll call, Malone said, "There is a handful of you here that are approaching your five-year mark. I know it's still a few months out, but we need to know what you decide. Let me know if you're going to re-enlist or not. We also need to know if you are choosing to stay out here in Stella or be reassigned on Earth. Either way, you'll get to take your leave and return home for a bit."

They all received the plan for the day from the Expeditor as Justus and Shorty headed out to check out the radar problems on Ship 1895. Specialist O'Reilly was getting the tools. As they walked, Justus' tablet dinged.

He read the message from Seth. "Memorial Day is almost here! At 1800, the Dirty Dozen and *only* the Dirty Dozen will meet at The Shack. I have reserved the entire bar for the event. See you there."

———————

Justus was walking up the steps to The Shack on Memorial Day thinking about Virginia. She'd left a couple months ago back to Earth. She was done with the military, but not with Justus. Her plan was to finish her degree and start teaching in Colorado. He missed her. He didn't think he'd miss her this much, but he really did. He felt a hurt he'd never felt before. He was thinking about her in the mile high city when his tablet rang.

Reading the message, Justus froze.

The message was from Nurse Beth and read, "Hey there, hot stuff! I'll be on your station for a week of training, two weeks from today. I was hoping we could meet up. *Smiley face.*"

Justus was unsure how to answer her. He was unsure of a lot of things.

———————

The Dirtbag Dozen, minus one, sat at one large circular table at The Shack. There was a huge spread of catered food and an open bar. They were all confused by the occasion.

"Well, what is this?" Merrick asked Seth.

Seth answered, "I have gathered you here for three reasons."

"This oughta be good," Maisie said.

Seth ensured everyone had a drink in their hands, then said, "First of all, I want to toast to Sam. It seems we all knew something different about him and will have those memories to cherish always. He was by far the smartest member in our group and I bet he would have enjoyed every moment here on station with us. His life was surely taken too soon. We all know that. To Sam!"

"To Sam!" everyone said, as they toasted and took a drink.

Seth continued, "There is lots of food, so dig in."

They started to eat as Lenny asked, "What's the second reason we're here?"

"Take your time. Right now, this moment is for Sam."

They ate and talked, enjoying the company of the just the Dozen. Justus was lost in thoughts of Virginia, as well as that recent message from Beth.

Flange looked up. "Hey, guys, check it out. Another news cast.

Larry appeared on the video displays and said, "New York City had a ticker-tape parade celebrating the return of someone lost to time. Many would not believe it until they saw it with their own eyes. Hello everyone, my name is Larry the Llama and this…is MTV News."

He continued, "Nikola Tesla returned to Earth today as it was celebrated across the globe and live from the Big Apple. Apparently, Tesla has been in and out of cryo-sleep for over a hundred years, living it up at Viridis, of all places. He said he is ecstatic to be back and can't wait to see how much everything has changed. We had an exclusive interview with him earlier detailing his journey. For the full interview, click here, or visit our site."

"In other news, tension has been building up with the moon of Viridis. They continually blame Earth, specifically the US, for the Ignotus force. They believe those drones have always been our technology and refuse to let it go. That is all for now. Stay tuned as we'll keep you updated on the latest news and stories from around the galaxy. *The Llama* is out…this has been an MTV News update."

Wilhelm said, "Wow, that's cool about Tesla. I'll have to check that out later."

"You think he'll keep up his Rip Van Winkle routine on Earth?" Pete asked.

"I don't see why not," Seth said. "He seems to enjoy living forever. However, I'm more worried about the Viridis situation."

Lenny asked, "Do you think it was them that tried to attack our bomber on the moon?"

"Good question. Good question," Maisie responded.

"Okay, Seth," Pepper said. "What's the second reason we're here?"

"Alright. It won't be released until next week, but I got accepted to become an officer. I'll start my training when we head back to Earth."

Everyone was happy, talking over each other and telling Seth how great it was.

Wilhelm said, "That explains this meal. Only an officer could afford this."

"You going to stay near the Flightline?" Justus asked. "Become a Maintenance Officer?"

"That's what I put in for," Seth answered. "I'm hoping, but you never know."

They continued to enjoy the company as they had more drinks and talked about the crazy adventures they had all experienced. A few of them displayed various videos they had taken and put them up on The Shack's displays. They watched the '*Racks*' music video again from Simon and Pete, and they *had* to see Manny running from the Grim Reaper again.

Finally, Seth said, "Alright. Last item on our agenda..."

Maisie interrupted. "Last item on the agenda—you're already starting to sound like an officer."

Everyone laughed.

Seth shook his head. "You got me there. Here it is. Final thoughts. We need to know what everyone's plan is. Are you going to extend and stay out here among the moons? Will you head to Earth and be stationed there, or will you call it quits and start a normal life?"

Manny asked, "Are you saying the Space Military isn't normal?"

"I don't think I need to answer that. Just go ask your girlfriend, Jamie."

Everyone was looking around the table. Justus sat there thinking.

Seth Harvard said, "Alright, I'll start, then go to my left. I plan on getting my *butter bars* and sticking to somewhere on Earth, preferably the US East Coast. It'll be nice to live closer to the family I grew up with. Lenny, you're next."

"You know, after I take leave, I'm coming back here. Sam was right. Life is good on station. Everywhere we go, someone is trying kill us, but this is exciting. I'm definitely staying here."

Everyone clapped and nodded their heads.

Burrt Wilhelm took a deep breath. "I never thought I would even make it past Boot Camp. Look how far I have come! I will never forget you all, but I think I'm done. I came for what I wanted. I'm ready to move on. I'm sorry, but this is it for me."

Seth responded, "Hey, don't be sorry. Look at all you did! That's way more than most people. You're going do great out there, as this experience has made you stronger than most. Enjoy life on the outside."

Wilhelm's eyes lifted. "Thanks, Seth."

Pete Ward said, "I take it I'm next. I'm done with Stella, but want to relocate to somewhere in the US. There are a few bomber bases that look good, as long as I don't get North Dakota I'll be alright."

Seth nodded to Simon.

Simon Ward put out down his drink and pointed to his brother. "Ditto."

Manny Eastern spoke. "It won't be the same without all of you here. I don't mind it. I'll try for another five years here on station."

Jack Flange stated, "You know, like Wilhelm, I believe I'm done, too. My father's got a construction business, and he's always said there'd be a position for me. This has all been more than I could have ever imagined, but I'm ready to move on."

Everyone nodded in agreement, raising their glasses.

Maisie hit Merrick. "Hey, you're next."

Phil Merrick said, "Oh, you know what? This place ain't so bad. I'll miss you all, but I wanna stay here."

Maisie Elton smiled. "I hate to say it, but I'm staying out here as well. Who else is gonna teach these new Franks how to run the Bully engines?"

"Here, here" said Seth. "Pepper?"

Patricia York looked around the room. "Even though my brother Matt is staying here, I'm ready to move on. I want to head back to the States. Maybe I'll get stationed somewhere near Nate. I'm staying in the military; I just want to see another aspect of it." Pepper was tearing up, but managed to hold it back. "I can't believe we are all separating, but I guess we knew this day would come."

Everyone felt the same way as they nodded.

Pepper wiped her eyes and turned to Justus. "So, what is it? What's your plan?"

Justus Johannes responded, "I think I'll go home and start a garage band."

Simon asked, "What'll you play?"

"Guitar has always been my forte. What do you say, Pepper, you on drums?"

Everyone laughed.

Justus took a deep breath, then talked slowly. "No, seriously. I am choosing...not to make a choice."

Seth asked, "How's that work?"

"I need a break. I need to figure things out. For now, I am getting out. I'm going home. I'll finish my degree in a couple years, *then* make a decision. I can always re-up and find one of you out there. I'm sure you'll outrank me, but I never cared about that. On the other hand, maybe I'll become an officer. Then again, maybe I'll just let you all have fun, as I find my life without the Space Military. Even as we sit here, we all still have a few months before we depart. Anything can happen. One thing is for certain, these memories will always be with me."

The rest of the night was full of laughs. They couldn't believe the Dirtbag Dozen would be only a memory. Only a memory of a group of Tech School grads that were put into an impossible situation and pulled through with remarkable results.

———————————

Justus headed back to his room in high spirits as his tablet dinged, then dinged, and continued to ding. He had a chill across his body, not knowing how to answer Beth's messages. To his surprise, it was *not* Beth.

He looked down to see the message. Justus stood there in shock reading each one.

0026 - GPS: RCVR ERROR 82% - NXT MSN.

0086 - COMM: FAIL 42% WITHIN NXT 5 MSNS.

0341 - NAV SYS: GPS ERROR 33%, INS ERROR 33%, CMPSS ERROR 33%.

DV5050 – SYS ERROR: UKNOWN, UNKNOWN, UKNOWN.

DV5050 – SYS ERROR: UKNOWN, UNKNOWN, UKNOWN.

DV5050 – SYS ERROR: UKNOWN, UNKNOWN, UKNOWN.

Epilogue

News agencies from around the world were in attendance. Dr. Henry Kirkland approached the podium, looked down at his notes, then ahead at the crowd.

Kirkland spoke in a serious tone. "I would like to thank you for this opportunity to speak the truth. I must say, for the first time in ages, I am not speaking on behalf of the Department of Defense. In fact, I resigned today due to irrefutable differences. What I am about to tell you will change the course of history, which is precisely why they wanted me to remain quiet. The information you are about to hear was never deemed classified, therefore I am in no way violating any security protocol. The truth must be heard!"

Kirkland continued. "I know what happened to LaMarche's lost transport. The reconnaissance effort recovered much from that planet. I headed the team that was trying to piece together all the evidence to uncover the truth. The truth, that some want to keep hidden from the rest. The truth, that I want to bring into the light for the world. A truth that I am still trying to wrap my head around."

A voice from the crowd yelled, "Get on with it!"

Dr. Kirkland continued. "Yes, yes, when I discovered the many secrets of the space bridge, I theorized the potential hazard of exceeding certain speeds. At the time I called it a *rift*. Something that would disrupt *time* itself. I now have evidence of the very rift I was so concerned with."

"LaMarche and his hundreds of thousands of passengers landed on the new planet," he continued. "However, they landed there over *five thousand years* ago. It was the fast speed they traveled that created the *time rift* that I only theorized. They assumed all went well and continued to track time as if nothing different had occurred. They tried to radio for Earth over and over again. No one was listening, since they were so far into our past."

"I have proof," he said. "We uncovered their logs. Electronic script whose dates went on for thousands of years. They may have been copied or transcribed on various devices, but the ones we found were entirely legible and contained a remarkable and detailed history. I will also add that these logs were in English for the most part, also encoded with in a computerized script."

"According to the logs," he explained, "they continued with their plan. At first, they lived on massive carriers, then ventured out. The planet was rich in resources. Clear blue skies. Fresh water streams, tons of vegetation and trees. There was some invasive wildlife, but not much. Years went by. LaMarche was correct—with their past knowledge and volumes of research, they were able to advance very quickly. In order to not lose sight of where they came from, they built a large structure out of stone. A structure that would point exactly where the space bridge was located. Today we call this structure a Stonehenge. We believe some of them were able take a space carrier back to Earth, only to find out they were in the past. We believe they created England's Stonehenge."

"Their ancestors even started working on defensive systems on their planet which became more and more automatic," he continued. "I need to look closer at the research, but I believe it was about sixty years ago when everything went to hell. The planet *LaMarche* as they described it had beautiful blue skies and lush vegetation. Something occurred, something drastic. I believe their advanced A.I. defensive system went rogue."

"Let me explain something else concerning Earth's system and these wormholes. We have recently discovered we are part of a triangle. Earth's solar system is one part, with Stella being the second. The third is where LaMarche's transport ventured. You may ask, where does Ignotus fall into all of this? Here is where it gets complicated."

"LaMarche's planet is in fact, the very same planet as Ignotus. This is where our recon team found all those logs. As was reported,

Ignotus looked very different. We believe the humans on LaMarche were exterminated, biologically. This would explain the drastic change in the environment for what we have been calling Ignotus, with its green-tainted skies. Our Space Military was in fact fighting the very A.I. defense system we created."

"I am sure many won't believe my claims. I can also assure you, if we were to venture across that new space bridge at a reasonable speed, you'll find yourself on Ignotus. The green sky planet with no life on it, only a reminder of a past civilization taken over by technology, then destroyed by ourselves. An endless loop, about which our conventional logic cannot fathom."

2nd Epilogue

I was looking up with my binoculars, but still saw no sign of them. I checked the GPS knowing they should come into view any moment now. It was a clear day with only a light cloud coverage in the blue sky over this Flightline in Arizona. I was pacing back and forth.

Being as impatient as I am, I tried the radio again. "Mama Bear, this is Lander-One. What's your position?"

"Lander-One, Mama Bear. We just passed the hill. We see the airfield."

"Hold on...yep, I can see you now. How's everything?"

"Everything is going great. The kid's a natural. We'll tell you all about it, after *he* lands."

I stood there looking up, nervous about it all. It would be his first attempt at landing, and anything could go wrong. I watched as they made their approach in the small twin-engine airplane. It looked like he was coming in too fast. *Slow down, slow down,* I kept thinking. The wings tilted a bit to the left, then to right. I was almost in a panic. Then it leveled out. The wheels hit the ground. Then the plane slowed down. A near perfect landing. I was so relieved.

I got back on the radio. "Well done. Very good!"

"Thanks, it was all him! I was just advising."

"Hey, I need you to have him taxi to the *Roger Cliff Memorial Hangar.*"

"Why not the main hangar?"

"I gotta surprise. Just pullup next to the hangar, I'll guide you in."

I marshalled the little twin-engine plane in and signaled him to cut the engines. After putting the chocks down, I saw the door open.

I smiled and asked, "How'd it go? You two looked amazing!"

"She answered, "Great, real great. **Martin** was born to fly."

Martin added, "Thanks, Mom. Just doing what you taught me."

I said, "Well, she did teach you almost everything you know."

"Can you believe I'll get my pilot's license before my eighteenth birthday?"

"Awesome!"

Martin asked, "What's this big surprise, and why is the hangar closed?"

"I didn't want to say anything while you two were flying. I didn't want you nervous."

"I would have been fine."

"I was talking about **Jo-Leia**, your mom."

Jo-Leia smiled and asked, "Yeah, okay, **Max**. What's the surprise?"

Martin asked, "Yeah Max, *I mean dad*, what's the surprise?"

I responded, "Just stand here while I open the hangar."

I peeked inside the small door and made sure everything was set up, including the balloons, streamers and of course the guests of honor. Giving them a thumbs up, I used the door controls on the outside of the hangar in order to see Jo-Leia's and Martin's expressions. The hangar doors slowly creeped open. Once Martin saw who it was, he ran fast towards his older brother. Jo-Leia was crying as she smiled at the sight of her son and ran to Justus.

There was a pretty woman next to Justus wearing a red dress. She looked happy watching Justus embrace his mom and brother. I approached them as well.

Justus said, "It's so great to be home. I want to introduce you to my fiancé. Her name is…"

Stay tuned for Episode III

The Flightline

For all that enjoyed my first book, *The Flightline*, here is some additional information and inspiration behind the ideas. (There are spoilers)

I wanted to write about many insane stories I encountered or heard in the military, yet at the same time, I needed it to be fiction. The cover picture was illustrated by my child, who is currently away in college at Northern Arizona University.

The Prologue: I started off by showing the Flightline from an Expeditor's perspective, knowing about every maintainer, career field and spaceship (airplane). I thought this would be the perfect overview for the book for both aircraft maintainers and those new to this subject.

Chapter 1 – Flying: The entire concept of this first chapter is a metaphor for military in-processing and Basic Training. Being among a huge group of strangers, herded like cattle, half naked and afraid. They are all put in a situation from which there is no turning back.

Who is Max Morgan? The town of Max is just south of Minot, North Dakota. My wife Erica and I would drive through there on our way to Bismarck. We even stopped there a couple times to visit the cemetery, which is the resting place of her grandmother. Early in our dating, Erica gave me a small stuffed dog. We named it Max. This little guy would find its way into my luggage on most of our vacations and even on my deployments. So yes, our lead character is named after the dog. Max is also a cool radio term, such as maximum volume. To go to the extreme and push the limits.

At first, Max's last name was Skylander. Yeah, that had to change. Then I realized, I needed a name that starts with 'M.' Many heroes have the same starting letters in their first and last name: Peter Parker, Bruce Banner, Marty McFly, Ronald Reagan, Luke Lander and so forth. It is noteworthy that Max Morgan is the only character in the book with double letters. I went through many "M" last names then came across Morgan. Arthur Morgan is the lead character in one of my favorite video games, Red Dead Redemption II. It fit perfectly.

Who is Roger? After a few chapters, I was hoping the reader would get a feeling that he's Max's psychiatrist. The name Roger is specific to the radio term which means *received and understood*. He is always there to understand the ones communicating. I grew to love the Roger character and started to imagine him being played by the actor Morgan Freeman.

Chapter 2 - Getting Hammered: Here we have the typical struggles of in-processing to a new job. Instead of having the nine enlisted military ranks, I kept things simple with only four ranks: specialist, sergeant, senior sergeant, and chief. I wasn't about to stop and acknowledge every time someone got promoted within the traditional system. I also didn't want to use the rank "airmen." I almost went with cadet (space cadet), then decided on specialist.

Who is Tillhammer? I needed a strong sounding name. I liked that his name contained the word hammer, which could be used as an expression. He is your typical mean sergeant. Always upset, always mad about something and always taking it out on the younger troops. He was probably never a very good maintainer.

Who is 'Flip' Samuel Dolphline? I knew a guy whose last name was the same as a certain type of fish. Naturally everyone called him 'Fish.' I thought it'd be cool to have someone named Dolphline and call him Flipper (from the TV show). In the early writings, Sam's name was Flipper. I later changed it just to Flip since I thought it sounded better and it was short and to the point. Plus, I thought a four-letter F-word suited him better. His first name, Sam, is also important since every main character needs a Sam as their right-hand man. Examples: Lord of the Rings - Sam Gamgee, Game of

Thrones - Sam Tarly, Supernatural - Sam Winchester, and Captain America's - Sam Wilson...to name a few.

Who is 'Turtle' Davy Michelangelo the Fourth? The comic relief, the little one, not the star, but always there as a loyal friend. The name Turtle just seemed to fit this type of character, small and strong. You don't expect him to do much, but it's good to keep him around. I added his last name Michelangelo, like the Teenage Mutant Ninja Turtle. Davy seemed like good first name since the artist Michelangelo sculpted the 'David.'

Chapter 3- Distant Neighbors: I used some history combined with fiction when talking about Nikola Tesla for this backstory. Originally, I thought the aliens would be all crazy looking like in *Star Wars* or *Star Trek*. I decided to make them look like humans, something we can relate to. All said and done, I wanted to focus on the *Flightline* and thought bringing in weird creatures would greatly distract from all that.

The three moons. I knew Max would deploy to various places, one being cold, one hot, and one tropical. I kept things simple by using Latin words. Nix = snow. Calidum = hot. Viridis = green. Even the star and planet follow this: Stella = star. Centrum = center.

I took my experience with working on B-52s and C-130s and combined them into one spaceship, the BC-76 which uses the birth year of America. I didn't explain the look of the ship in much detail for a reason. I wanted every maintainer reading to imagine it like the airframes they worked on. I also never talked about the landing gear. Do these have wheels or just static landing supports like many spaceships in movies? I left it out and let the reader pick.

Chapter 4 - Night One: Tool Counter (Consolidated Tool Kit, CTK) typical of any maintenance unit. I like the term 'Tool Counter' since it has a double meaning. Those that count tools and the counter you get them from. Early in the writing, I named one of the CTK guys 'Random Tool Guy' as a place holder. After several read-throughs, I came to like the name, so I kept it in there.

We had a saying in Little Rock: "On the line...all the time!" The idea of being literally chained to the Flightline stuck with me. I wondered how the ships in *Star Wars* departed without the maintainers being sucked out. I thought, wouldn't it be cool if there was a window that opened and everyone had to be chained down? I don't know if the physics would work for this, but I loved the idea and imagery it holds.

Introducing Quality Control, or Quality Assurance (QA) as vultures was key, since we all called them that. Having it as a drone was just adding some cool future stuff to it. We all know it'll happen someday...if it hasn't already. The prank of having a new kid wear aluminum foil in front of the plane was something I saw first-hand.

Chapter 5 – I Don't Have Three Arms: On the B-52, we had an A9005 Avionics Junction Box that was in the Hell Hole in front of the navigator's station. We would use a 2x4 wooded beam to aid us in the replacement effort.

The term nonner is how Air Force Maintainers describe non-critical career fields that sit around in offices all day. They are non-mission essential, thus a nonner. They hate that term, so we continue to use it.

Chapter 6 – No Show: Who is Mike Pechman? He's a Hydro troop we'll see a few times. I found one meaning of the word Pechman on the internet that means *bad luck*. He'll be the one that breaks his arm during the gravity shift, cleans up the piss he thinks is hydro, and gets his tablet stolen on Viridis.

Who is Chief Bob Rogowski? We don't see much of this guy. He is the chief that talks in riddles. I didn't like this chief, so he shares his last name with an ex-pro skateboarder that raped and murdered a woman. The story of 'gorilla hands' was similar to one I heard firsthand from one of my peers. No intent of racism was there. It was a learning opportunity for the young airmen and an amusing story to tell.

Other than this story, I never mention race. I figure the reader can decide what ethnicity they want for the characters. We all know that guy, or that girl, that these people remind us of. I want readers to put the people they know in these situations and go with it.

Chapter 7 – The Walk: FOD walk. One of many done on the Flightline. In this chapter, I also needed an opportunity to force some backstory out of Flip. I figured a long walk was perfect for this.

The radio D.J. thing was inspired by a student I taught during my time as a Tech School Instructor at Sheppard AFB. This young kid told us stories of his time working at a radio station. The story about diverting traffic through town and swimming in the mall fountain were totally his, including showing up at his parent's house in a wetsuit with a cop by his side. I still can't remember this guy's name or where he ended up.

Chapter 8 – Flying Beds: Who is Jo-Leia Zwarc? At first, I just made her another Avionics character that was part of the team. She is smart and a hard worker that never gets in trouble. Let me stop right now and describe something interesting. I have learned that once I develop a character's personality, they seem to take over. I put these fictional characters in a situation and the dialogue starts to flow, they seem to take over and say things how they want in my subconscious. They talk to each other while I am out jogging or trying to sleep. I wasn't intending to let Max fall in love with the Jo-Leia character, yet it seemed to happen for some reason while they were on Calidum. Once I decided to move toward this direction, I added some more stuff to the wedding chapter. Then I altered her name and came up with Jo-Leia Zwarc, which contains the same letters as my wife's maiden name, Erica Jo Walz.

The Mattress Exchange is one I witnessed firsthand, as many of us did. Usually, we'd get two or three airmen to do this and there would be lots of laughs. One day during my time as a student at Tech School, we actually received new mattresses. No one thought it was real until we saw a truck loaded with them. So yes, we had a real mattress exchange in 1998.

Max reveals that his birthday is 076 day. This is March 17th, Saint Patrick's Day. Also, my birthday.

Chapter 9 – Experience Points: Interactions with the extreme cold. I described new fancy de-icers with enclosed booms. These were similar to those our guys used in Little Rock. The old ones Max uses were the ones we had at Minot at the time, old and hard to use. I said the instructions were written in the Nix language of *Kereg*. These letters scrambled spell *Greek*. If you don't understand, it's Greek to you.

Max said the coldest temperature was "negative forty." Roger questions if this is "Celsius or Fahrenheit?" Max replied, "does this really matter?" Negative forty is the exact same temperature in both Celsius and Fahrenheit.

Chapter 10 – Heaters and Air Carts: This air cart situation was real in Minot; there seemed to be a constant discussion with QA over it. Yes, we were required to use an air cart so our Avionics parts didn't overheat. At the same time, during the winter, we would also bring up a heater. It was dumb and we all knew it.

Chapter 11 – Field Trip: Max learns that Nix has a Stonehenge. I wasn't sure where I was going with this at the time, then I ended up developing it more in the second book. I saw Stonehenge while I was deployed to England...It was cool.

Chapter 12 – Shenanigans: The story of Random Tool Guy getting deployed then being sent back actually happened. We had a Bomb-Nav troop in Minot that deployed overseas and was immediately sent back. He had gotten into computer hacking trouble in the past and was not allowed to leave the country. Apparently, the military and some outside agencies don't always talk. I found this interesting, yet troubling.

The disappearing room was a new one I came up with. There was a secrete storage room within the dorm at Sheppard that the MTLs (Dorm Sergeants) didn't know about. The airmen used it for parties and what not. I had to actually draw this scenario out to ensure I got the room placement correct. This section was difficult to write grammatically. I have Max telling Roger the story about a time when Flip told Max and Turtle his story. Within Flip's story there is dialogue between him and Belington. The correct use of quotation marks had everyone confused, including my editor.

Chapter 13 – Medical: Another short chapter, not too much here just poking fun at the medical facility.

Chapter 14 – Compass Check: Who is Diego? Sergeant Diego is the best supervisor you can want. He is what they call in Dungeons & Dragons, *Lawfully Good*. For three years I lived in San Diego; it's where I left to join the military. The city was named after Saint Diego de Alcala, a Franciscan monk. Diego in my story was to be the moral guide for Max and others.

The Cookie Bus was a real thing provided from the Chaplain's group while I was in Minot. Not sure if they still do it, but we all loved it when they drove around the Flightline handing out snacks.

Who is Chaplain Christopher McKinley? This character is based on three people. One being my brother Mark, who was a Catholic priest for nearly ten years. There was also a military Chaplain at Little Rock who had similar characteristics. However, the image in my mind for how McKinley looks and talks is that of Father Mulcahy from the T.V. show M.A.S.H. McKinley sounds like it could be an Irish Catholic name. Although I never called him Catholic in the book, I imagined him so.

Chapter 15 – Take me to Church: The 'Help Me' on the soles of Marcus' shoes is from a story I heard about my brother-in-law Khris, who was pranked with this during his wedding.

Chapter 16 – Turtle and the Cougar: Here we talk about 'deployment hot' which a real term used while deployed as described in the book. Who is Columbae? This is a waitress from Viridis that Turtle starts dating. The name Columbae is Latin for pigeon or dove. So, with them together we have a Turtle-Dove.

Chapter 17 – The Gravity of It All: Here we see Max's life turn upside down. Metaphorically and literally. It is midway through the book. I thought we'd all have some fun with an anti-gravity situation.

Chapter 18 – Preparations: Max gets Step-Promoted. In truth, this was very rare. I don't know any maintainers that were Step-Promoted. We all got ours the hard way.

Chapter 19 – Groundhogs Day One: The maintainers are stuck in time loop repeating the same day over and over again, like the movie *Groundhog Day*. We called every day this in the Middle East.

Who is Lieutenant Kirkland? Lt Kirkland is based on two people I know. If you didn't know, my father was a Lieutenant that served during the Vietnam War, first name Kirk. The other inspiration for Kirkland was a young Maintenance Officer I worked with.

Chapter 20 – Llama: Who is Larry Alma? Here we go, we all know that one guy. If you've been around long enough, you know several people that fit this description. Maybe they are slower than the rest, maybe they don't care, maybe they just need someone to trust and talk to. Larry in this book was *that* guy. The pranks with the K-9P and tags on boots I saw firsthand, as well as many others. Even watching a certain young troop chase crickets across the Flightline was a real thing.

Jumping to the ground during an attack and finding myself sloshed in smoke pit debris definitely happened to me in Iraq. I brought an extra T-shirt to work with me for the rest of that deployment.

Chapter 21 – Franksgiving: While at Little Rock, we had a term for new airmen, Franks. The acronym at the time was, *F'ing Retarded Ass New Kid*. I almost used this term in my book. I debated about it for about six months. I just didn't want to use the word *retarded*. I changed it to *rookie* for the book.

Chapter 22 and 23 – The Road, To Recovery: I knew early on I'd have a suicide be a major part of this book. Aircraft Maintenance has one of the highest rates of suicide in the military. Anyone within the maintenance career field in the Air Force has experienced someone within their section attempt, if not more. I felt I needed to talk about this and show the correct way of how a suicide should be handled. I believed Max's leadership team handled it correctly. Also, I wanted to express some emotions and talk about it.

Chapter 24 – Dinner Guests: This was a fun chapter. At the chow hall Flip and Max hear the cooks start to sing 'Feliz Navid.' I encountered this firsthand while getting my hair cut in Iraq near Christmas time. There were two Iraqi barbers, one had a guitar as they sang to that tune with altered lyrics, "*We want to wish you an American Christmas…*" It was great. I smile whenever I think of that moment.

Chapter 25 – Commanders: I went back and forth on this chapter. I almost deleted it entirely. I came up with this crazy story out of the blue. Of course, it's all fake, but then again that's how launch truck stories go. They talk about the new governor, Gwen Stefani. Funny side story…Gwen went to high school with my brother Joe. She was even on his swim team at Loara High School, Anaheim California, late eighties.

Chapter 26 – Tough Life: Who is Major Leroy Gatlin? I needed a strong Commander name. He was also a pilot in the past. My grandfather Leroy was a Coast Guard pilot. Gatlin sounded like a cool name, like a Gatling gun.

The story of Pechman cleaning up hydro fluid that was actually coming from the urinal is real. We had a hydro troop in Iraq that was doing just that. It took him a while to figure out the fluid was actually urine.

Chapter 27 – Island Hopping: To me this felt similar to many trips outside the US, trying to figure out where to go with the language problems and currency exchange rates. I felt we needed to close the loop with Turtle's finance and give her family an opportunity to make some money with the Rubik's Cube thing.

Chapter 28 – Birds of a Feather: This is my favorite chapter. Planes are breaking, everyone working together, time is a factor. This feels like every night as an Expeditor.

Who is Rose Caron? Rose is a Sheet Metal troop. I described her as a cross between Ronald McDonald and Chewbacca. Early in my career I met a Comm-Nav troop that worked in another section. She was described to me from someone else in this exact same manner. When I met her, I said to myself, *yeah, I can see that.*

Rose works in Sheet Metal, so she's named after Rosie the Riveter. The last name Caron is important, as well. In the book *Unsung Heroes – A History of the Enlisted Airmen from the Dawn of Flight to Desert Storm*, I read about Master Sergeant George B.

Caron in Vietnam. He is the one that fixed the plane using beer and soda cans; his last name is shared with Rose.

Chapter 29 – Flock Together: Just a bunch of maintainers hanging out downtown in a foreign place. Like Flip, in England we did have a Crew Chief beat the pub's record of the most drinks in a specific time frame...and this was on our first night out. Here we learn Flip's birthday is 110-day. This is April 20th, or 4-20 day. In recent culture, this is considered smoking weed day. This also happens to be my son's birthday, arrg...

Chapter 30 and 31 – Ground Control / Major Tom: Who is Major Thomas? Just as the song goes, one trapped out there in space with his circuits dead.

Who are pilots Hamilton and Chandler? Where I live there are two rival high schools. My kids go to Hamilton High School, while down the street is Chandler High. Who are the civilian pilots, Bill and Del? They share the names of my two great uncles, my grandpa's brothers. For some reason I think of them as Statler and Waldorf, the two old Muppets in the balcony.

Chapter 32 – Driving in Circles: There were a bunch of rocket attacks while I was deployed in Iraq and Afghanistan. Lucky for us, no one from our unit was hurt while I was there. I did get stopped by Security Forces for driving around in circles. The conversation was very similar to that in this chapter.

I wasn't there, but I heard everything about the foreign officer going on and on about his stolen chicken (cock). Apparently, he didn't know about the double meaning. I think he was from France. Lastly was the young officer trying to load her IFF codes. I experienced this firsthand, as I had to drive her and the Commander to their office to load new codes.

Chapter 33 – Standing in Line: The conversation with the cashier and man buying beer with his daughter was almost word for word from my own experience. This was at a Walmart about four years ago, while I was buying groceries with my daughter.

Who is Colonel Bucket? The name Bucket comes from the Air

Force term called deployment buckets, that were supposed to classify people into different buckets that deployed at specific set intervals. This concept looked good on paper but never worked.

Chapter 34 – The Slow Death: Who is Aaron York? Aaron is Marcus and Sharyn's boy. Just a baby, so not much going on. A-A-Ron comes from a Key and Peele skit. (A-A-Ron is in the prologue of the Flightline II).

The fake APR lines were similar to ones I wrote while writing EPRs. There is even one in my own EPR that states, "Fostered American/Greek holiday festival; coord'd transportation for 52 mbrs—fortified international relations." In other words, I was the designated driver for our group going to a winery on Easter while in Greece.

When I first wrote this section, each sentence fit exactly across the screen. Just like in a real EPR where we are forced to fit every thought into one line exactly. When I went into the publishing process, they wanted to change the font and so forth, and I realized this section would not have the same impact. With books being printed in paperback, or hard copy, or digital, there was no way to keep each line exact. I then added something in the *Outtakes* to explain about the intent of the lines. So, there you go...

Chapter 35 – Hello Darkness: This is the first time we hear Max cuss in the entire book. I wanted it to be impactful. He explains this world has changed so much he doesn't know how to live in it. For me this was another metaphor. Coming out of the military after twenty-one years was difficult. It was like living in a new world, and many things had changed. It was difficult adjusting to a new job with all the changes. I tried to show Max was struggling in a new environment like many do after getting out, with a feeling they have been away for decades.

Chapter 36 – My Old Friends: This title goes with the one in the previous chapter. The funeral was a quick recap of many of the events from the book. I was hoping to spark some memories and help readers appreciate what they read in the past.

Max meets up with Jo-Leia and of course they head off into the sunset. Wait, not the sunset, it wouldn't make sense for a small private aircraft to start flying at night. Okay, they head off into the wild blue yonder, no that is way too Air Force nerdy. Let's go with, "Jo-Leia had control of this marvel of flight as we took to the open blue skies." This also closed the bookends. In Chapter 1, Max is flying and is terrified of it. Now he is excited to get the plane to start his new journey.

Epilogue: Here we have a fictional hospital. Who is Doctor Dumas? He is in charge of all these doctors and thinks he is better than everyone. His name sounds like his personality, dumb-ass.

Another doctor brings up the situation concerning that dude in the cafeteria. At first, they say he talks to himself; some readers may think this whole thing is Max going crazy. In the end, Roger is just a random janitor. I wanted to show that it doesn't matter who you talk to, just talk to someone that will listen. We all need to be there for each other to listen and understand what they went through. Anyone of us can be 'Roger.'

Good Luck and God Bless.

About the Author

Timothy M. Lander was born in 1976 and raised in Southern California. In 1998, Tim joined the Air Force and served for over twenty-one years as an Avionics troop primarily working on B-52s and C-130s. He served alongside truly exceptional aircraft maintainers in North Dakota, Texas, and Arkansas; while also deploying to such places as England, Iraq, Greece and Afghanistan. Tim currently resides in Chandler, Arizona along with his amazing wife Erica as they raise their four awesome kids, currently guiding them through high school and college.

www.ingramcontent.com/pod-product-compliance
Lightning Source LLC
Chambersburg PA
CBHW070412310726
48977CB00003B/651